STORIES TO SING
IN THE DARK

ALSO BY MATTHEW BRIGHT:

(as author:)
Four Seasons
Between The Lines
(with Christopher Black)

(as editor:)
Threesome
The Myriad Carnival
Clockwork Cairo
Gents

STORIES
to
SING
in the
DARK

MATTHEW BRIGHT

LETHE PRESS
AMHERST, MA

Published by LETHE PRESS
lethepressbooks.com

ISBN: 9781590217047

Library of Congress Cataloging-in-Publication Data
available on request

Cover art
by GRANDFAILURE

Cover and Interior design
by INKSPIRAL DESIGN

———⁓⁓⁓———

For **STEVE BERMAN**,
for providing editorial notes
on his own birthday present.

———⁓⁓⁓———

CONTENTS

1 | *The Library of Lost Things*

23 | *In Search of Stars*

41 | *Golden Hair, Red Lips*

57 | *Croak Toad*

71 | *Nothing To Worry About*

85 | *Director's Cut*

103 | *The Concubine's Heart*

117 | *Antonia & Cleopatra*

147 | *By Chance, In The Dark*

165 | *The Last Drag Show On Earth*

177 | *No Sleep In Bethlehem*

FOREWORD

[To come]

THE LIBRARY OF LOST THINGS

THE LIBRARIAN TURNED his eyes upon me, reversed the single sheet of paper once, then neatly back again.

"An excellent candidate," he said.

And:

"Thomas Hardy. An apropos name. We have one of his, you know? No relation, I assume?"

And:

"'Favourite grammatical form: passive voice.'" He looked me up and down, pinprick eyes narrowed, and licked his dry bottom lip. "Marvellous."

"Sir?" I said.

The Librarian's tongue flickered. "So wonderfully *uninterested*. Most boys, well they come here with their nasty adverbs and their present tense, or, God forbid, *second person*." When he shuddered his spine cracked like an old hardback opened in one swift, cruel motion. "Quite unsuitable. You on the other hand…"

And, after some deliberation:

"Very well. The job is yours, young Thomas."

"Tom," I said and swallowed with relief that he hadn't asked me why I wanted to work for the Library. I'd prepared a response, but I doubted it would impress. The Librarian's eyes were sharp and astute, shadowed in the hollows beneath a foxed brow. He would have picked apart my half-truths, separating non-fiction from fiction and sniffed suspiciously around the superlative adjectives.

"Come along." He unfolded his eight-foot frame from the armchair, stick insect stretching. He led me out of his office, down a long hall which echoed our footsteps, and to a set of ornate double doors. "Through here," he said, "is the main hall of the Library. You must always treat this place with the utmost respect. We serve a greater good. Stay long and you will know this."

He guided me through the doors. On the other side, bookshelves reached the horizon.

The Librarian bent close to my ear. He reeked like damp second-hand bookshops, or comics left to moulder in the bottom of a wardrobe. "How would *you* describe it, *Tom*?"

I was still being tested. The interview was not truly over. Perhaps it never would be.

I looked from one behemoth shelf to the next: it was a graveyard of spines, leather, paper, string, the wormed carcasses of all those books, buried next to each other one after another into the dark. The feeling of disintegrated sentences hung in the air, a deadness of language, like a word abandoned mid-syllable.

"It's impressive," I said.

"Im-pres-sive." The Librarian outstretched his arms to the expectant hall. "It takes you three syllables to encompass all this?"

I had been memorizing *Roget's 1911*. "Large," I said.

He chuckled. "'Large'—*hmph!* Better to be faced with an eternity of literature and render it down to one uttered word, one brief sound. 'Large'—I think you'll be perfect."

From beneath a shelf of peeling grimoires, scratchy muttered sounds could be heard. At first I interpreted them as squeaks, then realized instead that they were voices. Words, in fact. "Stripling! Gangrel! Pilgarlic!" A scurry of grey tiny shapes crossed our path and disappeared among the nearest bookshelf.

"Ignore the rats," the Librarian said. "So bothersome. I try to keep them away from the books, but they over-run the place. They have a particular taste for the folios. I suppose it's only natural they've picked up some words. But such *bothersome* words." He licked a spindly forefinger and thumbed his lapel as if he could turn the page of his suit. "To work then, my unremarkable boy."

He led me through the stacks, past row upon row of books. Some were bound in leather, some gaudy, some decrepit, some little more than stapled paper, and some emanating a faint electric glow. Skittering around in the shadows, the rats could be heard in our wake: "Jackanape! Welkin!"

"*Voila!*" said the Librarian. "The Index."

Like a still pool in a forest, the library had given way to clear empty space containing a circle of doors, freestanding and unsupported, each unadorned apart from a single round window at head height. Narrow bookcases stood attendant by each, laid out like spokes within the wheel of doors.

"Observe." The Librarian plucked the first volume waiting on one of the bookcase-spokes. It was gently smoking; the Librarian carefully patted out its glowing embers. He inspected both of its covers. "*Sonnenfinsternis* by Arthur Koestler. You do know German? I've been waiting for this one. File this under Wartime Casualties."

And:

A sandy pile of barely bound papers. "*The Visions of Iddo the Seer*—fascinating. File under Myriad Apocrypha."

And:

A sheaf of laser-printed paper. "*Untitled Novel About a Boy with No Hands (Incomplete)* by S. Berman. That's one for the Self-Doubt section—half a novel deleted in a crisis of confidence, if I'm not mistaken." He coughed. No, it was a laugh. "I'm never mistaken."

And:

A threadbare exercise book missing one of its staples. "*The Collected Works of the Poet Jeremiah Blenkinsop, Aged 13-and-Three-Quarters.* Much as I regret that we must collect such ephemeral dross: file under Adolescent Verse. Do I make the task at hand clear? Take the volume, examine its cover, file in the appropriate section."

I nodded.

"Under no circumstances do you *open the book*. Is that clear?"

When I was late in responding, he peered at me. "You are not a curious boy are you? I insist on no aspirations, no predilections. Books are not to be read."

"I haven't read a word since my GCSEs, sir."

He smiled. I suppressed a shudder. His teeth were spotted, like the acid foxing on old paper.

In the round window of the door directly behind the Librarian, a face appeared. It was a wide, flat face, that of a rag doll's, or a scarecrow's—the look emphasized further by thick stitches that shut his eyes. The door opened to admit the lumpish creature. Behind it, I saw a vista: not the Library stretching away but a courtyard at night. A mound of books burned and the silhouettes of men watched from below scarlet flags. At the sound of a bugle, each figure raised their right arms high in salute.

The Librarian noted how I stared. "1943 Common Era," he said in a grave tone. "So many books lost forever. We were understaffed—had been since the Great Pandemic."

The rag-doll creature unloaded an armful of still-smoldering books onto the case before turning back to the door. The Librarian stopped it. "This is a Collector," he said, then added, squinting at the nametag sewed on his chest, "Gadzooks."

"Why are his eyes sewn shut?"

The Librarian scowled. "That's only a metaphor." He squinted at me. "You know...symbolic? *Not real?*" He sighed and bent an arm around my shoulder. "Gadzooks, this is Thomas Hardy. Passive voice, mind you. He's our new Indexer."

Gadzooks bowed his head.

"I trust you'll show him the ropes," said the Librarian, "and then to his chambers at the end of the day." He picked up the next book on the shelf. "Misguided Pornography," he said, then placed it into my hands and shuffled away.

So:

I worked, for an indeterminate number of hours, filing away the books as they were deposited on the stands for my inspection. I saw many more Collectors, barging in and out of their respective doors, carrying armfuls of books; through the frames, I caught glimpses of a multitude of places—a sun-baked Jerusalem, a Scottish highland under water, the underwear-strewn floor of a teenager's bedroom. 1943 remained where it was even as the others changed; clearly there was much work to be done there. Gadzooks lumbered around gloomily beside me, pointing in the right direction for each department: "Censored Tracts? By the fountain. Suicide? Fourth on

your left. Hard Drive Failure? Up the ladders by Rejected First Novels."
His gentle voice belied his maimed face.

Occasionally on my journeys I would spy the rats. One might dash close and spit out a forgotten word at me—"Nidgery! Boyborygmus!"— then skitter away back beneath the stacks. Gadzooks grunted and chased them away. "They seem to like you," he said.

And then:

The day closed, Collectors unloaded their last piles and vanished. All but Gadzooks, who gestured for me to follow him. I did so, because I *was* a curious boy, and let him lead me into the deep warren of the Library. We arrived at a rickety spiral staircase at the back of Reformation Sermons. The small room at the top was drafty and sparsely furnished, nothing much more than an unmade bed and a little writing table.

"Your room," said Gadzooks.

I thanked him, expecting him to leave. Instead he hovered in the doorway, wringing his massive and scarred hands.

"Yes?" I asked.

"Sometimes at night, we—well, I wondered if you might like to come…to a party?"

And then:

A trio of Collectors recited couplets from *Love's Labour's Won*, regaling each other with smutty double entendres. In another corner, a gaggle of Collectors poured over Byron's diaries, pausing frequently to *ooh* and *ahh*. Another group gathered in armchairs, pouring absinthe over sugar cubes into their glasses, and repeating lines to each other from Rimbaud's *La Chasse Spirituelle*. "Welcome to the Speakeasy." Gadzooks moved with a bit of mirth.

He led me to the bar, introducing me to those we passed on the way, a series of names—Tango, Philtrum, Esperanza, Pushkin—that I immediately failed to correctly attribute to their proper owners. "This is Tom, the new Indexer," he said, and they all earnestly shook my hand and recited couplets for me by way of introduction.

"Whiskey," said Gadzooks at the bar. "You do drink whiskey?"

I felt bold. "Naturally." A glass was pressed into my hand.

Perched on a bar stool atop a table, there was another boy, who looked older than me because of his long silvery hair. He played an elegant tune on the violin. "From the Library of Music across the Silent Canyon." Gadzooks caught me looking, and perhaps mistook the expression on my face. "They sneak across when the Librarian isn't looking. That tune he's playing—Mozart and Salieri's *Per la Ricuperata Salute di Ophelia*. One of their prize possessions." But I wasn't thinking of a boy from the halls of lost music; instead, I was remembering a boy from a place far more ordinary and humdrum, though his fingers were no less nimble on the strings.

Still—he was a long way away, and I was here, in the Library, and that was the price I had paid.

They refilled my glass a second, then a third time, and I gladly accepted.

The door burst open and two Collectors entered, flanking a man covered entirely by a threadbare blanket. The door safely closed behind him, he threw off his covering, and spread his arms; he was greeted with a cheer. At first glance he appeared emaciated, almost consumptive, resembling a child's pipe-cleaner puppet, but he had a flamboyant assertiveness that belied the wispiness of his physical presence. "Ladies and gentlethings, I am *here*! Quite enough of the sad songs, don't you think?"

The musician switched to a guitar and launched into a rendition of David Bowie's "Jean Genie," though this version of the lyrics weren't those Tom remembered; a lost version, he supposed, like everything else here. The song seemed to prompt a sea-change in the party; a Collector with beautiful silver stitching climbed up beside him and swayed her hips, the bartender began acrobatically tossing bottles, the patrons starting to turn around the dancefloor with a newly giddy energy.

"That's more like it," said the man, sauntering to the bar. "And, why *hello* to *you*! Gadzooks, who might this handsome fellow be?"

"Tom—the new Indexer," said Gadzooks.

Although I had known the man was referring to me, I feigned surprised.

"A shame—one must never fall for an Indexer; the lamps are lit, but there's never anyone home." The man seized a glass from the bar, and tapped me on the nose. "Lovely you might be…but I require a tryst to possess a modicum of intelligence. What comes out of a mouth is just as vital as what goes in." He gave me a lingering look and then left for the swell of partiers.

"Who's he?"

Gadzooks looked at me as if I'd spat on his paws. "Jean Genet. We recovered the original *Notre Dame des Fleurs*. The Librarian has no idea."

Genet perched himself atop a suitcase in the centre of the room, thumbing theatrically through a sheaf of papers in his hand. "Shall I *read?*" he called out to the crowd, who cheered and held their drinks aloft. "Very well, very well. *'I wanted to swallow myself by opening my mouth very wide and turning it over my head…'* Oh, this is one of my favourite bits! I remembered it word for word—got this one just right!"

Gadzooks handed me another glass. "That's Hemingway's suitcase that he's standing on," he said, with great import.

When I did not react with awe, he sighed and abandoned me.

I didn't remain alone for long.

Genet plucked at my shirt-sleeve. "Remarkably, I find it easier as the night wears on to ignore your lack of discursive faculties. Animals rut, and *they* cannot reason."

I sipped from my glass, holding it as a meagre barricade between myself and him. I had been with men. I preferred it. But never with a Genet.

He summoned two tall conical glasses from the barman, and placed a slotted spoon across each one, on which he placed a sugar cube. His fingers—contrary to his otherwise louche presence—were long and nimble, executing his actions with quiet delicacy. I found the practiced nature of his preparations reassuring.

Absinthe trickled over the cube, dissolving the sugar, and pooling in the bottom of the glass. Genet interlinked his arm through mine, bending it back around to reach his mouth. "Thank goodness you're not Rimbaud," he said before taking a gulp. I sipped and coughed. He laughed. His warm breath traced across my cheek before he kissed me hard. He drank again, and determined, this time, I matched him sip for sip. It lit an emerald fire in my belly.

There were boisterous shouts rippling around the Speakeasy—Genet wheeled around, discarding his empty glass. "What's that? You want me to go on a *night run?*"

I swayed on my stool. "What's a night run?" Was it the longest sentence I had said all day? It felt marvelous.

"Wait and see," said Genet. I caught a glimpse of Gadzooks across the room. He shook his head, and I wondered if the gesture indicated disappointment or a warning. No matter—Genet took my hand and pulled me up. "I'm hearing...'The Ocean to Cynthia' by Walter Raleigh? Any other offers?"

Calls sounded from around the room.

"*The Romance of the Devil's Fart!*" "*Inventio Fortunata!*" "*A Time for George Stavros!*" "*The Poor Man and the Lady!*"

Genet gestured as if he had tasted a bad oyster. "Boring!"

"Plath's *Double Exposure*!"

Genet grinned. "Excellent. Come along, my handsome witling!"

And then:

The overhead gas lamps were extinguished, but a kind of luminescence, much the same lustre as moonlight, emanated from the stitching of the oldest books on the shelves like silvery skeletons. I crouched low.

Genet swaggered ahead of me. I half expected him to burst into song, or start skipping.

At the Index firelight still burned in one door window, casting a lone spot of colour across the flagstones. Genet stood and looked through, waiting for me to catch up. "1943," he said. "I escaped from one hell into another."

He spun on his heel. "Just through that door and a few streets away there is a room above a tavern. And in that room is a bed with springs that sing as you fuck. Would you like to discover conjugating?"

A rat scurried. I jumped, startled, which he mistook for virginal anxieties.

Genet laughed. "Relax. We must forge a path to Plath." He led me away from the ring of doors. He seemed to have a knack for moving without eliciting noise; I did not share it. Each footfall of my own rang back at me from the shelves. I fell behind. Genet had vanished, leaving lazy spirals of disturbed dust in the air, and I was on my own.

I anticipated he would be thumbing through the Suicide section, but I arrived and found it solemn. Rather than being alphabetized, here the shelves were organized by methods of dispatch. Most works were incomplete. I traced my finger along the shelves, moving from gas oven to hanging, then finally to razorblade. I squatted, tilted my head to read the spines.

And there it was:

The Sum of All Our Tales. Barnabus Hardy. A single slim volume, it seemed insignificant in the vastness of the Library. I pulled it carefully from the shelf, and ran my fingers over the plain cover. The type was raised; my skin prickled. To hold the book in my hands had been worth the exhausting pretenses of the day.

A tiny voice spoke in the dark, inches from my ear. "Swivet."

I nearly fainted.

I envisioned the Librarian leaning down from the ceiling, his hands armed with a needle and cord with which to sew my eyes shut.

The rat sat bolt upright on the fourth shelf, grooming its snout. "Zamzodden."

I looked around cautiously before uttering "Rumblegumption." The sheer delight of multiple syllables, held dammed up inside me all day, burst onto my tongue. I added another for good measure. "Falstaffian."

It paused and cocked its head. Shiny black eyes stared at me. "Anopisthograph."

I thought for a second. "Sardoodledom."

The rat twitched its nose and long whiskers and dashed away, throwing back over its scaly fine tail a disgruntled, "Ninnyhammer." It dislodged a book, which fell with a ponderous thud.

"Well now, my handsome library boy. This is a surprise." Genet was leaning casually against Shotgun/A–G, watching me. He stepped close to me. In the moonlight, it was almost possible to describe his gaunt face as handsome. "I was injurious in my dismissal of your mind. Hiding such an"—he reached out and grabbed at the crotch of my trousers—"impressive vocabulary would be grounds for"—he squeezed and I gasped (truth be told, I was hard, rigid, *tumescent* then, both by the wickedness of the man and my discovery)—"termination."

I stepped back and he released me. His scuffed shoe nudged the fallen book. *Double Exposure*. "Of course," I said. "We should go back."

He tsked. "Say it right."

I sighed. "It would be auspicious for us to return to the Speakeasy before our mischief is discovered by a certain overseer." Somewhere within me a door opened.

THE LIBRARIAN FOUND me on the morning of my second day's employment hungover and only a few breaths short of whimpering at every book deposited by the Collectors for me to index.

"How's our young man doing?" he said, unfolding his papery frame from between the stacks.

Behind him, Gadzooks mumbled something. He had barely glanced at me beyond the necessary since the night before, when Genet and I had burst into the Speakeasy out of breath and disheveled and sweaty.

"Fine," I said, enunciating the single syllable with care.

"Tremendous, tremendous," he said, rubbing his endpapers together. "The Index is looking pleasingly sparse. Fine job, fine job." He paused, mid-flow, and looked around, wrinkling his nose. "Hmmm."

And:

"*Hmmmmm.*"

I rubbed my bleary eyes. "What's wrong?"

Gadzooks looked away.

The Librarian took a deep breath which expanded his torso like an accordion. "Something smells amiss," he said. "No. Something smells... *missing.*"

I risked a glance over his shoulder, to where the slim pink spine of *Double Exposure* sat on the shelf.

The Librarian sniffed again. "Most incomprehensible." He departed, dragging his long coat on the ground, which rather than wiping them bare instead lined the flagstones with dust in his wake.

⁓⁓⁓

I FRETTED ALL the day. Shelving volume after volume of lost books, I slipped more than a few times on the cold brass ladders. Behind texts, the rats devoured the deracinated and the archaic. Gadzooks labored next to me, but he still avoided conversation.

That night he did not invite me back to the Speakeasy. I didn't mind: I had other things to occupy my time. Before he had been smuggled back to 1943, Genet had pressed the worn copy of *Our Lady of the Flowers* into my arms, suggesting that it might make good bedtime reading, and departing with a lascivious wink. (Thinking on it later, his precise words had been, "Take this and think of me in bed," which I supposed wasn't quite the same thing.)

And so it was for a week or so. The Librarian would appear unbidden and unnoticed, sniffing the air before vanishing, leaving me to dreary tasks—filing the assembled works of a seven-volume fantasy epic into Doubt , box after box stuffed into Teenage Diaries, navigating the complex organization of Pantos/Variations/Peter Pan.

Gadzooks had been correct about the rats' fondness for me; they would appear amongst whatever shelf I was tending. "Anopisthograph!" said one in particular. I was convinced it was the very same rodent with which I had exchanged words on the night run. "You've already had that one," I said, and shooed it away.

The next day I saw the Librarian sniffing around the display that featured famous luggage—the Library must have had other workers, still unseen, who tended to the glass-enclosed exhibitions of the detritus of authors—and with that long finger tapped by Hemingway's suitcase. I was thankful that—for tonight at least—Genet's manuscript was not hidden within as it usually was, with such fragrant prose that the Librarian could not have failed to scent its presence.

Yet, for all his strange behavior, the Librarian didn't seem to once suspect I possessed an intellect.

Eventually Gadzooks thawed, and reappeared at my bedroom door. "Would you like to—y'know...?"

At the Speakeasy, Genet regaled the crowd from atop the suitcase. (I wondered what had Hemingway done to Genet to deserve such roughshod disregard for his possessions, and eventually asked him; he said only "The man is famous for writing about a fish. Not a whale but a fish.") Genet greeted me loudly. "Witling! I don't suppose you have my book on you? I've drunk enough to chase away the memory of what I wrote ages ago. That I can remember my own name is a wonder."

He pirouetted drunkenly, and toppled over. He chuckled. "Perhaps I shall just be Jean tonight and let Genet stay on the shelf."

I helped him to the bar. I arranged two glasses, placed spoons over them, and a sugar cube atop each. Genet watched my hands as I poured the absinthe over it.

"Why do you leave it here?" I said.

"It? Pronouns are the weakest of words. Even an adverb has more panache."

I leaned into him. He thought I meant to kiss him and I moved at the last moment so my lips touched his ear. "Your book," I whispered into it, and felt Genet press vigorously against me; after all, what words could be more seductive to a writer? "They smuggle you in, they smuggle you out— couldn't you take it with you?"

Genet held my face in his hands and blinked a while. "A first draft—a mere masturbatory fantasy. It belongs right here, one more lost book. It's a dirty rag for my spent fantasies, written in the throes. What was published is superior." He frowned. "At least, that's what the Collectors say. I've only sold..." He let go of me and began to count on his fingers but quickly lost his way. "Well, not many, but they tell me that one day—"

I kissed him. Our teeth clicked and thankfully parted. We had yet to even drink the sugared absinthe but I found his mouth so pleasing that I did not notice someone tugging at the cuff of my trousers.

No, not someone. A rising wave of noise broke the familiar chatter. The minstrel faltered in his song; the assembled revelers bloomed into panic. The single rat at my feet let go of the fabric and leapt for my knee, claws digging through my trousers into the skin. "Anopisthograph. *Anopisthograph!*" and then at the doors the noise crescendoed with a tumult of panicked rats spilling through and across the floor.

Genet cursed. I shouted, "The Librarian!"

And:

"Run!"

And:

We dashed, and it was hard not to laugh with how Genet smiled as we escaped. I pulled him towards the Index; he pulled me towards the staircase; in the tension between the two we spun in each other's arms as if we were dancing. In the end, I did not deny him another night spent in my bed. I shut the door fast, almost crushing the rat that scampered in and took refuge in my writing desk.

"Ow," Genet said as we collapsed onto the mattress. "How can you sleep? What is in this? Horsehair?" He wet my lips. "Have you ever eaten *cheval*?" He groped me. "It's an acquired taste."

Authors were indeed.

———～———

I NIBBLED ON the sweet rolls they fed us. I had pocketed an extra one for Gadzooks.

"The last Indexer would give me his meals," Gadzooks said as he chewed. "He never came to the Speakeasy. He wasted away in his room."

"Lost in a book?" I said.

"Oh, no. He didn't dare read. I think that's why he faded to nothing. Every time he spoke he lost the words in his head." Gadzooks rapped on his misshapen skull. "If you don't replace that with something...even feelings, then you stop."

I had so many words in my head but I wasn't sure if there would be enough feelings if I lost my vocabulary.

A rat scurried into the middle of the Index.

"Anopisthograph."

And then:

"Thomas Hardy," said the Librarian. His fingers traced down my cheek and neck, and far from the brittle dryness I had imagined, they felt sharp, as if they might leave a trail of papercuts on my skin. "Quite fascinating. Such a faultless resume should have been enough to make me doubt. Clever boy...I was lulled by the passive voice. I should have checked your references."

The rat turned slowly, almost apologetically, and backed away beneath the stacks. I sighed.

"Indeed," I said. "That would have been prudent of you. Judicious. Shrewd. Discerning, even."

The Librarian winced.

Gadzooks attempted to fade away into the shelves. "Ah-ah-ah," said the Librarian. He beckoned Gadzooks closer with a crooked finger. "Surreptitious sneaking—I'm afraid I cannot allow that."

With one hand the Librarian covered my face. I feared he meant to smother me; his skin against my nose smelt of spilt ink, the emaciated palm against my mouth made me choke with its taste of glue.

Then I heard Gadzooks scream.

The Librarian released me. All that remained of my Collector friend was a large hessian sack and some old wooden toys. A yo-yo stopped spinning, its thread a last umbilical cord.

"Don't think of it as murder," said the Librarian. "Think of it as a *metaphor* for murder."

I swallowed.

"The old beak warned me. Something missing. Boys before you sneaked into Unwarranted Adventures or Illegal Pornography. But you went *there*." He gestured at the door. Neither of us needed to say aloud the section.

"What am I to do with you?" He plucked from his coat pocket a book that made my heart sink. "And more importantly, what am I to do with *this*, found in your mattress?" He inspected the spine. "*The Sum of All Our Tales*, by Barnabus Hardy. Father? Grandsire? Brother?" He leered. "Lover?"

"Father."

"Pity," the Librarian said. "You must have been so young. The age when you were warned about razorblades in Halloween candy—not the bathtub."

I stiffened.

"No note. Just his final manuscript. Did the literary world mourn his loss?"

"Stop."

The Librarian shut the book hard enough that his clothes rippled. "By all means. But tell me, young Hardy, have you ever heard the word 'deaccession.' Not so common any more, which is a shame." He opened the grate of the nearest gas lamp. I screamed at him to cease, to desist, but still he poked one corner of my father's only book into the flame.

He dropped the papers curling into ash as the fire spread.

"A lesson, a dear lesson in realizing what a lost book is," he said.

The Librarian's immense arm pressed me back, anticipating me wrestling free, though I didn't know what I would do even if I could escape his grasp—perhaps throw myself on the fire in hopes of extinguishing it, rescuing the scorched remnants of the manuscript from the ashes? But it would be futile: it does not take long for poetry to burn. Verses are highly flammable—it's because they were dear fuel in someone's imagination.

"Consider that a written warning—obviously it cannot be filed away, but...well, I am a practical man. With the elder Hardy's *esprit* in ashes perhaps you will no longer want to open a book again." The Librarian straightened his bow-tie. "You may take the rest of the day off. If I find you at the Index in the morning, I will know your decision to stay with us. At a reduction in salary."

Perhaps my gaze was too wet with tears to set his retreating backside ablaze.

I trudged to my room. The Librarian's search had torn apart bed and desk. I sat down on the floor and wrapped my arms around my knees.

Something climbed up my back and to my ear. "Empressement."

I stroked the rat with two fingers. It chirped and then nipped gently at my earlobe. "Frantling." It leapt to the ground and ran towards the door, stopped and looked over its shoulder at me and squeaked. "Usative."

I followed it through the maze of the Library. The lighting where we tread was dimmer. I had not been everywhere. Some subjects were unknown to me. Down one path I saw a familiar figure reclining on the penultimate shelf devoid of books. The rat scampered away as Genet peered up at me.

"Sometimes I do not go back," he said, looking chagrinned. He handed me the book his head had been resting on. *A Scheme for a New Alphabet and a Reformed Mode of Spelling* by Benjamin Franklin. "How he loved whores. Once they brought him to the Speakeasy and all he wanted to do was steal a boy's glasses and find the door leading to ancient Lesbos."

Genet stretched, a gesture that was part exercise and part pretense to embrace me suddenly. "I doubt more than a handful of authors end up in Wasted Graphemes so it is safe here." He touched my face, my cheeks. "Ahh, but you recently had a terrible encounter with the wicked regent, I see."

I told him of my father, of his poetry. It had been years since I spoke of being away at school when they found his body, of life at the homes of distant relatives who could not look at me without seeing a debt to family they wanted little part of. My last name was all I had of my father's until I learned of the Library.

"You must feel his loss keenly."

I shrugged. "My father is a long-closed chapter."

"Ah, I see. The book, then—you mourn the loss of the book."

"Something like that."

"We shall toast to both the man and his book at the Speakeasy tonight," Genet said, laying a hand on my shoulder.

I rested my cheek against Genet's fingers. "Actually—I had another thought. If you don't mind."

And finally:

1943 smelt of fire and paper. Feet stamped in unison, close by; voices intoned, "Heil Hitler!"; the books of Germany burnt in the courtyard, a gout of gluttonous smoke bearing their words into a sky already thick with many volumes. I backed away from the bonfire as fast as I could, pushing through the crowds that railed against the soldiers, shouldering my way through and away. Away from the crowd, away from the noise. Ducking into an alleyway, I paused to breathe, heaving against the damp wall.

One hand was in Genet's as I pulled him along behind me; the other clutched tight to the worn leather handle of Hemingway's suitcase. Several street corners away, I pulled Genet into an alleyway. "You said you had a room near here—the room above the tavern, where the bed-springs sing?"

He pressed against me, mouth close to my ear. "How forward of you—I like it."

He led me a few streets further, arriving at a narrow doorway in the shadow of rotting tenements, the tavern windows the only warm thing in sight. He fumbled with a key, whilst I wrapped my arms tight around myself and shivered. Away from the book-burning, the city was freezing. Eventually, Genet persuaded the door to open, and he led me up rickety stairs to a room reminiscent of my chambers at the Library: sparse, furnished with a bed and a writing table. The greying sheets were balled on a threadbare mattress, and the table was strewn with papers. The floorboards creaked and wobbled beneath our feet.

There was a murine flicker by the doorway, and a scaly tail darted between my feet. A whispered word floated back in its wake. "Anopisthograph!"

I sat on the bed, still shivering. Genet watched the rat depart and closed the door. The sound of the key in the lock released me; the tension of weeks in the Library, fumbling around under the Librarian's watchful eye, drained away. I sank back.

Genet lay down beside me, his skin warm against mine. He smelt of absinthe and book dust; I had the urge to bury my face in his chest, but my bone-weary limbs wouldn't co-operate.

"Will you read to me?" I said.

He arched an eyebrow, and nuzzled against my shoulder. "My handsome witling—foreplay, is it?"

"This isn't foreplay."

"I have nothing to—"

"The suitcase."

The bed-springs sang as he arose; I heard the grate of the lock opening, and the rustle of papers, then Genet returned to me with the contents of the suitcase in his hands: the first manuscript of *Our Lady of the Flowers*, where I had returned it when I had finished.

Genet smiled faintly. "My slack-handed first draft—but if you insist…" He cleared his throat, and raised the first page to his eyes. "'*Wiedmann appeared before you in the five o'clock edition*,'" he began.

"No," I said. "Turn it over."

He did as I asked, squinting at the fresh scrawl that coated the reverse of his pages.

"Sorry about my handwriting," I said. There had not been light in my Library chambers, or much space with which to work. My letters had been shrunk to the smallest I could manage to cram in everything I needed to write on the pale underside of Genet's own pages.

Genet sat up on the bed, crossed his legs, looked from the page, to me, and to the page again. He cleared his throat theatrically. "'*The Sum of All Our Tales*, by Barnabus Hardy'," he began.

IN SEARCH OF STARS

IT STARTS WITH a secret place, as many stories do.

On the outside, it is a laundrette. The printed letters on the plate glass are peeling, but still legible: *Whites*. Below it, a list of numbers is scraped away, leaving the cost of a wash a mystery. Occasionally, I pass it in daylight. During the day, the door is propped open by a rickety stool, and I peer inside. It is filled by graying women with rumpled, dishcloth skin who talk quietly amongst themselves about their children and their husbands.

Once, I dare to take my clothes there to wash. An innocent errand, I reason; no shadow of suspicion could fall on a man simply doing his laundry. This does not prevent the women from eyeing me as if the mere presence of a man amongst them is suspect. To compound this, I am unprepared, and am forced to swap a nickel for a palmful of powder, a foolish error met with sad tuts.

As I empty the powder into the drum, I study the door in the corner.

It takes me several weeks to get the courage to return at night. The front door is no longer propped open advertising itself, but it hangs ajar, distinctly not *closed*. Inside it is dark, and quiet—none of the machines are awake. But men pass in and out of the doorway with regularity, briefly spilling light from the door in the back across the machines; they are not carrying clothes.

I do not know whatever password it is that would grant me access, and neither do I have the will to ask. Perhaps were I to be bold—simply walk up to the door in the back of the laundrette and go in—I might be able to talk my way upstairs. But when my foot breaks the curb to cross the street, my stomach churns, noxious with fear, and I step back.

Tonight, it is cold, and so I cross the alley to the diner. The waitress there—a pretty girl, like the small-town ones from back home—knows me by name now. "Usual, Albert?" she says, and I enjoy being someone who has a "usual." I imagine that perhaps she does too—this is not the sort of diner with regulars. I sit in a booth by the window and drink coffee, covertly watch the laundrette, and the men that come and go. I don't know what I imagine is on the other side of the door, but I know I want to find out. Perhaps the waitress knows—it seems unlikely that she works here night after night and doesn't have some idea what is going on opposite. The thought makes me uncomfortable, but I remind myself there is nothing wrong with a man drinking coffee—or a man washing his clothes.

There is someone waiting outside the laundrette. He leans against the window-frame, making insolent eye-contact with any man who enters. His boldness—starkly opposite to my own reticence—tugs at me; I dowse the feeling with coffee and look at the chipped table-top. The jukebox is playing music—rock and roll, tinny and weak. It clanks and whirs when the records are changed.

After a while, I can feel—in that skin-pricking way that comes from a sense other than sight or hearing—that the man is looking at me. I chance a look, and meet his eyes.

The waitress is serving an old man in the corner, her back turned. I gather my coat, and step out into the cold. At the end of the road the city exhales a blare of cars, distant music, police whistles, but its cacophony falters at the corner. Our street is still like midwinter, and the man waits for me in the middle.

We exchange words. It doesn't matter what they are. Suffice it to say, I have spoken similar words before; I am a man who knows their real meanings, just as he.

The walk is a few wet streets away. He talks, and I interject enough answers into the conversation to keep it from stagnating. I keep a proprietary distance from him, glance nervously at the darkened windows around us, any one of which might contain a watcher who knows my face—*I saw that scientist from round the corner*, they might say, *and you'll never guess what?* He tells me he is a musician—saxophone, because all the other boys in this city are playing guitar, he says. I picture the pads of his fingers stroking the keys, and the cold reed leeching the moisture from his bottom lip.

I ask him if he's ever played *inside*, meaning the secret place above the laundrette, hoping he'll say yes so he can describe it to me. He shakes his head. "I've never been in," he says. We are at the foot of my building, and I fumble in my pocket for keys. He leans in close to me. "Have you?"

"I don't know the password."

A second, then he laughs. "Password? You don't need a password." He looks me up and down. He is mentally reconfiguring me from a man of experience to a naïf who imagines cloak-and-dagger, film-noir secrecy. He hesitates.

"Come in," I say.

I let him climb the stairs first. With the door closed, my stomach spins in anticipation, as if permission is granted by the cloak of privacy—nobody to see us now, not even if I were to pull his clothes off right here on the stairs.

But I don't—I jam my hands in my pockets and follow his shadow upwards.

At the top, he looks around the detritus of my apartment, and asks me what I do. "I'm an artist," I say, which is not *exactly* a lie. He looks for a light-switch, but I point him through the door to the bedroom. I pull dustclothes over my work, then follow him. He is already naked on the bed, his clothes a gray pool by the nightstand.

He tastes of something I can't describe.

Afterwards he rolls to the cold side of the bed, pulling the damp sheets with him. He looks appraisingly at me, and he is re-evaluating me all over again—perhaps tallying up the number of men that added up to the expertise I had displayed. He looks at me for some time. An endless parade, he must conclude—all those other men.

My chest congeals into a thick, black, furtive shame, soul-deep.

I offer him a cigarette, but he refuses, rolls onto his back and closes his eyes. At first the lids are tense, like a child pretending to be asleep after curfew, and then they relax. He breathes slowly.

I place the cigarette between my lips, but leave it unlit. Tentative dawn is creeping over the horizon, silvering the rooftops. I left the curtains undrawn when I left earlier, the window fully open—not a conscious choice, but it fortuitous: the window grates on opening, loud enough to wake someone sleeping.

I arise quietly, pad into the other room, and pull aside the dustclothes. The paint is where I left it, viscous and silver in its vat. Its clean, sterile smell stings my eyes. I open a drawer, select the right brush—hog bristle, which is soft and delicate, and will not wake him.

On the bed, I kneel, apply the paint gently. I cover him in reverse order of the skin touched by my tongue and fingers, turning it warm pink to cold blue. By the time I have covered his chest and thighs, he is lighter, rising up from the bed. When I cover his arms, they rise above him, as if he is reaching for an embrace. I run the brush to his feet.

When I am finished, he floats a foot above the bed, rising. When I lay my hand on his belly, he is light as a feather, and my touch guides him across the room as if he were a leaf on a still pond. He passes below the lintel soundlessly, not waking even when his steady ascendance nudges his shoulder against the frame.

My hands on his cheeks anchor him, like a child clutching a balloon that tugs against its string. His feet lift, inverting him. His eyes open when I kiss him gently on the lips. He smiles, and I release him.

He turns as he floats up, alternating blue then pink in the watery dawn, and then is higher than I can see any longer, beyond my sight with all the others.

I lie down on the bed, pull the still-warm bedsheets around me, and light my cigarette. The smoke rises in clouds, and vanishes as if it was never there.

THE STORY CONTINUES with the morning after, as many stories do.

Firm block capitals in my diary prevent from lying abed long into the afternoon: I have an appointment to make. I meet Eugene in the foyer of the Mayfair. I wonder exactly how much Eugene has been told about my present circumstances, and whether his choice of venue is a deliberate statement of his success. It would be just like Eugene, though it would be intended without malice.

He presses whiskey into my hand, and greets me as if we have never been apart. "Such a surprise when old Selwyn told me you were in LA!" he says. He ushers me to an armchair, and gestures for the discretely hovering waiter to refill our glasses. Eugene has aged well—with a thin, fashionable moustache that I am pained to admit suits him well. I briefly wonder if our mutual acquaintance—Selwyn Cavor, the starchily British professor who pushed us through five years of boarding school—is pushing for something other than the reunion of old school friends; it is he, after all, who told me about the laundrette.

But then Eugene tells me about his wife—an ice-queen blonde, so he says, by the name of Marilyn, though aren't all the blondes called Marilyn these days? Perhaps Selwyn is not as calculated as I imagine.

"So, how are you ticking, Mister C?" he asks—habitually, for this was how Eugene had opened nearly every conversation between us since we were both eleven and meeting for the first time in a draughty dormitory. "Finally cracked and come out chasing stars in the city of angels, have we?"

I try to smile warmly, and shake my head. "Not exactly," I say, and try to explain something about my work. I tell him about the two publications that took my reports. I fail to mention that my laboratory consists of a worktop hauled from a garbage tip, and basins purloined from the ruins of a barbers that had burnt down. Those particular details do not jibe well with the foyer of the Mayfair, or the two-hundred-dollar whiskey.

"And what is it you're trying to build?" he asks, though his attention is on the whiskey bottle as he tops it up.

"Space travel," I say, though this hardly covers it.

"Smart boy!" Eugene says. "Space—they're all at it. Give it ten years, and we'll get there ourselves. But I tell you what though—Hollywood is damn well going to get there first."

I think of my saxophonist, turning lazily on the edge of the atmosphere. Out loud, I point out that Hollywood has been going to space for some time. I remind him of the Saturday afternoons we would sneak from school to the nearest town, and the showing in particular of *Woman in the Moon*, sucking down ice cream floats and salted caramels.

He waves it away. "Oh, Hollywood has moved on since then. Special effects!" He is practically shouting, and heads are turning. I shrink in my seat. "That's what the studios are excited about. And they want everything to be *two* hundred per cent accurate at all times. *Suspension of disbelief*, and all that. That's why they hired me—an 'expert consultant,' that's me."

He leans forward. I realize he is already a little drunk.

"Do you know what one of the directors asked me—he asks, 'What does space *smell* like?'"

"Goodness," I say. "Why would they need to know that? It's only film."

"Some new technology they're working on—a *full* experience, you know? Squirt the audience with water, shake the seats, all that lot. And they want to use scent. It's what we've all been waiting for—not only can you *watch* cinema, you'll be able to *smell* it."

He looks pleased with himself. The ice clinks in his glass as he waves it.

"What *does* space smell like?" I ask.

He considers. "Gunpowder," he says. "By all accounts."

LATER, I GO to the laundrette. The gray women look at me once when I enter, then disregard me. I am an insignificant little man encroaching on their world, and not worth the energy of observation when there are hampers of clothes to be washed. I run a finger along the grimy edge of a washer, and my fingertip comes away blackened. It satisfies me; in a perverse way, the laundrette, with its washed-out women and secret doorways, makes me feel scrubbed clean of all the gilt decadence Eugene has subjected me to that day.

I do not look at the door in the back, although I itch to go through it.

This visit is an inoculation: a brief sojourn in the laundrette during the day and then I will not be tempted to return after dark. I will remain in my apartment for the night hours; a small amount of exposure that defends against a greater illness.

I empty the bag of clothing into the drum. At the bottom are the saxophonist's discarded clothes. Turning away so as to go unobserved by the women, I press his undergarments to my face and inhale. I half expect the smell of gunpowder but of course that is absurd—his clothes remained with me. I smell only cotton, soap, and the faint linger of sweat.

I drop them in the drum, and pay my cents. The machine starts up, spiralling our clothes together in a wet rush.

In the Lucky Seven diner, I order coffee. By the time it has arrived, I know the inoculation is not enough; I will be returning tonight.

The waitress squeezes into the booth opposite me. "I have a half-hour break," she says.

"Right," I say, not quite sure why she's telling me this.

She bites her lip; I recognize this from movies, the coquettish seduction. Only hers is awkward, as if she isn't used to being this forward. Perhaps she isn't: she works amongst bottom-squeezes and drawled *darlin*'s all day; I doubt she ever has to ask. "I have half an hour," she says. "I was thinking you could take me home and fuck me."

I notice a grease-spot on her lapel, just a few inches above her bare breast. It is just to the left of the name-tag: 'Marilyn' in uncertain capitals. It makes me think of Eugene's ice-blonde wife, and his big job up amongst the stars. Eugene would say yes without hesitation.

I could just say no, I tell myself, and then, *inoculation*.

Afterwards, she looks around the detritus of my room and asks what I do. "I'm an engineer," I tell her, which is not *exactly* a lie, and go to wash myself in the dirty sink. She remains on the bed, smoking the cigarette I offer her. Naked, I had been able to feel a week of diner grease on her skin. She tasted of the bitter coffee at the bottom of a pot, and my usual expertise had deserted me.

I wonder if she washes her clothes at the laundrette. I feel the usual nausea arising, though it is a different kind; this is a physical nausea in the pit of my stomach, as if I have swallowed something rotten.

"Good old American filth," Eugene said to me earlier, as we were leaving the Mayfair, him paused on the curb to hail a cab, me turning my coat collar up for the long walk home. "I'm tired of all the glamour. You know— mansions, cars and movie stars. The whole city's coming down with a case of shallow—even my Marilyn's picking it up; won't fuck without doing her makeup first."

He wanted me to take him out in *my* parts of the city, with all the implications of what *my* part of the city entailed. "Well—you're here amongst it all, aren't you? Think it's about time you and I went out on the town. I want some *squalor*, you know what I'm saying?"

I imagine he'd be pleased with me right now.

I walk her back to the laundrette with five minutes of her break to spare. On the way, she tells me that she picked me because I didn't *ask*. All day long, men suggest things, demand things of her. But I never did, and she liked that. I ignore the bitter irony. We part in the middle of the street, her kissing me quickly on the cheek.

In the washing machine drum, I find my white clothes stained blue. I hold up a once-pale vest and wring pastel water from it. One of the gray women looks at me and shakes her head. I bundle my clothing back into my knapsack, and leave the saxophone player's articles—dark blue shirt, pants, underwear—in a sopping pool at the bottom of the lost and found basket.

Two weeks until the threat of itch to visit the laundrette again outweighs awkwardly encountering Marilyn in the Lucky Seven. Sitting at my work-bench, listlessly tracing paint along a series of pencils so that they float and turn in the air, I reason with myself. If I am to risk facing the woman with whom I have had less than satisfactory relations with—and not seen since—then it must be for a greater gain than watching from afar.

The queasy light of the diner is an oasis that beckons—but tonight I ignore it, although I look long enough to realize that Marilyn is not to be seen. It does nothing to calm me; my hair, still damp from the cold shower I took before leaving, hangs in clammy lumps against my forehead. I feel unwashed—wrapped up tight against the night, I am immediately overheated, sweat springing up in the folds of my body. I cannot imagine anyone wanting to touch me.

"There is no password," the saxophonist told me. No secret or phrase: just the confidence to walk through the door.

I end up in the diner, breathing heavily to calm my pulse. There is a stinging pain in the palms of my hands that spreads up my arms and worms its way into my ribcage. The laundrette stares balefully at me across the street.

An older waitress materializes beside me. She is dumpy and string-haired. Her name-tag says Marilyn. Eugene was right—*every woman in Los Angeles...*

She fills my cup and putters on to the next booth to serve a hulk of a man who I think I faintly recognize. He is looking down at a newspaper spread on the table, his face lost in a tangle of beard, but when Marilyn the Second departs, he looks up at me. He is round faced, and despite the beard, oddly boyish. "Not brave enough, huh?" he says to me.

"Excuse me?"

He nods over at Whites. "You go in, you come out," he says. "Been there, done that."

The itch in my palm redoubles. "Have you?"

<hr />

HE IS MORE discreet than the saxophonist; he maintains a respectful distance from me as we pass through the streets, hangs back as I open the door, and remains three steps behind me as I climb the stairs. As soon as we cross the threshold, the gentleman vanishes—his hands are on me, yanking away my coat and scrabbling at the clothes beneath. With my shirt tangled over my head he is already moving to touch my body before I am free; his fingertips are rough on my skin, and as his mouth skates down my body, his beard scratches like the wire wool I use to scrub away paint. His teeth nip at my belly.

I back away, lead him to the bedroom. He disrobes as he follows, revealing a heavy-set body swathed in hair, and a stubby penis peeking from the shadow cast by his bulk. The pale light from the window sweeps around the heavy sphere of his stomach, and I am struck by an absurd image of a fast-motion film of light's passage around the moon that I dimly remembered from a visit to the planetarium with Selwyn.

He pushes me onto the bed and straddles me. He is commanding, guiding my hands where he wants them, tangling my fingers in the hair on his chest and thighs, and then as he pins my shoulders with his knees, thrusts my hand behind him where my fingers slide, sweat-slicked, into him. I open my mouth to receive him and for a second I picture myself outside my own body looking down on us—the same position as the watchers I imagine at my windows. The image is clear: this beast of a man, crouched ursine on his haunches over me, my head and shoulders lost in the dark shadow between his legs.

Afterwards, he kisses me.

<hr />

HE DOES NOT go as easily as the saxophonist. Firstly, he awakens. None of the others have ever done this. His legs are already several inches off the bed, the room suffused with the anodyne hospital smell of the paint. My mistake is in selecting my brush; still sore and tender, I find poetic justice in selecting the largest, roughest of them.

Secondly, he struggles. I doubt he comprehends what I am doing to him, but he has awoken in a panic to sensations he doesn't understand, and so he lashes out like the animal I pictured. He strikes a blow across my face, and I fall to the floor, tasting blood in my mouth. The time for gentle artistry is past: I upend the tub. It coats his chest, tiny bubbles bursting amongst the strands of my hirsute canvas. There is blind panic in his eyes as he rises, spittle at the corner of his mouth turning blue where it mixes with the paint. He flails, claws at my sheets, but they can't prevent his ascent and simply rise with him, a useless tether.

I jostle him out of the window, which stands open as always. He clings to my bed-sheet and we reach an impasse—him upside down, fist wrapped tight around the cotton and me at the other end, pulling back with all my strength. For a minute, we remain connected.

Then his fingers open, and he soars up, up to where the air smells of gunpowder.

"Pineapple!" says Eugene. "Goddamn pineapple. Can you believe it?"

Six weeks pass—six weeks in which my frantic scuffle squashes the itch to visit the laundrette, though the image of a door opening to a crowd of men waiting for me slowly recurs nightly in my dreams. Six weeks in which I bury myself in work, in which I dodge the landlord knocking for rent, and in which I write three-quarters of a paper on the gravity-negating properties of an as-yet-unnamed viscous solution of my own devising. Six weeks, and then Eugene.

"Gunpowder is too hard to synthesize, apparently, and anyway— it's not like anyone's going to know. So according to the head honchos of Paramount Pictures, space will smell of pineapple." Eugene is on his third Singapore Sling, and already blurring into intoxication. He speaks at great length about his Hollywood consultation business. He tells me I should come advise on engineering, build robots for the *flicks*. He doesn't understand why I'm mouldering away in a poxy flat in the cheap end of town. I try to explain what I'm working on—tell him about my three-quarters-written paper—but he doesn't listen. He starts talking about space flight again.

In each bar we go to a pattern repeats: the girls flock at first to his expensive suit, gold watch and big tips, and then, when his generosity has dried up and he has done little beyond leerily grope a behind or two, they ghost away to search for more forthcoming targets. And at each bar, he complains that the place is 'too swanky' or 'too bogus' and demands I take him somewhere *real*.

Deep in a whiskey glass in a honky-tonk bar that still carried more than a whiff of speakeasy about it, I watch Eugene flirt with a sour-faced woman leaning against the bar. She is lit by neon, and has a look similar to his: rich, but slumming it for the night. He won't pick her, I know, but flirtation is a habit of his. Even in a single-sex boarding school, he had never had much trouble finding women where he needed them—a couple of the maids, girls from the town. Sneaking back into the dormitory at night, he would describe his latest sexual exploit to me in a low whisper, and I would stiffen under the covers.

One night he claimed to have conquered one of the schoolmistresses— new to the school, and on temporary assignment. One of those long evenings in his study I relayed Eugene's story to Selwyn who laughed quietly, and said, "I don't doubt. Frightful, really—students and teachers." We laughed together, conspiratorial.

Not for the first time, I wonder why Selwyn has thrust Eugene and I back into each other's lives.

If I focus, I begin to wonder if Eugene's heart is really in it tonight. He's effusive with everyone we meet, expounding upon his personal theories of life, love and pleasure, and the opportunity to sneak off and spend himself in a furtive tumble has presented itself on multiple occasions. And yet he seems to be dodging every offer, returning to me with freshly charged glasses. As we descend into that strata of intoxication in which profundity insists itself in half-complete sentences, I wonder if perhaps Eugene fears the same as I: that in the post-orgasmic chill the squalor of a back-alley screw loses its grimy glamour and becomes something furtive and shameful instead. And so he postpones it as long as possible—perhaps indefinitely.

Eventually, there are no more bars to go to—or none that will allow two such stumbling fools entry. Early dawn is pricking the horizon, and, like a magnet, I draw us to the Lucky Seven. My waitress is there—Marilyn the First—glimpsed through the kitchen hatch but I am too drunk to care.

Besides—it has been two months.

We collapse into a booth. Eugene rests his head on the table. I lean against the glass; it is cool and soothing. Across the road, I cannot tell if the laundrette is open or closed—I am too unfocused to make out if the door stands open or not. I suppose even such a place as Whites closes.

"Usual?" I squint up at her. She doesn't sound upset. This is good.

Eugene, hearing a female voice, rears up. He strikes what I imagine he believes is a charming smile. "Darla!" he says. "How pleas—pleas—*pleas*ant to meet you."

I blink. "Darla?"

She taps her name-badge.

"I thought your name was Marilyn?"

She leans in close, ruffles my hair, matronly. "No, darling. I forgot my badge, had to borrow one. But at least you *remembered* my name—I'm flattered."

Darla. Somehow the name changes her. Marilyn is a girl daintily upset when a man does not call her the morning after. Darla takes a man home to screw because she wants to.

She leaves to serve the only other customer in the diner, down the opposite end of the window. I lean into Eugene, and tell him—in a whisper that is almost certainly not really a whisper at all—about what Darla and I did in my bed. I don't know why I did it: I have never been one to brag, but recasting our limp splutter of an encounter as erotic exploit gives me a fraternal thrill I have rarely felt.

Eugene grips my wrists and shakes them victoriously. "Albert, my man," he says. "I *knew* you had it in you."

For a second I see me as he does now: earthy man of the people, slipping it to waitresses on a nightly basis. And then the image bursts like over-inflated bubble-gum as I look past Darla. She is bending over, pouring coffee, and behind her is a noticeboard. *Protest march, singing lessons, artist seeking model, poetry reading* and *MISSING*. Below it a photo of a hulking man, round-faced and boyish despite the beard.

Darla sways past us again. "You boys had a good night, then?"

Eugene reaches out a hand to her, pulls her back to sit on his knee. His fingers snag on her sash. "Darlin', not nearly good enough. Not *yet*..."

For the poster to be here in the Lucky Seven, he must be a regular. *We've all been there*, he said, as if he too had sat for long hours in this diner, getting up the nerve to cross the road. And then there is Marilyn and Darla, who see every man and every face.

Darla looks at me. It isn't a look asking for help, to rescue her from my lairy friend, just a calmly assessing look. Eugene's fingers make it clear what he wants.

I do not ask. I know what she likes.

"I get off in half an hour," she says.

THE STORY ENDS with a decision, as many do.

Darla leaves, and I return to the bed as if she is still there, a cold ghost between Eugene and I. Her female presence granted permission: for our naked bodies to share the same space, for my fingers to touch him, provided mine were not the only ones.

I wonder if this is where he wanted the night to go: his life, so drearily decadent, that the only thing to jolt him out of his drudgery is the taboo touch of a man. Perhaps he had marked me out as an easy target—the sexless boy from school, the one who spent a bit too much time with Professor Cavor.

I realize the room is silent. His snoring has stopped. When I look at him, his eyes are open.

Afterwards, I anchor us both to the bed with the sheets, wrapped around our wrists and fixed loosely to the bedpost. I paint him first, until he has risen, tipped on his side, free of gravity but strung by one rebellious limb to the ground. The alcohol in his veins that deadens him to the feeling of my awkward brush-strokes. He hovers above me, eyes closed, like a statue.

Then, disjointed with my off-hand, I coat myself. I float to meet him, the front of our bodies pressed together, lips close enough to kiss.

I wrestle the knot loose, and we are released. I wrap my arms around him, and press my face into his chest. It is difficult to guide him across the room to the window—I have to kick off against the walls and the ceiling, as one does in deep water.

My feet alight on the windowsill. I push away.

Light breaks across the city. If my phantom watchers in the windows opposite are looking, they will see us as we rise into the sky, one man clinging tight to another as they ascend like balloons that have slipped from your grasp, until the atmosphere becomes rarefied and thin, and breath freezes before our faces. I catch a glimpse of the sun rising over the edge of the world before I close my eyes and rise up, to where the air smells of gunpowder, and men are waiting for me.

GOLDEN HAIR, RED LIPS

I'M NOT IN the photograph. I was off to the side, picture of disinterest, smoking a cigarette, watching passers-by. That was how I passed my days in that part of the century, hovering on the street corner in sight of all those colours. I remember the photographer—button-down shirt, round glasses, mussed hair, the look of someone born away from this city. He was beautiful.

The men were clenched around the window, where the sign had been taped. The photographer's camera clicked, and there they were, stock still in black and white forever. You might have seen the photograph. There's a good chance, now that we good men of the Castro are the immortalised nameless. Books, documentaries—hell, postcards, probably. This photograph was the vanguard, you see. The seraph's trumpet. Bad times, they were a-coming.

The photographer lowered his camera to roll on the film, and I drew close, unobserved. My eye was on one of the men of the gathering, a hand on his waist as I read, but when I stepped into their circle that feeling—that incessant dressing down, dressing up, undressing behind the eyes—drained away.

There were three photographs, close-ups of body parts, inflicted with vicious looking welts, dark and sick. I'd never seen anything like them before, and I'd lived through them all. TB, scarlet fever, influenza—all the greats. Lesions, they're called. Sarcoma. We didn't know that at the time.

Instead, the poster was labelled, in neat felt-tip capitals, "GAY CANCER." The photographs were of the man who had made the poster, whoever who was. These were the symptoms inflicted on him, all over his narrow body. The poster was a warning.

The camera whirred again, and I turned to face the photographer. He snapped another.

I've seen that photograph, although you won't have. I've tossed back my long hair, and I'm looking straight into the camera. My eyes are quietly confident in the shadows of the sockets. I look fabulous. The other men are still behind me, reading the poster. Concern and fear is in their frame, their worried looks at each other. They're all dead now.

"Good morning," I said to the photographer. "If it's not too bold, sir, I'd like to tell you that you are an uncommonly beautiful specimen of manhood."

"I know," he said, and matched my smile. "But I appreciate hearing it in such an English way." He raised the camera, but I put a hand up to block it, lifting it out of his hands. "You're a long way from home, Lord Fauntleroy."

"I always am," I said, "though that's not my name." I circled him, and lifted the camera up to my eye, pressing the button and capturing him in the frame.

In that one, you can see what's not quite clear in that first—more famous—photograph. The words at the bottom of the page. "Be warned," the felt tip letters read. "There's something out there."

———⁓———

THOMAS MOVES HIS head infinitesimally to rest against my cheek. His skin is cool and clammy, and his face is drawn as if the skin has been pulled inch by inch into every crevice of his skull, the muscle melted away. Every movement feels brittle, as if something will break any second. He looks like a skeleton. He's not the only one in the Castro.

I touch my lips briefly to his forehead. "If it's not too bold, sir," I say, throat tight, "I'd like to tell you that you are an *uncommonly* beautiful specimen of manhood."

The lesions are all over his face, crawling steadily closer to his eyes and nose, as if he's drowning slowly in his own rebellious skin.

"I know," he says, a papery whisper on his shrunken tongue. "But it's nice to hear it in—" He chokes, and there is blood on the pillow. "You're a long way from home, Dorian Gray."

"I always am," I say.

His blood was in my mouth when I stalked the Castro later that night. I had kissed him on the lips until he was gone. He sputtered out, and the beep of the machine solidified. The nurse appeared. She was horrified when she saw the blood on my lips—she pushed my head into the sink, and shrieked words at me that I didn't listen to. They were unnecessary for me, but the poor woman couldn't have guessed.

I wasn't the only one lurking in the corridor outside the ward. Others had been marooned there, dead-eyed and confused. I could hear the electronic fanfare of more lives ending, up and down the ward.

It was no different in the Castro—flatlines everywhere, dressed in their tight shirts and jeans, handkerchiefs in their pockets, sunglasses covering their already dead eyes. I moved between them, brushing against their cadaverous skins, imagining the lesions crawling on their bodies, squirming to escape, to crawl into the pigmentation of my own supple skin.

I found tequila in Twin Peaks, and I found Lewis in the Rooftop Lounge. I was mostly past words by then, but so was he. I kissed him against the bar, and he led me by the hand down the back-stairs, along the alley. In the doorway of Sankeys he slipped his hand down the front of my trousers and gripped me tight, jerking me hard. I breathed hard against his neck.

"Who's he?" Lewis asked.

"Who?"

He bit my neck and jerked a head across the street.

A man was watching us. Golden-blond hair, red lips, flawless skin, half-lost in the shadow.

"Ex-boyfriend?"

"No," I said. I had never seen him before, and yet he seemed curiously familiar.

The blond man moved toward us. "Aren't you afraid?" he asked us.

Lewis laughed, and pulled me deeper into the doorway of Sankeys. "Dizzy queen," he said. "Leave her be." I let him pull me into Sankeys. The gap in the door, at the whim of a slow-close mechanism, narrowed around the blond man, shrinking him from elegant broad shoulders to a glimpse of a piercing face as he followed us.

Sankeys kept up its pretence, mostly; thus, the naked bodies rutting in the damp were lost amongst jets of steam. Lewis pulled me to a corner, pushed me down between his ebony thighs.

"Aren't you afraid?" The blond man had followed us in, taken a place next to Lewis, who hadn't noticed, his eyes closed in ecstasy.

I was. Afraid. Illogically, irrationally. Afraid.

Perhaps the sickness would crawl down my throat, rot my stomach, split my veins into a thousand slender hairs, let me paint the disease in savage brush-strokes over the body of my painting. In my attic by the park, the painting would crawl with lesions like fat, hungry slugs, until there was nothing but the white of my eyes left staring out into the shrouded dark of the sheet that hides it from view.

Whilst I fucked my way from sauna to sauna, my painting would wither and die night after night. And it wouldn't be alone; around it, strung from wall to wall, were hundreds of Thomas' photographs, the ageless black and white faces silently thronged around the decrepitude of my own painted visage—the invert of my own sojourn here on the streets of the Castro.

The blond man watched me defiantly sink to my task, smiled faintly as Lewis filled my mouth. The taste was still slick in my throat when I stumbled home, dragging my aching body up the stairs. I looked in every direction but my covered portrait as I methodically pulled down each of Thomas's photographs, stacked them in a developing tray, and lit the corner with a *snick* of my lighter.

I left only one untouched—the very first one. The one you've seen, the one that's gone down in history. The men gathered around that sign, back before the real cannibal horror of it all had gripped the street, the words at the bottom of the sheet illegible but stuck fast in my mind.

Especially as, glancing out the window for a moment, I was sure I could see the blond man watching from a doorway.

Be warned. There's something out there.

⁓

"I DON'T KNOW how you do it, honey," Lewis said, touching the end of his cigarette to mine. I breathed in deeply to ignite, and I could smell the stale undertone to his aftershave. I wasn't certain, but I could guess. He was perhaps—what?—a few pounds lighter than when I saw him last week. Nothing too noticeable right then. But it wouldn't take long. Six months, and he wouldn't be here either.

"Do what, good sir?" I asked him. They loved the upperclass British schtick here, and it was nice to relax into old patterns of speech. Henry would have been proud. They thought my name was just a part of the act.

"So *handsome*. All the time. Lordy, honey, I wish I knew your secret."

"A deal with the devil," I told him.

Lewis struck a pose, pouting. "'Faustian Pact—for men!'" he quoted. "'Because youth doesn't come cheap.'"

The flower-seller swept up to our table. Lewis scrabbled for a dollar and purchased a rose.

"For the new paramour?" I asked.

"You know it, darling. He's *totally* worth it. I think he might be—" self-consciously dramatic, "—*the one*."

I pointed at the door. "Is that him?"

It would have been easy to mistake the man who had entered for another Castro clone, but on him the flannel shirt and sandboots had a ring of authenticity, as if he had just stepped right off the farm. Ruddy faced, running a little to fat in a homefed sort of way, blinking in disorientation in the gaudy lights of the bar as I could imagine him blinking as he stepped off the train into the circus of San Francisco. Just my type.

"That's him," said Lewis, and bustled to sweep him into our orbit. "Honey, let me introduce my—" with a schoolgirl giggle "—boyfriend, Luke."

I extended a hand. "A *pleasure*," I said. "And if it's not too bold . . ."

<hr />

". . . SIR, I'D LIKE to tell you that you are an *uncommonly* beautiful specimen of manhood."

Luke moves his head infinitesimally to rest against my cheek. His skin is cool and clammy, and his face is drawn as if the skin has been pulled inch by inch into every crevice of his skull, the muscle melted away. Every movement feels brittle, as if something will break any second. He looks like a skeleton. He's not the only one in the Castro. He's not the only one in San Francisco.

The lesions are all over his face, crawling steadily closer to his eyes and nose, as if he's drowning slowly in his own rebellious skin.

"Tell Lewis," he says, a papery whisper on his shrunken tongue. "Tell him I'm sorry for what we—" He chokes, and there is blood on the pillow.

"I love you," I tell him. I don't know if I'm lying.

"I'm sure you do, Dorian," he says.

I kiss him, long and hard, and he doesn't fight back.

I CAUGHT SIGHT of Lewis in the hospital waiting room as I passed through. He locked his eyes with me fiercely; his anger was livid and bright, powering the husk of his body. I felt like storming over to him, shaking his bony shoulders, telling him that these days, we should be used to losing things. You can't get too attached to your toys.

He looked rough—bagged eyes, concave chest. Not a sign of the godlike figure between whose legs I had worshipped months ago in Sankeys. But credit to him: he'd lasted more than the six month prognosis I gave him.

Outside, I paused to light a cigarette, and blessed the brush-and-oil lungs of my distant counterpart as I inhaled deeply.

"Aren't you afraid?"

The blond man stepped up to me, though I had counted myself alone on the steps of the hospital.

I exhaled. "Of what?"

He indicated the cigarette. "Dying."

I laughed. "Not really."

The blond man smiled. "That's good," he said.

"Look," I said, "I don't mean to be rude, but you're possessing of a pretty poor sense of timing."

"Oh, my apologies," he said, looking up at the hospital doors. "Another one dead, is it?"

I was too exhausted for anger. "Something like that," I said.

"You'd think you'd be used to it by now, wouldn't you?" the blond man said. He stepped closer, produced his own cigarette from his pocket, motioned to me to light it for him. I extended my lighter. "All those people dying around you. Old hat. The corpses piling up around your *beautiful* face."

He leaned in closer to me, shielding the nascent cherry of the cigarette against the wind. His hand touched mine for a second.

It was as if I had been licked by the slimy, bristly tongue of some foul, preternatural creature; every inch of my skin felt as if it had been turned inside out to puke its stinking contents in the gutter. For a moment his face, leant close to mine, was no longer beautiful; his pale white skin was the hue of maggots in a soldier's wound, his lips the sheets between a miscarried mother's legs.

"Oh, Dorian!" he shouted after me, as I beat a hasty retreat. "Surely you don't believe there's anywhere far enough to run away from all this?"

I MEET FREDDIE in the Rooftop Lounge, and fuck him in Sankeys. Five months later, he moves his head infinitesimally to rest against my cheek. His skin is cool and clammy, and his face is drawn as if the skin has been pulled inch by inch into every crevice of his skull, the muscle melted away. When it's all over, I stalk morosely away from the hospital, and don't dare look to see if the blond man is on the steps.

Leon I meet in the Castro Theatre, his cock in his hand to a grainy video of two bears fucking in a workshop, furtive with the thrill of it. He takes me home to his house on the other side of the city, a respectable, shady tree-lined street, and we pull each other's clothes off as soon as we're in the safety of the cool hallway. We're together for seven months, until his movements become brittle, as if something will break any second. He looks like a skeleton. He's not the only one in the Castro. He's not the only one in San Francisco. He's not the only one in America.

I wonder what my portrait looks like now.

Aimlessly walking the blank corridors of the hospital, I run into Lewis. We hug, anger forgotten, and he introduces me to his new boyfriend, a boisterous drag queen by the name of Tallulah Travesty. I summon the spark of humour to plaster on a charming smile, take her hand, and say, "Why, madam, if I might be so bold as to say . . ." but then Lewis elbows me in the ribs and I laugh it off. She's not my type anyway.

"Aren't you going to introduce me to your friends?" the blond man asks me, when I pass him on the steps, but I ignore him, and sweep Lewis and Tallulah past him, before he can lay a pestilent finger on either one of them.

I meet Nelson in the dark-room of The View, and the low light hides things for a while. He's fresh in the city and I'm the older man—oh, if he only knew. But when he moves into the light, I can see his naked body is already pricked with black patches. As I take him, he reaches behind to hold me, as if marvelling that anyone is touching him. When we're done, I pull my clothes on, kiss him on the forehead, and escape onto the street. I can already see the shape of the hospital bed forming around him.

I search out Lewis and Tallulah in Las Playas, and we go dancing.

The music in the club was hardly what my erstwhile Lord Wooton would have envisioned at even the most debauched of his parties. As we danced in the strobe lights, three drunken men at the centre of a visibly emptying dancefloor, I closed my eyes, and pictured myself eighteen again, clean-cut and freshly enamoured with the indulgences of life. There was Henry, in leather chaps dancing in the corner. Basil, dizzy on poppers, grinding with the leather queens. Sybil a towering drag queen with candy-cane hair piled high. We'd really outdone ourselves, hadn't we?

I could feel the eyes of men on men, but tonight I shrugged it off. I am, and always have been, desirable. I'd already had my fill tonight, and I could still feel the shudder of it, lubricated by fingers and tongues, creasing the lines of my portrait. I'd rather not lay more burden upon it tonight; in fact, it quite appealed, to be dancing there in the centre of the dance floor, an incandescent beauty for all the good men of the Castro to lust after, fruitlessly.

Come on gentlemen, I thought. *Dance to keep the wolf at the door.*

In the gap between lights, I was sure, for a moment, I saw the blond man smiling to himself, waiting for my gaze to alight upon him.

THE LESIONS ARE all over his face, crawling steadily closer to his eyes and nose, as if he's drowning slowly in his own rebellious skin.

"I love you, Lewis," he says, a papery whisper on his shrunken tongue. "I love you—" He chokes, and there is blood on the pillow.

"I love you," Lewis tells him.

"Me too, Tallulah," I say.

Lewis kisses him, long and hard. Neither of them have any fight left in them.

When the nurse draws a sheet over Tallulah's face, and ushers us from the room, I escort him to a forgotten corner of the hospital, and let him slump into a heap. We're both getting used to this routine, but I'm still the more experienced.

"It's not fair," he says.

"I know," I said. "He was too young."

"Not that," he said. "You. Untouched. God, you're still so *beautiful*. How have you escaped this . . . this . . . this fucking *thing?*"

I put an arm around his shoulder. It's angular and weak. I wonder how he's still here. He wonders the same thing about me.

"Do you want me to die?" I ask.

"No," he says, and leans into my chest to get the afternoon's sobbing out of the way before we go dancing.

———

IN MY ATTIC, I stood in front of the covered portrait. My finger twitched at the corner, ready to fling it away, unveil my face.

I could picture it clearly.

My skin would be cool and clammy, and my face drawn as if the skin had been pulled inch by inch into every crevice of my skull, the muscle melted away. Brittle, as if something would break any second. I would look like a skeleton.

The lesions would be all over my face, crawling closer to my eyes and nose, nothing but the whites of my eyes left. As if I was drowning slowly in my own rebellious skin. But then, I'd felt that way for years.

One thought kept me from pulling it away, showing me to myself.

What if it wasn't? What if my face was exactly as it had been the last I saw it? Aged, yes, sick, yes, but not laid low by the plague that had, one by one, snuffed out the lives of all my lovers. What if the portrait had nothing to do with it? What if I had just *survived?*

———

"HERE HE IS!" Lewis announced giddily. He was practically skipping along the street. It would have been hard to credit that it was only three months since Tallulah's death, but this was a sight common in the Castro these days—nothing lasted long, so you grabbed hold quickly.

"Him?" I asked, and tightened my grip on Lewis' skinny wrist.

"That's the one," Lewis said.

The blond man extended a hand to shake mine.

"I'd rather not," I said.

"Dorian!" Lewis was shocked—properly shocked, not his usual pantomime version. He looked at me pleadingly, shaking himself loose of my hold and wrapping himself around the blond man's arm. I was momentarily torn, but the hurt in Lewis' eyes swayed me. I extended a hand and shook, feeling my skin crawl.

"A pleasure to meet you, Dorian," the blond man said.

"It always is," I said.

"Right, ladies," Lewis said, stringing an arm around each of our shoulders, "it's time to *party!*"

He led us, awkward but compliant, from the street up the spiral steps to the Rooftop Lounge. It was busy that night. In fact, I can tell you exactly how many people were there. Sixty-six. Sixty-seven including me. That's what the newspapers said.

The music was pounding, the drink flowing, but as many shots as Lewis thrust into my hand, nothing could coax me into the party mood. I prowled the floor, placing myself as far away from the blond man as I could at any cost, watching the evening ramp up.

Be warned. There's something out there.

Lewis and the blond man were dancing, increasingly lairy as the night wore on. His fingertips on my friend's bare chest made me shudder, slithering across the corrugated ripple of his ribcage, the crater of his belly.

I couldn't begrudge Lewis his happiness, but I didn't have to participate. At eleven, I slipped down the stairs to the bohemian hubbub of the street, seeking solitude amongst the crowds, and lit a cigarette. It was more than the usual partying tonight—the seeds of a protest parade were gathering, marching with placards. *Save our lives! Save our lives!*

I vowed that when I got home, I would uncover my portrait, look and see what damage should have been done to my body.

"Aren't you afraid?"

I didn't turn.

"I said, aren't you afraid?"

I sighed, and sucked on the cigarette. "Of what?"

"That it's your fault they keep dying?"

"That's not me," I said. "It might be you, though."

"That it might," the blond man said. "But even you couldn't possibly take the blame for all of those bodies in the morgues. But some of them? Maybe." He lit his own cigarette. "Thomas. Luke. Freddie. Leon. Nelson. Tallulah. Lewis—soon."

"It wasn't me," I said. "I'm not sick."

"No," he said. "You certainly don't look as if you are."

We were both quiet for a moment, watching the world go buy. A moustached man in tight leather shorts and denim shirt ran his eyes appreciatively up and down the length of me. I returned the gaze, and then his eyes flicked to the blond man; he practically licked his lips with lascivious delight. I sneered inwardly, and mentally rejected him, added him to the stockpile of Men I Would Not Deign To Fuck. He marched on down the road, the placard wavering. *Save our lives! Save our lives!*

"I wonder who *could* take the blame?" the blond man said. "The first rotten seed. Who could possibly be responsible for *all of this*." The last three words fell from his lips lightly, like a schoolboy proud of his science fair project, beckoning eagerly to his parents to come see.

I didn't answer.

"The devil perhaps?" The blond man smiled. "I don't know, Dorian. You're on better terms with him than I."

I grated the last of my cigarette into the ground.

"If the preachers in the city squares are anything to go by," the blond man said, "then it's God. But I don't really believe in him. I don't think there's anything out there."

I opened my mouth to speak, but I couldn't form a full sentence. Instead, only one word rattled out of my throat, amidst phlegm and spittle. "Monster."

"Probably," he said. "You'd be the one to know." He stepped close to me, and rested a hand against my cheek. Beneath his skin, the maggots squirmed. "It's really not fair, is it?" he said. "Your face. So pretty, whilst everyone else's wastes away."

He kissed me firmly on the lips, and I vomited sourly in the back of my throat.

I STOOD IN front of my painting, with the lighter burning in my hand. It was not the first time in my century of living I had considered sending my frame up in flames, but I had never been so tempted. You can clean a wound by burning away the dead skin and cauterizing the hole. You can stop an infection spreading.

At the foot of the Rooftop Lounge, I'd laid a thin line of fluid across the doorstep and stepped back. Behind me, people marched, frothing with oblivious indignation.

Lewis nearly made it out alive. He'd squeezed through a window—

many of them did. Thirty-two of them, if we're talking numbers. But Lewis went back in, to save his lover, the blond man. His blackened body was found, arms wrapped tight around the blond man to protect him from the engulfing flames.

He wasn't the only one to die. Two brothers, and their mother. A reverend. The man who, trying desperately to squeeze between the bars of the upstairs windows, died screaming, fused to the searing metal.

The cremated bodies of Lewis and the blond man were photographed. You can hang them in a museum with Thomas' last remaining photo.

And here I was, in my attic, squaring up against my painting.

I'm sure I don't need to tell you that the death of the blond man changed nothing. History isn't on my side. You know as well as I that the sickness carried right on spreading. I didn't save anyone. I never do.

I'd branded him a monster, but his skin had crisped and turned to charcoal like any man's would. Except mine. On the streets of the Castro— and the streets of hundreds, thousands of cities across the world—men (and women, and children) were still dying. Their skin would be cool and clammy, and their faces drawn as if the skin had been pulled inch by inch into every crevice of their skulls, the muscle melted away. Their movements would be brittle, as if something would break any second. They would look like skeletons, all the skeletons of the world gathered in adoration around the beautiful monster, Dorian Gray.

Be warned, I thought, as I pulled away the sheet. *There's something out there.*

CROAK TOAD

I BET YOU'RE wondering how we got here?

A cell is not where we meant to be. Well, that's a lie, if we're going per-dant-ic. We *did* mean to be in a cell, but we *didn't* mean to be locked in. And there wasn't meant to a dead body.

Well, okay, it wasn't meant to be *this* dead body.

Badger is *not* helping. He's pacing, which he always does when he's angry. Or frustrated. Or nervous. Or bored. Point is, he paces a lot, and it's doing none of our nerves any favours. And with those big beast legs of his its barely two steps across the whole cell anyway.

Mole is looking pretty worse for wear. He never looks exactly what you'd call *stable*, but right now he's about six thunderous badger-steps away from blubbing, and that won't do any of us any good. He looks at me all pleading-like. I'd just as soon stick my fingers in a mangle as try talking to Badger right now, but hell if I've ever been able to refuse Mole when he does that soft, wet quivering thing with that cute pink beezer of his.

"Hey—Badger, could we maybe just—"

Badger stopped, and slowly craned his neck to fix his one good eye on me. His snout twitched, baring one sharp yellow tooth. He growled.

"'Course," I said hurriedly. "Go right ahead."

Anyways, like I said, I bet you're wondering how we got here, right?

Buckle up then, pups, it's story time.

FIRST OFF, MOLE turned up on my doorstep. Not unusual, but since everything went down the way it did when—when, well, *you know*--this place had a strict guestlist of one. Somehow he'd found his way to my deepest, hidiest hole, the one that takes two boats, three sewers, and twenty minutes of crawling under the boardwalk to get to. Just the kind of hole a dirty rat runs to lie low.

Mole's always had an excellent nose for this kind of thing.

I greeted him like an old friend, handing him a glass of whiskey, and pointing a shotgun at him.

"We had an agreement," I said.

He trembled. Apart from his nose, that's his main talent. Well, and the other thing.

"I know," he said mournfully. He took off his little round glasses and polished them on his waistcoat, though it did no good; he was soaked in sewer filth right to the fur. "But I had no choice."

I cocked the trigger. It had a good, scary *clunk*, this particular beanshooter. It's why I chose it. It's my intruder-threatening gun. "You better be about to give a damn good reason, pup."

He peered miserably through his glasses. "Gingham," he said.

I snatched the whiskey out of his claws, and knocked it back, ice-cubes and all.

Here's the thing you gotta know. Gingham—gingham is capital-b Bad. Gingham's the last thing an animal wants to see in this town. You see gingham, you're about to get popped by the Kingpen.

LOOK, I'M NOT speciesist, but it really rankles that the Kingpen isn't exactly an animal from *round 'ere*. But *round 'ere* don't count for a dime here in the Smoke. Cross the Kingpen, you end up bundled in a hamper and sinking six feet down. Usually when the bodies end up good and gassy, they float back up. Cross the North Bridge early, before the buttons have been out dragging the river, you'll see a bunch floating along. Just these wicker squares, done up in a gingham bow, another good boy off to the Great Big Hunt.

You don't cross the Kingpen. And you don't screw up a job for him, but I guess we missed that memo.

Some heavies tossed Mole's den in the Stacks. Low-level thugs—stoats and weasels, nothing that would concern me, but Mole's *Mole*. They said they were carol-singers, and I guess nobody told Mole that in this town carol-singers give you three hard choruses then charge you protection afterwards. He let them in, and that's why *I'm* the brains in this team.

They knocked him around a bit, threatened to turn him into a notebook, and told him what we had to do if we didn't want to get picnicked. "They left a bow right on the door," Mole sniffed. "Where *everyone* could see."

I was already digging in the ammo drawer, stowing slugs into all my trench pockets. "And what does the nasty ol' flipper want?"

"It's Toad," Mole said. "We've gotta croak Toad."

A job goes south, you go to ground, hibernate for a bit. If the elbows come sniffing, keep your mouth shut and don't say a single thing about which criminal overlord may or may not have hired you. We'd have been hitting on all eight, if it wasn't for Toad getting sent down. And if there's anything Toad is, it's a loose mouth in a crowded room.

"We need Badger," I said.

Mole's rheumy eyes filled up. "But I don't know where he *iiiiiiiiiis*," he wailed.

"I do," I said. "We gotta go to the Wild Wood, and we gotta see a skunk about some mushrooms."

The Wild Wood isn't somewhere I frequent. Too many streets, all too narrow, and a knife in every alley. And look—I *said* I'm not speciesist, and I *know* not every skunk is a mycologist, but I'm also *just* saying that the first one we met in the Wild Wood—well, you know.

"Chew them," I told Mole. His snout wrinkled in disgust. "We won't find Badger's place unless we get good and *lost*." What I *mean* is, to find Badger we gotta look like we're easy marks who won't remember anything in the morning.

So we tripped around the Wild Wood like happy, dumb hopheads who can't tell downstream from up, until eventually a fieldmouse in a fedora came sidling up to us. "You party animals looking for a bit of skin?" he squeaked.

I tweak his tail. "Sure as spinach we are," I said.

Badger's shake joint isn't for your average palooka. Drop a dime in the wrong ear and this is the kind of place that'd be up to its whiskers in the fuzz in no time. Not that there aren't always a few of those in there on the regular, but there won't be a badge in sight.

Badger's has everything you want from a dive. It's got whiskey, got music, and got girls. But Badger's is where you come if you like your hoochie girls with a little... less.

And look, I am *not* speciesist, but between you and me, *I just don't get it.*

Here the girls are dressed for a unique audience. The kind that like humans, not animals. They bundle everything up inside these disgusting pink skin-suits and freaky smooth masks, pout those weird-shaped mouths and shake their hairless behinds in the punter's faces. Gives me the heebies just being in the room; call me old-fashioned, but I need a bit of furry for the purring.

Mole was trembling. I think it was a badtime trembling, not a goodtime trembling, but I don't judge.

The minute Badger saw us, I knew we were in trouble. He was sat on the balcony, up above the fug and noise, in his throne. (Yeah, he's the kind of guy to have a throne.) Soon as we locked eyes, I saw his teeth. The fieldmouse took one look and scarpered—smart pup knew when he'd made a mistake.

Then in swooped the heavies.

<hr />

"I've told you," I said, twitching like bait on a hook, "not to use these guys on me. I see wings and a beak, I freak. Scratch any one of us and we still bleed woodlander." I glared up at the sparrowhawk that had me dangling from its beak, doing my best to look tough. Maybe I shouldn't have mentioned *bleeding*.

Badger bared his teeth. "Ten seconds."

"Gingham," I said. "Call off your birds."

"So here's the sitch," I said, when I had been unceremoniously dropped. And I told him.

"Killed?"

"Yep. Dead before he can talk. And I'm guessing Kingpen doesn't have any moles inside Chokey, otherwise they'd have Toad in the hole already. Which leaves us. The fall guys."

"But if we break in..."

I was ahead of him, as always. (Brains of the operation, remember?) "Why not break him out with us? Thought of that. But something tells me that ain't gonna get the big gingham target off our backs."

Badger paced. It took a while. Badger's got one of those faces you can't read. Either that or he really *is* just angry all the time.

I ventured a paw. He didn't bite it off, so that was a start. "Badger," I said softly, "you know as well as I do, Toad should *not* be in *that* prison. You know what they do to a creatures like Toad there."

Badger bared a fang. I'd won. "Fine. You got a plan?"

I grinned. "*Do* I got a plan?"

———

I DIDN'T HAVE a plan.

It took several hours and a satisfying puke in the gutter before I was clear-headed enough to make one. I squatted in the alley, smoked my way through a whole deck of luckies, and form-you-late-d as the sun oozed up.

The way creatures think in this town is: wanna keep your house safe, you keep it bristling with tin. Keep everything outside your four precious walls at bay. But none of these lunkheaded idiots ever think about the *ground*.

Which is where Mole and his champion digging claws came in.

Step 1: dig a hole, a really, really long hole.

It didn't emerge in Chokey—too simple, and besides: Chokey's in the middle of a moat too deep to dig under—but that wasn't the plan. When a beast gets a 'first class ticket to the chokey express' it's not a euphemism. The train is the only way in and out of Chokey. Anything that comes and goes has to do it by rail—guards, prisoners, food, you name it. The station is guarded so closely you can't twitch a whisker without catching heat, but that didn't matter.

We came right up between the tracks.

I poked my snout up and sniffed the air. We were just where I planned: under the back of the train. Ten or more guards on the platform, but we were invisible. We were also late—the engine was already gunning, and a whistle was blowing above us. "Badger!" I shouted down. "Haul fur."

————

STEP 2: BRAWN over brains. Badger rips out a few non-essential bits of engine, and we go up. *If all goes according to plan, we emerge completely unobserved in an empty laundry carriage.*

It did not go according to plan. We came up right between two fancy-uniformed stoats playing poker. Thankfully, the element of surprise gave us precious seconds between gaping and gats, and that was all Badger needed. A bit more of brawn over brains and things were back under control.

"Mole," I said, without even bothering to look. "Stop trembling."

Step 3: laundry carriage. Mole and I halfinch some drudge uniforms. Badger goes in the—

"Absolutely. Not." Badger licked blood off his chops, and shook his head.

"Absolutely *yes*." I pointed firmly into the empty laundry hamper.

Step 4: roll Badger right past the Chokey guards. No-one bats an eyelid.

Step 5: get a bit 'lost'.

Here's where the plan was wobbly. We could only skulk around inside for so long without someone noticing us, and we had to get to where we were going fast. Real fast.

Step 6: encounter a lock, Mole cracks out his toys.

I swear, the only time Mole doesn't tremble is when he's rigging up wires to explosives.

Step 7: encounter a guard, crack out a Badger.

Step 8...

"What do we have *you* for?" Badger asked me, when I'd finishing laying out the plan.

I gritted my teeth. "Easy," I said, "*I'm* the only one with the acorns to kill Toad."

⟋⟋⟍

THE SMOKE MAKES you hard. If you pups are wondering how I could think about bumping off someone I might rightfully call a friend, you've not spent enough time in this town. You have to do what keeps you safe, what keeps your skin on your bones and not curing on a hook somewhere--or floating down the river done up in a bow. Someone like the Kingpen comes after you, you're in a trap. Not the nice kind where you get released and put outside where you can't do anyone harm. The kind where you have to gnaw off your own leg to get free.

Or somebody else's leg, if it comes to that.

And if you can look me in the eye and tell me you don't remember the wild, what it was like to feel blood and gristle in your teeth, I'll smack you on the schnozz and call you a liar anyway.

I don't mind saying though, as we worked our way up the prison quick as a hare on hunt day, I felt a twinge in my stomach. It was like when you've eaten bad worms, but I guess it was probably guilt. Chokey sits over the whole Smoke and its casts a long shadow. There's not a single boy in a single street that doesn't live under that fear. But inside...

...it was so, so much worse than I'd imagined.

This was a terrible place for all of us, but for Toad most of all.

———

A PADLOCK. *A padlock.*

Here we three chumps were risking hide *and* hair, and Toad's secured with nothing but a *padlock*? I was almost offended. Professionals like us could get a padlock open faster than a mayfly hits puberty. And I include Badger in that, even though he's got paws like a pair of ribeye steaks.

Adding insult to injury, Toad was *snoozing*.

A narrow beam of moonlight shafted through the window opposite. It illuminated Toad curled up facing the back of the cell on a small, narrow bench. I goggled. I wouldn't sleep a wink if I was banged up in this hellhole. I'd expected to find Toad wide-eyed and sleep-deprived, hopping at every noise.

Still, as any good hitman knows, *it's easier when they're sleeping.* I fingered the popgun hidden inside my drudge uniform. Mole was shaking so much now that he was even giving *me* the jitters. I pressed a stick of dynamite into his hand. "Stroke that and breathe." I cracked out my lockpicks.

Thirty seconds later—embarrassingly slow—we were in.

Which was around about when we realised our mistake.

The first mistake was Toad. Or to be more specific, the sleeping body that was neither sleeping, nor Toad. I reached to smother its face with my paw. It rolled over, and what I saw staring dead-eyed up at me was not at all amphibian.

The second mistake was that we had all stepped inside the cell. But we didn't realise that until the door slammed shut.

⁓

YOU'RE GOING TO fall in love. Don't feel bad—hell, we've all been there the first time. Toad's just that kind of dame. One kiss, and we've all swooned, and that's not just down to the venomous toxin she secretes. It takes talent to look good in stolen washerwoman's clothes, but she always knew how to work backlighting, even as a bug-eyed boy fresh out of the spawn.

She sucked long on a cigarette, exhaled a cloud of white smoke. A misty halo of moonlight ballooned around her. "Well well, chaps," she said.

I'm the brains. Badger's the muscle. Mole's the tech. And Toad?

Every story like this needs a femme fatale.

I looked down at the not-Toad. "You bopped an innocent broad just to get out? That's cold-blooded."

She batted one beautiful lid at me. "You're one to talk." She had me there, I had to admit.

Badger slammed against the bars, claws flailing. "Let us the hell out!"

Toad didn't even flinch. Just out of Badger's reach, she silkily exhaled into his face. That's Toad for you: untouchable. No matter how much you want to.

"Well, as much as this reunion has been *thrilling*, chaps..." The cigarette dropped to the floor and was ground out. I knew how it felt. She swished away, pushing the laundry-cart.

"You can't leave us here!" Mole called after her.

She turned and looked back, lost in the shadow between cells. "Sorry boys. I've a train to catch." She blew a kiss. "Poop poop."

～∕∕∕～

So THAT'S HOW we got here. Just your standard-issue misguided tale of woe, and if you're lucky enough to have avoided fate playing you her own little melody of chin music yet, that just means it's coming your way sometime soon. Sorry. That's just how the cards fall for beasts like you and me in the Smoke.

Step 1: throw the book at us, plus some kicks and punches.

Step 2: drag us out of prison by our ears.

Step 3: haul us in front of the Beak.

Step 4: send us right back to Chokey where we belong.

So there we were handcuffed in the back of a cattle-wagon doing a shifty fifty across town. Mole was shaking so much he's hurting himself in the bracelets. I could never bear it when he sniffled. "Mole, hey," I whispered. "Could be worse. At least the Kingpen can't get to us now."

From my lips to Pan's treacherous lugholes, apparently.

A cacophonous bang like summer thunder. Something lurched beneath the wheel. Suddenly the wagon was upside down. Mole was bouncing off the ceiling, and I was using Badger's furry chest as a trampoline. The wagon flipped, doors bursting open, and we were spat out the back like so much gristle.

After that it's all a bit wonky. I remember Mole wailing as two stoats grabbed his back legs. I remember Badger thundering towards me swinging two bloody ferrets from his jaws. I remember something heavy smashed across my vision, then nothing.

I KNEW WE were dutched as soon as the hood came off. This wasn't going to be a simple henchman knockaround. We were going to be cucumber sandwiches before dawn.

I blinked around. We were *in* Toad Hall, I realised. Judging by the junk, the bastards had taken it over.

"Hey, Badger," I said. "He's got a throne too. Creature after your own heart."

Badger growled. He's never appreciated gallows humour.

The Kingpen laughed. The big black-and-white fishsack actually *laughed*. It was this squelchy sound like he's trying to cough up fishbones.

I squinted. "I thought you'd be bigger. But I guess a King ain't quite an Emperor."

He didn't laugh at that, at least not until a couple of stoat-stooges had finished playing kickabout with my face. *Then* he laughed, this *yuckyuckyuck* noise.

I spat blood between his flippers.

He poked his beak against my snout. "One simple little question. Where does a Toad go to ground?"

"Is that a riddle?"

Yukyukyukyukyuk. "Fine." He wiggled a fin.

Mole screamed behind me. I squirmed, twisted and snapped, but I couldn't see him. "Mole!" I squawled. "Mole! Just—just—."

"*Raaaaaaaaattyyyyyyyyyyy!* They're going to skin me!"

Kingpen bobbed his head apologetically. "We're going to skin him," he confirmed.

MATTHEW BRIGHT

"They're not," I shouted. "We're gonna get out of this. I'll take you out to the country. We'll get a boat, we'll go rowing. We'll go find your house. This will all be—"

A ten tonne truck hit me and all the lights went out.

"You've all made a very grave mistake," said a voice. And oh, that voice. It was the voice of mother midnight, of an uncatchable moonbeam, of a deep dark current that sweeps you to the riverbed.

These idiots have dug their own graves. See, grow up like Toad, people think your body is for breaking and entering; when you make your den, you make it so no-one ever, *ever* gets that chance again.

"But…" The voice was moving above, fast. "You're forgiven."

A cold wind zipped past my neck. All around me, beasts squealed as they were crushed beneath an exquisitely coutured heel.

Afterwards there was only Badger, Mole and I—and Toad, atop a furry pile of groaning bodies, in one hand a gleaming sword, the other a cigarette. "Hello chaps," she purred.

"Toad… I…" Badger began. It's honestly as far as I've ever seen him get into an apology.

"Oh, darlings, no hard feelings. I leave hard feelings to men. Love heals everything." Sticking up from an open hamper was something black, white and wriggling. "For example…" Toad's lips coloured a deep, poisonous turquoise, "right now just a little kiss would solve our problems."

When the flippers fell still, I finally breathed.

Toad stalked down the pile. "I think I'm over this decor," she said.

"We could all use a little holiday, don't you think? Somewhere warm, with willow trees."

I wrapped my arm around a trembling Mole and hugged him close. "I know just the place," I said.

NOTHING TO
WORRY ABOUT

I T'S PROBABLY NO accident that they look like grandmothers; Tasha
thinks this the morning Miss Stowe knocks on her door. Briefcases full
of knitting perhaps, alongside the stacks of casefiles. Tasha's friend Caitlin
over the road (who failed her Inspection six months back) reckons it's part
and parcel of the whole thing, their appearance—there's no reason why
the Birth Inspectors can't be six foot bodybuilders, but they never are.
Innocuous, kindly even, yet the whisper travels up a street in seconds the
same way they used to shudder about the bogeyman when they were kids; a
Nanna is coming, a Nanna is coming.

"Miss Jackson?"

"Yes?"

"My name is Miss Stowe, and I'm from the Department of Family
Control, I've come for your Home Inspection."

The Nanna pokes her ID up towards Tasha's sleep-fuddled face.
Beside the department logo-- a stork in a dark red circle—the head-and-
shoulders photo is of a much younger, rumpled-looking woman, less severe,
less impatient than the woman on her doorstop. Miss Stowe-now seems to

have vacated the creased on her younger self's dress to her face, and now her face looks creased and forbidding, like a letter balled up in frustration and thrown in the bin. She taps her stylus on the clipboard screen. "You were expecting us, I presume? We did send a letter."

Caitlin's curtains twitch, Tasha notices. She's watching. In the kitchen, Tasha's phone will be lighting up. There'll be someone behind every curtain in the street this morning, if she knows Barff Road like she thinks she does.

"Er—yes," Tasha says, "we were expecting you." They are, though not e"xactly today. The letters specify a three week period. Today is only four days into it. Caitlin's Nanna hadn't turned up until the penultimate.

The Nanna blinks at her from behind her half-moon spectacles, and Tasha thinks briefly about how vampires have to wait to be invited in.

Tasha pushes back Jason's muddy work shoes with her foot, out of sight of Miss Stowe, and then steps back to open the door fully. "Come on in," she says, as sweetly as her nervous stomach will allow her.

The Inspector folds down her umbrella, shakes it, and steps inside. Jason's work boots have left a thick, gooey trail of dirt across the exposed floorboards; she fastidiously props her umbrella between them, leaning against the cold radiator.

Tasha dithers. "Sorry about the mess," she says. She feels her accent thickening the words, and tries to rearrange the syllables on her tongue. (Careful, she thinks, don't lay it on too thick.) "'Ere, let me move them for you. Bloody Jason always leaving his stuff lying around." She gives the boots a powerful kick, and they ricochet down the hall, landing against an open box of power tools.

Tasha and her guest watch the blades rock in their box, and then Miss Stowe makes a note on her clipboard.

"Sorry," Tasha says, and realises she's almost whispering. (We aren't prepared, she thinks, the thought stomping around her head insistently. We aren't ready, we aren't ready.)

"Oh, don't you worry, dear," the Inspector clucks. "Don't need to go to any special effort for me. The Inspection is about seeing your day-to-day life; you wouldn't believe the number of couples who put on a special performance to try and fool us. But no--" the creases in her face pull out for a moment, like a fabric stretched suddenly tight "--we can always tell, dear."

"Tea?" Tasha asks, leading the woman into the kitchen.

"That would be lovely, dear," the Nanna says, casting an appraising look around the room. Swallowing nervously, Tasha tries to sees all there is to see through Miss Stowe's keen eyes, imagining she has her own clipboard to tick off the house's inadequacies: grubby skirting boards, can of paint in the doorway, bottle of bleach by the stove, empty beer cans in a row by the back door. Miss Stowe's stylus skates smoothly down the screen.

"Paint," notes Miss Stowe, recapping her pen. "Confident, are we?"

Tasha turns to the kettle to hide her face. "We just wanted to be prepared," she mutters, clicking on the kettle. There are two empty whiskey bottles on the counter; she pushes them away behind the toaster so they clank against each other loudly.

"I'll just pop myself in the living room and get all the paperwork up and running, shall I?" says the Inspector, and off she toddles down the hall before Tasha can say anything. The kettle takes an age to boil, I should go after her, Tasha thinks. If the whiskey bottles weren't empty, she'd sneak a mouthful to calm her.

In the living room, the Inspector is introducing herself to Jason. He grunts an acknowledgement, and takes his hands out from the crotch of his tracksuit bottoms for long enough to politely mute the TV. Tasha can't see from the doorway what is onscreen; when the bell had run he was still deciding between his two favourite films, Dykes with Drills 4 or Licking Lucy's Lips. The Nanna looks everywhere but at the TV, and taps on her screen. It's full of text, Tasha can just about see.

Tasha catches Jason's eyes, and makes a furious head gesture at the open can of lager in his other hand. He grimaces, and takes an exaggerated slurp. Tasha roles her eyes and stomps back the kitchen, listing all the imaginative ways she can think of to punish Jason if he screws this up for them.

"Two sugars," calls Miss Stowe after her down the hall. "I like it extra sweet."

The kettle steams and clicks off. Tasha pours the water into mugs and dunks a teabag into one. She hears the Nanna introduce herself to Jason—Inspector Lucy Stowe, but she prefers Miss Stowe if that's alright, and you must be the husband-no-pardon-me-boyfriend—and Jason responds with a loud belch. If she knows Jason, he'll have accompanied it with a good rummage in his boxers. She briefly glances at her phone on the side, the screen crammed with messages. Caitlin has messaged fourteen times. She recognises the names of other neighbours too. Word travels fast.

She transfers the teabag briefly to the second cup, then throws in some milk.

"Here you are," she says, returning with the mugs, setting them down perilously close to the edge of the table. "One sugar, wasn't it?"

"It was two, love, but don't worry yourself about it." Miss Stowe beams at both of them. "Now, let me just stress before we start, this Home Inspection is nothing to worry about. I just have to read you out some standard wording so we're all on the same page—now where was it?" She rummages through the papers. "Here we go—right. 'This Home Inspection will be conducted by INSERT NAME HERE—that's me—to establish your eligibility for Paragraph 93b under the Family Control Act 2031, Section

4, Parts 15-21. You have the right to withdraw from the procedure at any time without prejudice, but you will not be permitted with the necessary permits until successful completion of the process.'" The Nanna adjusts her glasses. "Now, I understand one of our counsellors has spoken to you on the telephone and you fully understand both stages of the procedure?"

Tasha glances at Jason for support, but he continues to stare pointedly at the jumble of breasts on the screen. Based on the level of gadgetry, Tasha reckons it's probably the first film. She looks back at Miss Stowe, who is smiled benignly at her.

"Well—I was sort of hoping we wouldn't have to get past the first stage, like?"

The Nanna's smile thins. "Well, of course, dear; most couples feel the same. And that's certainly a possibility, but we at the Department have to make sure we're thorough."

Tasha bobs her head. "Yeah. Of course."

"Right then, well, as I'm sure you know, we'll just start with a brief interview. Let me stress again—absolutely nothing to worry about." She taps at her clipboard screen a few times, and words flash across it. "These are just a few questions, designed to give me an indication of whether you'd be like to be unfit or not; nothing to worry about and no decision is final at this stage based on your answers. The questions are selected randomly, but please answer as honestly as you can. Don't be try to think of what you should say to convince me—far too many couples fall into that trap. Understand?"

Tasha nods again. Jason is studiously not catching her eye.

"Right—number one; ooh! One of my favourites this one. 'What are your feelings about physical discipline of a child?'"

Tasha takes a mouthful of her insipid tea while she searches for an answer. "Well—I dunno, I mean, it never did me no harm. My mam used to give me a smack if I wasn't doing what I was meant to. At the end of the day, it teaches you, doesn't it?" Miss Stowe scribbles something down, and Tasha panics. "I mean, I'm not saying you should bear your kid black and blue or anything, but--" She tails of hopelessly. "Well, I guess it's easy to get it wrong, isn't it? So I say don't lay a finger on them. Best way."

She nods, pleased with her final answer. Miss Stowe makes another note. Jason catches Tasha's eye and frowns. Tasha glares at the remote, be he still isn't getting the picture.

"Right-o, Miss Jackson. Second question." Questions cycle across the screen. "'What are your feelings on a child doing chores in exchange for pocket money?'"

Taska practically gulps. What is she supposed to say to that? "Weelllll," she ventures, "I suppose it could be... good? Like, it could teach them responsibility and value of money, and that." Miss Stowe stares at her expectantly. Tasha winces, visibly. Is that the right answer? It had almost sounded parental and considered, hadn't it? It sounded convincing. She pastes a confident smile onto her face, though inside she feels like nothing of the sort.

Miss Stowe sigh heavily, and puts down her clipboard.

"Look, Miss Jackson--"

"Tasha," she tries desperately.

"--Miss Jackson, I'm going to be frank with you. I see countless people like you every week—on their own, in couples, in triads, all manner. And it's clear that you've gone to... some... effort. But I'm afraid I'm going to need a little bit more than that." Miss Stowe leans forward. "I'm going to take my notes back to the Department to review with my colleagues, but I'm afraid it's likely that we'll need to move to the second stage."

Tasha goes cold. "I--is--is that necessary?" She wants to cry all of a sudden, this rush of frustrated tears, like when she was a child, when they built up like a physical pain and you couldn't stop them even though you knew if you cried everyone would laugh at you, and you'd want to cry even more. She ached. "I mean—look--we tried."

"Yes," says Miss Stowe. "You tried." With those two words, she imparts a wealth of disappointment, and Tasha fully understands why the Department hires women like her. This whole thing wouldn't be complete without an extra dollop of shame, after all, she thinks, bitter but powerless.

"How long til we hear?" she says.

THE LETTER COMES in three days; as they predict, they are progressed to the second stage. They have three weeks to prepare. This time, a date is given. When the letter arrives, Jason comes into the kitchen and puts his arms around her from behind, one hand cupping her belly, his chin resting on her shoulder and rubs his nose against her earlobe in the way that usually calms her. She imagines her body full beneath his hand, and Tasha shrugs him off. She is inexplicably angry with him, even though she has to remind her it's not his fault, not really. Not all his fault anyway.

She doesn't message Caitlin to tell her, because she can't quite face it, but she'll know. As soon as she sees the paint, she'll know.

MISS STOWE IS below an umbrella once more, though on this occasion there isn't a cloud in the sky. She folds it away, and follows Tasha into the hall.

Though she's had plenty of other things to think about leading up today, she'd made at least a half-attempt at tidying the hall—the shoes are lined up neatly, at least, and the power tools are back in the garage where they belong. She sees Miss Stowe notice, but doesn't really care at this point. Everyone knows once you've got this far, it's only about one thing.

"Tea?" Tasha asks, though the question is in fact moot, as the cups are made and ready; she'd put the kettle on as soon as the whisper had reached her up the street.

"Not today," Miss Stowe says. She rests a comforting hand on Tasha's arm, but Tasha recoils and backs out of reach.

"It's upstairs," Tasha says. Her stomach is bubbling, her own breath tasting sour and fearful. She picks up her own cup, and holds it like a shield.

"Mr... Jason? Will you be accompanying us?"

Jason is sat in the living room, watching cautiously. The TV is dark today.

"It's okay," Tasha says. "I can speak for both of us. This way."

She leads Miss Stowe upstairs. At the top of the landing the door to their bedroom is open, and glancing in she sees that this morning Jason has tidied; there are freshly laundered sheets on the bed, a scented candle set out on the nightstand, clothes neatly folded away in the cupboard. She closes the door before Miss Stowe can reach it and see in, though she supposes it hardly matters by now. The next door stands open too. She leads Miss Stowe in.

"Here," she says, dully.

"Well! It's lovely!" Miss Stowe steps across the threshold, looking around appreciatively. Tasha nods dumbly. "A boy, I take it?"

Tasha nods and tentatively steps in. She runs a hand along the spine of the books on the bookshelf that they've placed by the window. Miss Stowe circles the room, clucking delightedly. "Did you know—blue used to be for girls and and the boys' colour was pink? Strange how these things change. That was centuries ago, of course. I absolutely love the moon and stars."

"Jason painted them," Tasha says. The constellation run up the wall and opens over the ceiling, glinting silver in the afternoon light filtering through the soft curtains.

"They're really lovely, dear—and they match the curtains! How wonderful!" Miss Stowe pauses in the middle of the room. "Well, I must say—this is one of the nicest cribs I've seen. Will you be donating it to the Department when you're finished with it?"

Tasha shakes her head, looking down at the floor. "No—it was mine. We had to get it out of my mam's garage. She wants it back, eventually." She feels self-conscious, still referring to her mother as 'mam' in a situation like this; and talking about it brings to mind her mother's expression when she'd had to go an ask for the crib, and explain why. She fiddles with the spines of the books to keep herself distracted.

"Oh, well, that's a real shame, but understandable I suppose," Miss Stowe says. "Never mind, we're not short on them. And The Wind in the Willows—yours too?"

Tasha looks up in surprise and meets Miss Stowe's eyes; she hasn't even realised she's stroking the spine of that book in particular. She smiles weakly. "Yes—that was mine too. It was my my favourite. Still is."

"I see. Well—it certainly looks like you've made the necessary arrangements." Miss Stowe ticks off something on her clipboard. "Now—a few more questions, if you don't mind. Name?"

"Robert Allan, after our dads."

"Oh, lovely! And which school?"

"St. Matthews. It's down the road. I went there too."

"Christened?"

"We don't believe in it."

"Favourite subject?"

"Science."

"Best friend?"

"Bridget O'Brien. My friend Caitlin's daughter. She's due soon."

"First kiss."

"Bridget again. In the treehouse that Jason's going to build."

Miss Stowe opens her mouth to ask another question, but Tasha cuts across her. "When the treehouse blows down in a storm he'll feel sad because it's the first time he realises that things from when he was young will disappear. He'll date Bridget for a bit, until Bridget tells him she's a lesbian. They'll stay good friends and introduce each other to girls. He'll go to sixth form and then he'll plan to go to university, but he'll mess up one of his exams and we'll think he can't go on to university, but then he'll get an offer from Portsmouth and he'll go there and study Physics and fall in love with the sea and with a girl and then another and briefly with a boy and and he'll get drunk and have sex and think he's a grown-up. He'll get a job in a laboratory researching things he doesn't care about but it won't matter because he'll meet a woman that he falls in love with. She'll be called Rebecca and her parents came to this country for a better life forty years ago before we closed the borders and all they want for their daughter is for just that and they'll think Robert will make that happen for her, but Rebecca will dream of travelling around the world, and Robert will want to go with her, so when he brings her home I'll disapprove, and so will Bridget because she's going to take us away from him, but Jason and Auntie Caitlin will adore her and they'll tell us to let him go. They'll get married, and I'll cry when Robert makes a speech, and at the party I'm going to catch him along in the dark garden and remind him that when he was a baby we painted his walls blue, and put moons and stars on his ceiling, and then I used to read him The Wind in the Willows." Tasha takes a long, calming breath. "Is that enough detail for you, Miss Stowe?"

Miss Stowe's stylus has ceased writing long ago. She looks at Tasha for a long, long time. After a time, she says: "Perhaps you'd like to sit down, dear."

"No," says Tasha. "I'm fine, thank you. I just have one question."

"Of course."

"Do you have a child, Miss Stowe?"

Miss Stowe looks down at the clipboard. "I never got to be a mother," she says, after a moment. "But I got to be a Nanna instead."

Tasha manages not to laugh in her face; it's not a done deal yet, she reminds herself.

"Sit down," Miss Stowe said, and this time it's a command. Tasha squats onto the small child's chair. "Miss Jackson, I'll be frank with you. I've seen a lot of women in your position, as I'm sure you well know. Don't be under any illusion that I have seen the same tricks you tried on the first inspection a thousand times. They always put on such a show. But I mean, really—whiskey bottles, power tools, good god even porn. You really went for it, didn't you? Your boyfriend was really quite spectacular. But it takes so much more than that to prove yourself fit—or unfit. Do you really think any of this stuff makes any difference?"

Tasha manages a wan smile. Miss Stowe pats her leg.

"It's all down to the nursery, I'm afraid. Nothing quite like the nursery for proving your commitment." She taps on her clipboard. "So I have to formally ask—are you still willing to go through with it?"

Tasha nods.

"I'll need that out loud, if you would."

Tasha meets her eyes. "I'm committed," she says, and believes it.

"And your signature, just here—and here—fantastic, that concludes your inspection."

Miss Stowe pats Tasha's leg again, and Tasha feels a white hot flash of anger that here and now she dares to be comforting. "I should have put the bleach in your tea," she says, surprising even herself.

"I didn't drink it," Miss Stowe says without looking up.

The formalities are disappointingly banal. Miss Stowe presses her ID against the clipboard, it beeps and a small window opens, dispensing a foil packet stamped with the familiar stork logo. It contains a single blue pill. She passes it to Tasha. "Here you are, dear. Now, I must warn you, there will be bleeding. It's going to be like the worst period you've ever had. Understandable really, it can't just vanish into thin air, can it? My advice—pop yourself on the loo for a couple of hours, take a good book, and put everything out of your head. Then it'll be all over and you can get to repainting this room. Before you know it, it'll all be gone, and you'll have nothing to worry about."

Tasha took the wrapped and tore it open. She inspected the pill. It's stamped with a white icon.

"A heart?" She almost laughs again. "Really?"

"Don't blame me, dear, I don't make the drugs. I just do the inspections. I'll let myself out, shall I?"

"Yep."

"Any questions, give me a ring, okay dear?"

"I won't."

"Bye then."

On the street, Miss Stowe She marks the Jackson household file as resolved, looks back at the house, and thinks about the woman she has left behind in the nursery, the woman who know doubt thinks she's fooled them all. Perhaps she has, Miss Stowe thinks, perhaps she has, and taps at her clipboard until the next case-file appears. Four streets over. It's a busy area. She puts up her umbrella again, though there is still no rain, and departs.

Across the street, Caitlin watches the Nanna leave from her upstairs window, one hand wrapped around her bulging belly, the other clutching a paintbrush. Their nursery is very nearly ready now. Just a few weeks to go, and they still don't have a name.

Jason opens the cupboard in the living room below the clock, and pours himself a whiskey from an unmarked plastic bottle. He hates whiskey, but it had seemed a waste to just pour it down the drain. He wonders if he should go upstairs, but thinks he should not. If we ever have a child, he thinks, I'm going to call it George, after my dad.

In the bedroom, Tasha sat on the tiny child's chair, in a room with blue walls, and moons and stars on the ceiling, and The Wind in the Willows in the bookcase. She put the pill in her mouth, rolled it around her tongue. It felt small and hard and simple.

Nothing to worry about, she thought, and swallowed it down with a large mouthful of tea.

DIRECTOR'S CUT

*C**lack.*

EUGENE WATKINS HAS a problem, though no-one talks about it. It is a nasty little worm of a problem. It takes up all the space in Eugene's head every hour of every day. For everyone else his problem is nothing more than an unspoken whisper, caught on the inside of the mouth and swallowed. *It will sort itself out*, they think. *One way or the other.*

Fanny Watkins also has a problem, though it is of an entirely different hue, and *everyone* talks about it, most notably Fanny herself. The problem is of her husband's new job overseas—a consulate position, very well-paid she'll have you know, but with all that time spent away from home, she will miss him dearly. But of course, she couldn't complain, because it's an embarrassment of riches really, but still one cannot help but...

The delicate matter of children is raised at the wedding reception; Fanny and Eugene's mother dismisses it with her customer matriarchal candour. "There is plenty of time on the honeymoon," she says, and later, to Eugune, "Fanny will make a wonderful mother." She straightens his cravat. "And you would have made a wonderful father too."

Eugene does not think of the significance of that *would* until later in the evening; at the time he is distracted by one of the guests—a man glimpsed frequently between head and shoulders, and who Eugene cannot remember seeing seated anywhere during the meal and the speeches. The man looks different to all the other guests somehow, though Eugene cannot quite distinguish how. In a darker hours of the evening, dancing with cousin Cecily, then cousin Georgina and later cousin Effrygia—we do so *love* dancing with you, Eugie, they squeal—the *would* settles in the back of his head, and *would* that has solidified from a *will* only a few months ago. It is his sister's marriage, he realises—he has been released from familial expectation, free to become the broken branch on the family tree, the confirmed bachelor that no-one quite talks about.

He looks for Fanny; she is nowhere to be seen. Perhaps she is upstairs, already conceiving the next generation.

There is the man again—at the door, watching Eugene. Or, no, perhaps not; when he looks again there is no man to be seen.

Eugene excuses himself, retreats to the cool solemnity of the hall. Four marble busts—the grim visages of his grandfather, great-grandfather, and so forth—are white and judgmental in the gloom. The door closes, the sound of the quarter and the stamp of dancing feet muted. In the back of his head, Eugene's nasty little problem squirms for attention.

"Brother?" When he looks up, Fanny is on the stairs, ghostlike in her dress.

"Sister." He sips from his whiskey glass; the bitter dregs bite his tongue.

She glares at him. "Well—aren't you going to congratulate me?"

He smiles; the smile is to himself, and not to her. "My heartiest of congratulations, sister darling. You have netted yourself a fine man."

She stands up. "If you're going to be like that, Eugie." She makes away up the stairs, then stops and turns on him. "Honestly—you are foul, you know that? It's my wedding day—why can't you behave as you should?"

Then she is gone, and Eugene finds he is in his bedroom, alone.

You would have made a wonderful father, whispers the room, and *we love dancing with you, Eugie*. He reaches under the bed. There is a carpet bag he has stashed there; until now he wasn't certain that he was going to open it, but now…

Inside is a rope. It is a thick rope, but easy to knot. Eugene has tested it. Standing on the dressing stool, he loops one end over the light fitting and pulls the knot tight. He holds the other end, already tied in a loop, in his hands. The rough fibres scratch his fingertips. His nasty little problem is awake; it's scratching with its nasty little fingernails and chattering with its nasty little tongue. *You're foul*, whispers the rope.

At first it is pain, and then there is a rush of white, and then there is black, and finally there is colour.

This is what it was, thinks Eugene. There are arms around him, lifting him, and fingers at his neck. When he opens his eyes, there is a face close to him. *Colour*, he thinks. It is the man from the reception. *It's as if he's in colour, and we're in black and white.*

He finds he is laid on his bed. His neck is sore, and breathing hurts. The man in colour is knelt beside him. "This is not how your story ends," he says. "Do you understand?"

Eugene struggles to sit. His neck is sore, and its hurts to breathe. "I'm sorry, but who…?"

The man shakes his head. "Doesn't matter," he says. "Just listen to me. It's very important. *This is not how your story ends.* Agreed?" Eugene tries to protest, but the man cuts him off. "Agreed?"

Eugene can do nothing but nod.

Clack.

HE AWAKES THE next morning to what feels the worst hangover he has ever experienced. He washes his face, and ties a fresh cravat tighter around his neck to obscure the marks. In the mirror, he looks into his own grey eyes and shivers; he feels disconnected from the day, as if the morning light from the window should pass straight through him rather than alight upon his beaded brow and pallid cheeks.

Making his way downstairs, he pauses at the door to the dining room. He hears his sister's voice from within, plaintive. "It's so sad, of course it is, but quite honestly—why that day of all days? It was my *wedding*..." More voices join hers—the cousins, comforting her.

He steps through the door. "Good morning!" he announces brightly.

Fanny freezes mid-sentence; Eugene almost laughs. His sister isn't moving; none of them are. They are a tableaux of confusion, and it is *ridiculous*. He is discovering today—as he piles high his plate with eggs, bacon and mushrooms—that many things are.

As one, their pause unspools. "Brother," says Fanny. "I thought you were—we believed you to be—" She casts around, looking to the left and right. It is as if she is in a play, Eugene thinks, and has forgotten her lines. He cranes his neck for the prompter, but there is no-one. Finally, she says: "I was given to understand you were indisposed."

"Nonsense," he says, taking a seat at the end of the table. "Why would anyone think that?"

Cecily's cheeks are streaked with tears. She looks at him uncomprehendingly. "You know, I couldn't say, Eugie darling. The idea had quite gotten into our heads... but nevermind! You're here! I was thinking, perhaps we could go boating today? The weather is really delightful."

Eugene bit into a slice of toast. "Top idea, old sport," he says. "I'd love to."

They watch him eat in silence.

"I say," he says when he has finished his plate, "did any of you notice a gentlemen at the reception last night. I didn't recognise him. He was sort of…" He tries to think of a way to describe the man in colour such that they will understand the description. "…handsome."

Fanny's mouth sucks in a moue of discontent. "No," she says, with finality. "No-one of that *nature*." That word, *nature*, drips with the same oily accusation of *would* but Eugene is astonished to feel the word pass in one ear and out the other. His nasty little problem doesn't stir to claw for the word to chew upon.

"Never mind," he says. "I'll look for him myself."

Fanny stands abruptly, hurling her napkin to the table in disgust. "If you're going to be like that, Eugie." She makes for the door, then stops and turns on him. "Honestly—you are foul, you know that? It's my wedding day—why can't you behave as you should?"

He waves at her as she sweeps out of the door, then turns his attention to the scrambled eggs.

Clack.

HE IS THE good kind of tired after a day boating with Cecily. The girl had been a delight; she had quickly forgotten her upset over breakfast and arrived at the lake fresh-faced and excitable. His legs and arms ache as he ascends the stairs and walks the corridor to his chamber.

The chambermaid has made his bed. She has helpfully neatly folded his pyjamas, dusted the dressing table and the mirror, opened the curtains. With forethought, she has provided Eugene with everything he will need for the evening: a fresh bar of soap, the bowl refilled with cold water, and a hanging rope from the light fitting.

The loop hangs there, empty, waiting for his neck.

This is now how your story ends. Agreed?

Eugene pulls the dressing stool to the centre of the room and climbs onto it. He runs his fingers the length of the rope, then unknots it from the light fitting, opens the window, and drops it out. He leans out: the rope curls in the flower beds below like a snake. Satisfied, he closes the window, and draws the curtains again.

That night he sleeps deeply, with not a movement from his nasty little problem.

———————

Clack.

"HELLO SISTER DARLING," Eugene says, sitting down for breakfast.

They pause, though they recover faster this morning. Cecily wipes the tears from her face. "Eugie! We thought you were…"

"Indisposed?"

Cecily rubs at her forehead. "Honestly, we must be quite mad. Here you are, right as rain."

"Yes," says Eugene. "Right as rain. Fanny, I was meaning to ask you—a gentleman at your reception. I want to find him. I'm sure you'd have noticed him, he was astonishingly handsome. Quite frankly, he was the most beautiful specimen of humanity I've ever seen."

Fanny doesn't look at him. "I don't recall anyone of the story. What on earth do you want with him, anyway?" she asks.

"Well," says Eugene, "he was in my bedchamber the night before last, and I really have to thank him for what he did for me."

The napkin rebounds from her water glass, which spills, dousing the table. "If you're going to be like that, Eugie…"

He is left with the cousins, staring out of the window. It's curious, he thinks, how the grounds look from here. Almost as if they are a painting outside the window, rather than real gardens and trees.

———※———

Clack.

THERE IS NO trace of mud on the hang-rope, nor indeed any sign of its sojourn in the garden. He opens the window and peers out—the flower-beds are empty. Someone must have retrieved the rope and returned it to his room; whoever did so must also have washed it.

He pulls the dressing stool to the centre of the room and climbs up.

"You should do it, you know."

Fanny is in the doorway, in her dressing gown. She glares at him from beneath long lashes.

"Shouldn't you be on your honeymoon by now?" says Eugene. "It's been two days."

She blinks in confusion, and looks left and right. *For the prompter.* "You should do it, you know," she repeats.

Eugene sighs. "Do what?"

Her lip curls. "Hang yourself. It's the only decent thing. Everyone knows people like *you* can't be happy. You *have* to kill yourself, it's the only thing, isn't it? That's what mother says."

"And that wouldn't trouble you?"

She frowns. "Of course it would trouble me, darling brother. I would be heartbroken from the rest of my life. But surely you understand—there isn't any other ending?"

He sits down on the stool. "These aren't your words, Fanny."

She shrugs. "You should do it, you know," she repeats for a third time, and leaves.

Eugene waits, inspecting his nails.

"You should do it, you know."

"Hello, mother."

Eugene sighs. "Do what?"

Her lip curls. "Hang yourself. It's the only decent thing. Everyone knows people like *you* can't be happy. You *have* to kill yourself, it's the only thing, isn't it? That's what your sister says."

"Well, if it's quite alright by you, I'm not going to do that."

His mother freezes—at first for long enough that it appears she is merely thinking of the next thing to say, and then longer until Eugene realises she is neither blinking, nor breathing. She has become a still photograph, unmoving.

It is then he notices the men. There are two of them. They wear black suits, and black bowler hats, and Eugene realises they have been standing in the room the whole time and yet he has not quite noticed.

"Perhaps you were right," says one.

"I'm always right," says the other.

Eugene grips the stool. "Who are you?"

The tall one smiles. His teeth glint silver, sharp, like scalpels. "How rude of me. My name is Mr. Text, and this—" he indicates his shorter companion "—is my brother, Mr. Subtext."

Mr. Subtext clenches his jaw, and looms.

"Now, it seems to me," says Mr. Text, "that we have a problem here.

You see, the thing is, you've gone *off script*."

"Ex—excuse me?"

"Off script, Mr. Watkins. You see, you were meant to hang yourself two nights ago. The night of your sister's wedding no less—very melodramatic." Mr. Text tuts to himself; his teeth clack together. "The script is very clear about these things, I'm afraid. We certainly can't have you gallivanting around the estate, boating and eating and being *happy*, can we? That won't do at all. No, I'm afraid your ending has already been decided, and a happy ending is simply not an option."

Eugene loosens his cravat; the bruises are still there, mottled and purpling. "Why not?" he says. "I *am* happy! I don't see why…"

Mr. Text steps forward. His shadow falls across Eugene. "Perhaps I haven't been making myself clear, Mr. Watkins. Frankly, you have received an abnormal amount of latitude already. A happy ending is not permitted for you. It's all because of your *nasty little problem*, I'm afraid."

"I don't see…"

Mr. Subtext cracks his knuckles. "You're queer," he says.

Mr. Text sighs. "My brother is rather blunt, but he does have a knack for getting to the truth of things, I'm afraid. That is it in a nut shell, Mr. Watkins. You are an invert—homosexual, if you prefer—and thus your ending has been decided already. The Whitehouse Institute are very firm on the matter."

"You're queer," repeats Mr. Subtext, for clarity.

"I had sought simply to nudge you in the right direction," says Mr. Text. "My brother thought you were made of sterner stuff. Still: I am a gentleman, if nothing else. I would like to offer you one more chance to co-operate."

"And what if I don't… co-operate. What if I don't hang myself?"

Mr. Text smiles. The scalpel teeth catch the light; Eugene thinks of sharks, with their razor teeth and dead eyes. "Then we will *cut* you, Mr. Watkins."

Clack.

AT BREAKFAST, EUGENE can think only of the rope hanging in his bedroom. He does not speak to the girls at breakfast; they pause as he is accustomed to, then wipe away their tears and continue as if nothing has happened. Fanny watches him reproachfully from the other end of the table.

A happy ending is not permitted for you, says the shadow of the rope, and when he tries to push it away it snaps, and says, *you should do it, you know* and somewhere in the back of his head he feels his nasty little problem stirring again.

On the lake with Cecily, he finds himself unable to enjoy the sunshine or her chatter, and stares moodily across the water until she reprimands him. Yesterday's daring has been punctured; today he dare not tell her that he scans the shoreline for a flash of colour amidst the grey.

Clack.

Ascending the stairs, he looks around, hoping the handsome man will appear, like a gallows reprieve, but the hall is silent and still. Not even Fanny appears to argue with him.

Clack.

The rope hangs as it always has. Eugene drags the stool to the middle of the room.

He holds the loop in his hand. *I'm not doing this for you,* he tells his nasty little problem. *I'm doing it because they say I have to. I don't have a choice.*

His nasty little problem licks its greasy lips, and curls tighter. *That is what it always has been,* it replies.

Eugene puts the loop around his neck.

"Good boy," says his mother. She is standing at the door; Fanny is beside her. "We'll miss you terrible," they say. "But it's the only ending."

He kicks away the stool.

At first it is pain, and then there is a rush of white, and then there is black, and finally there is colour. "I'm sorry," says the handsome man, "I'm so, so sorry." There are arms around him, embracing him. Eugene sags against them, feels himself caught, and held. He sobs, like a child in its mothers arms. He realises the man in colour is crying too, bright technicolour tears; they weep together.

Eventually, he is laid on the bed. The man in colour lies beside him. He traces a warm finger over the bruises on Eugene's neck. "The Censors came," he whisper. "I'm so, so sorry." The man in colour closes his eyes. "I wanted more for you. I wanted me—you—to be happy, but they won't let me."

Eugene runs his hand over the man in colours cheek. He is young, he realises—only a few years older than Eugene. In fact, they look similar. "Who are you?" he asks.

The man in colour opens his eyes. He laughs; it is to himself, not to Eugene. "What a complicated question, coming from you," he says. "Tell me—do you frequent the moving pictures?"

Eugene shrugs. "Not often," he says. "But I have on occasion."

The man in colour looks at him; his eyes are an impossible green, so green that it as if someone has painted them, Eugene notices. "I am the Director," the man in colour says. "Or perhaps not *The* director. Certainly *A*."

"I see," Eugene says, and he thinks he does.

"I wanted a different story for you," says the man in colour. "I truly did. I thought I could this time. But the Institute disagreed. And so it seems they have sent their agents... for that I'm truly sorry."

Eugene lays back. "They said I had gone *off-script*."

The man in colour's fingers are on his chest. "Indeed. Perhaps you should find solace in the fact that in that, you are not alone."

Eugene shivered at his touch. Looking down at his chest, he fancied for a second he saw colour spreading from the man's fingertips across Eugene's chest: a burst of pink skin, a shocking red nipple. He turns his face towards the man in colour, and their lips meet.

The room slides—the bed, the dressing table, the stool fall sideways, until all that can be seen is the open fire, the flames drawing closer as everything begins to fade—

"—no," says the man in colour, and suddenly it is he that fills Eugene's vision. "I will not permit them to turn away—no pan, no fade. If they will not permit the ending to be happy, I will not them look away now."

Clack.

FANNY DOES NOT seem to notice Mr. Text and Mr. Subtext sat on either side of her at the breakfast table. Eugene does, though. The sight is enough to turn the scrambled eggs to ash in his mouth, but he soldiers on.

Cecily wipes away tears. "Forgive me, cousin—I don't know where such silly notions have sprung from. I'm afraid we were given to understand that you were..."

"Indisposed," says Mr. Text.

"Dead," says Mr. Subtext, who is sharpening silverware.

"Absolutely not," says Eugene. "I'll admit I had a late night. I was up 'til the wee hours making love to a handsome man."

They freeze; Eugene waits for the prompter to supply their next lines.

"That's sounds lovely," says Cecily, after some time. "Would you like to go boating this afternoon? The weather is delightful."

Fanny is still frozen; it takes her a little longer to come unstuck. When she does, she stands up, and flings her napkin. Disgust is written across her face with the subtlety of an actress playing to the back of the hall. "If you're going to be like that, Eugie." She storms off. "Honestly—you are foul, you know that? It's my wedding day—why can't you behave as you should?"

"Yes," says Mr. Text. "Behave as you should."

"Kill yourself," says Mr. Subtext.

"You'd have to put the noose around my neck first," says Eugene cheerfully.

"That," says Mr. Text, "can be arranged."

Clack.

"I do so love being out on the water," says Cecily, trailing her fingers in the water.

"One admits it is rather pleasant," says Mr. Text, who is sat primly in the bows. "Water: the unheeded elixir of our continued existence. Its uses are endless."

"Good for drowning in," says Mr. Subtext.

Clack.

"Beautiful stairs, these."

"A broken neck is very quick."

Clack.

"Ah, Mr. Watkins. Kind of you to join us again. I trust you have had a nice day."

"Your *last* day."

"Thank you, Mr. Subtext. I think we are perhaps a little past that now. Mr. Watkins… perhaps you would like to take a seat, as it were."

Eugene climbed onto the stool. He ran his fingers over the rough rope. The light fitting trembled.

"Well done, Mr. Watkins. Now—if you would be so kind as to place the loop over your head."

This is not how your story ends. Eugene closed his eyes and offered a silent apology to the man in colour. "I already told you," he said. "I'm not doing it. You'll have to do it yourself."

Mr. Text crosses to him so fast Eugene does not see him move. Thin lips expose the scalpel teeth leaning in close to Eugene's face; his breath smells vinegary and sharp. "Nothing could give me greater pleasure, *Mr. Watkins.*"

Mr. Subtext is cleaning his nails. "Nothing would give him greater pleasure," he explains. "He hates queers."

Mr. Text pulls the rope tight around Eugene's neck. The rope chafes against his already bruised and sore skin. He closes his eyes. "Thank you for your co-operation, Mr. Watkins," says Mr. Text, close enough for him to feel the consonants scratch across his skin.

At first it is pain, and then there is a rush of white, and then there is black, and finally there is colour.

"This way," says the handsome man, and grips Eugene's hand. He pulls him across the room.

Mr. Text and Mr. Subtext watch dolefully across the room. "Honestly, children, this is quite beyond a joke. What hope do you have of escaping? The door is locked, and my brother and I will not stop pursuing you."

"We're going to murder you, and chop you into pieces," agrees Mr. Subtext.

"This way," says the man in colour, and he pulls Eugene in a direction that's he's never quite looked, and they are stepping out of his bedroom through the wall that Eugene realises has never really been there at all. And then he is running through corridors full of items that Eugene cannot comprehend, in fleet pursuit of the man in colour.

"We will *cut* you," calls Mr. Text from somewhere behind, unhurried.

"We will cut you and you will bleed," adds Mr. Subtext.

Eugene dashes to keep up. "Where are we?" he asks.

The man in colour chances a look at him. "Let's call it *behind the scenes*," he says. "Through hear." They duck beneath cameras and lights, leaping cables, and then they are at the wedding. The tables are crammed full of guests, and at the centre of the table his mother is making her speech. "Her father is sadly unable..." she begins, and then they are off, darting through the crowd. Behind them, Mr. Text and Mr. Subtext cut a swathe, and they are pursued by the sound of tables crashing and crockery smashing.

"Follow me," says the man in colour, and the duck from one scene to another, to another: now here they are in the rain when Fanny meets her husband-to-be, and now here in the maze during the comical misunderstanding that briefly separates them. And then, opening a door in a spectacular sunset, the man in colour leads them into blackness.

They sink as in deep water, and then Eugene finds his feet, steadying himself against his companion. The dark is absolute at first, and then there is both light and sound: enormous white letters that appear above their heads, and an orchestra that swells to a rousing crescendo.

"End credits," says the man in colour. "We're nearly there."

"Don't think this stops us," says Mr. Text from somewhere in the darkness.

"We can cut anything," says Mr. Subtext.

"Run," says the man in colour, and they do, plunging through the darkness, ducking below letters and leapfrogging names until they reach what can only be the end of this crawl, the white outline of a horse rearing on its hind legs.

"Stop!" calls Mr. Text. "This game has gone on quite enough. Surely you realise at this point that you have no hope of your story ending how you want it to?"

Mr. Subtext shuffles towards them. He clutches thin, sharp scissors between his meaty fingers. "You're ungrateful," he says. "We showed the first bit of your nasty little story, and then you throw it back in our faces when we try to give you the ending you deserve."

"Quite right, brother," says Mr. Text. "I'm disappointed. How can we show you... *homosexuals* if we cannot show the truth? Misery and death, I'm afraid—it's the only way."

"Now," says Mr. Subtext. "We've reached the end of your showing. Nowhere else to run." The scissors flash. Behind him, Mr. Text holds up the rope, already knotted.

The man in colour places himself between Eugene and the Censors. "If you want him, you'll have to take me first," he says.

"Not a problem," says Mr. Text.

"Not a problem at all," says Mr. Subtext.

Clack.

THEY CUT ME *from the credits, you know? It wasn't until 2013 that anyone even knew I'd directed that film. It was a different time I supposed, but they didn't like what I'd done with Eugene. I didn't want him to die you see, but the censors said he had to. I wasn't allowed all that stuff that went beforehand if I did... oh, I don't know... punish him, I suppose. I like to think we've moved past that sort of archaic story now, but... well. That's why I'm so thankful for this opportunity—I never thought I'd live to see the day. That's what this deleted scene is all about: this was the ending I thought Eugene deserved. The censors didn't agree with me...*

...but then again. Where are they *now?*

Eugene lies on his bed, the warm sunlight from the window casting his skin gold. Beside him, the handsome man from the reception turns beneath the sheet, opens his eyes.

"Morning," says Eugene.

"Morning," says the man, and kisses him. Then he leans closer, and whispers in Eugene's ear.

Lots of people have asked me what he says, but I've always kept it a secret. I suppose, given it's the anniversary... Here you go—an exclusive then!

"This is how your story ends," says the man in colour.

Eugene wraps his arms around him, and kisses him again. "Thank you," he says.

Clack.

THE CONCUBINE'S HEART

THE TOMB OF the Empress has breath, and bone, and muscle. I can feel her shiver and moan beneath my hands, and though my fingers tremble I know the vibrations are more than my own weakness; they are a pulse that runs deep to the caverns of her far-off ventricles and atria. The tomb of the Empress lives, and we live inside her.

There is one window before which the Empress's coffin lies at rest. The coffin is gold, the only bright embellishment amid the hall of greys and silvers and coppers, and it bathes in the reflected light of the passing planets. When there are no planets to be seen, and no suns, the window is black and cold, the coffin shadowed.

"That star," whispers Baozhai to me on the first night, pointing out the window at a distant dot of white. "It is our destination, set in place by the astrologers and the architects as it has been for every Empress. We sail directly for its centre, and the seven of us will kneel before our Empress's coffin until the window cracks and we burn in a crucible of white fire."

Else, we will all starve first.

FOR THREE NIGHTS we can hear the sound of the engineers. At first the sounds are angry and male, and then they are wet and bloody, and finally they are silent. As the astrologers and the architects intended, the secrets of the Empress's tomb lie unspoken by the engineers' bodies—or at least, such I imagine, for we can see nothing but the metal door behind which the men are locked. We press our ears to the door, but we can neither see nor hear anything any longer.

"Such fools are men," says Yanmei. "To beat themselves bloody; if they only followed our example, they would yet live."

The white star hangs in the window; today it is but a single bright point amidst a black ocean.

"Come," says Suyin. "Come back to the Empress."

She shuffles to the tomb, kneels beside the coffin and bows her head. The others follow her, kneeling beside her in a neat row, each girl perfectly equidistant from the other. My place remains empty. I turn back to the door, and run my fingers over its hinges.

"Qiaolian," says Suyin without opening her eyes. "Come back to the Empress."

I do as she bids.

AT FIRST THERE is thirst, but this is a matter easily rectified. The tomb of the Empress is encased in water, its skin beaded with tanks that absorb the light of the universe and shield us from its heat. The engineers knew this, and I know this, and so perhaps this knowledge remains only mine, but irrespectively the evidence is before our eyes: the window to the stars ripples and bends with the weight of water on the other side. Is is a contradictory effect, the sensation that we are both submerged and airborne.

Yanmei kneels before it and prays that the gift of water might be granted to us to wet our dry tongues. She presses her head against the cool glass. Her lips move silently, begging.

While they sleep, I arise from my knees and scavenge the ship. As with any great machine, there are parts that seem to serve no utility, and I select one such part—a long, sharp part—and coax it free of its fastenings.

When my sisters awake, it is to a small hole and a thin stream of water. They quench their thirst, and I wait until they are done to drink.

<hr />

SECOND THERE IS hunger, such hunger as is impossible to describe in words.

The tomb groans. I wonder if, with the engineers grown still in her belly, the ship also feels empty. When my sisters kneel, I kneel, but when my sisters sleep, I search, examining every gantry and balustrade. I press my ear to its veins, hear steam roaring inside. I follow the sound into its ribcage to where shadows press tight around gears and motors.

I have always been the one to watch and listen, to determine the single necessary word of influence; human or machine, there is little difference.

"Qiaolian."

I startle. Wenling has awoken, come looking for me. I am thankful that it is her, for she is mild and unwearied by the world—on occasion, she has shown me kindness. Better her than the pious Suyin, or the capricious Baozhai. Or Yanmei—that thought does not bear consideration.

"Qiaolian, come," she says. "You know you must not exert yourself."

She looks at the gargantuan mechanica atop which I crouch, and shivers. "You must rest."

Perhaps she is right. My heart is quivering; the blood sings through its rebellious hole.

I follow her back to the Empress.

———

MY FIRST TIME before the Empress, I can barely breathe nor stand. I have been taught the proper stance in which to appear: hands held supplicatory before me, head bowed. "At first, you must not look above her feet," I am told, and so I do not. She has such beautiful lily feet—the size of a child's, enclosed in delicate shoes embroidered with lotus flowers. Between the edge of the shoe and the hem of her robe is alabaster skin that I imagine cool as porcelain to the touch.

"Approach," she says.

I am led forward by the men, as if I am theirs to give.

She places two fingertips on my chin and raises my face to hers. I am wrong; her skin is warm.

"Come," she says.

There is a filigreed elm-bed, draped in rich fabrics—not a bed for sleeping but a bed for pleasure. The men respectfully close a screen behind us; only my new sisters remain, lined up, gazes decorously averted. Baozhai, Dongmei, Wenling, Liu, Suyin, Yanmei—soon I will know their names as intimately as my own.

Liu reaches around to disrobe the Empress. First I see white, and then I see black.

SUCH A HUNGER as is impossible to describe in words can be described in looks.

"There's meat," Suyin says, "if we could only open the door."

"The men have been dead six days," says Yanmei. "They will be spoiled now. We would die if we partook of their flesh."

Perhaps the hunger is hardest on me; I am frail and small already, and so my veins ring as hollow as my stomach. But then again perhaps it is easiest for me; I am accustomed to the weakness of my body, and how to push it away and carry on.

"Meat must be fresh, or else you will be poisoned," Yanmei says. Though she is not the oldest, she was the first, and wears this fact like a crown. "The flesh must be living, or near to."

She does not look at me, nor do any of them.

Fear chokes my frail heart, a candle guttering in a night wind.

I pray to the Empress to stave off my hunger, and theirs. *I was your favourite*, I remind her. *I could not be touched then, and I would not be touched now.*

I cannot hear what lies in my sisters' prayers.

I BECOME THE girl without use—after all, what is a concubine who can give neither pleasure nor utility without fainting? But somehow, the Empress's interest in me does not wane. She brings me before her physicians, who diagnose me with myriad conditions that none can agree on. One suggests that my heart is a weak vessel pierced at birth; the other physicians mock his description, but there is an echo inside my chest that convinces me he is right.

I petition the Empress to permit me to touch her as the others do; even if my heart bursts, it is the purpose for which I was brought, but she refuses. She will not allow me to die for her pleasure.

I am dispensed to help the calligraphers, the astrologers, and the engineers. I learn to write, I learn to read the stars, and I learn the intricacies of automata.

"You are lucky," Wenling tells me one day, catching me lying beneath a flock of mechanical birds to which I have given flight. Her hair is combed and shiny; she is on her way to meet a summons from the Empress.

I do not feel lucky, but I say nothing.

—◆—

IT TAKES SEVERAL days before they come for me, when the hunger has grown to a howl that cannot be ignored. I have anticipated, and apportioned my time accordingly.

It is not murder, they reason. Qiaolian, the girl who trembles in the presence of her Empress, the girl who can neither climb nor carry nor scrub. She is a candle already out; is it our fault if in her terror she falls down dead? As is it our fault if we choose not to waste the gift of flesh before us?

It is Wenling who knows where I will hide; it is Yanmei who leads them; it is Suyin who calls out to me to come back to pray before our Empress. "It is your duty," she says.

I slip between gears into the heart of the machine. I have learned my way around but I cannot hide forever; every crevice of the ship is familiar to me, and I have tested every chink in the perimeter to no avail. Today they may give up, but tomorrow they will be hungrier.

I straddle the metal veins of the ship. My heart races fit to burst.

"I am here," I call.

You know the story of Wu Yueniang, of course? The blacksmith's daughter? The beautiful concubine of an immoral man, toiling beside her ninety-nine sisters to tow his boat along the river. You know about her beautiful bound feet too, of course, in her delicate shoes embroidered in lotus flowers. Shoes so beautiful they could not help but draw the man's attention—a fatal mistake, for Wu Yueniang had concealed a small sword inside the bindings of her feet, and when he came close, she drew out the sword and stabbed him.

My bindings do not contain a sword; the engineers taught me tools as weapons.

It is unwise to underestimate the one who can do nothing but listen and learn. I watched the calligraphers, the astronomers, and, most importantly, the engineers. I have learned how to fashion metal into birds, into language, into oceans, into ships. The tomb of the empress has breath, and bone, and muscle, and I am its physician.

I press my face against its pipes, grip its rivets, whisper words that sink into its blood-stream and fly a-quiver to the heart of this ship, my beloved Empress's resting place. *They are coming for me*, I say.

THE STEAM SCREAMS when I release the bolts. For a second I am reminded of my Empress arising from her baths, steam wreathing around her, my sisters shuffling forward with oils and robes. Then the steam turns bloody, and Yanmei's screams meet it in chorus.

My heart convulses; the killing of Yanmei took nothing more than the flick of a wrist, but still my body is rebelling. I breathe, calm myself. I have coaxed the ship into a new shape to suit my own rebel physiognomy, but it can do nothing to combat the battery of emotion.

I pull the lever; metal grinds closed. The vent seals. Yanmei's body falls to the ground, and the smell fills the room.

Forgive me, but she smells… *delicious.*

My sisters back away. Suyin is clutching a metal pipe, torn from the ship. She drops it.

I point to Yanmei. "Meat," I tell them. "Food."

I delve amongst my robes, pull out one of my tools, a file sharpened to a point. It is not strong, but it is enough to cut flesh. I throw it down to them; it bounces across the floor and skitters to rest against Yanmei's body.

"Food," I repeat.

———

THEY CARVE HER into portions, and when those portions aren't fit for eating, they place them in front of the vent and I pull the lever. I am fair; I do not eat more than they do.

They feed to near-delirium, then return to the Empress. First is Suyin; her piety is expanding into Yanmei's absence, and the rest fall into her pattern. But I see the cracks spread: first through my sisters, and then around the splintering hole in the window, as if manifested by their pain.

One night the window breaks, and a great deluge of water bursts across the deck. My sisters, though sheltered from the worst by the coffin, still emerge soaked and coughing.

Perhaps they imagine themselves washed clean by the wave, absolved of their guilt, but with that gone there is room once more for the hunger.

I do not climb down to bathe in the water; I do not share their concern. Perhaps it is because I value my survival more highly than my soul, or perhaps it is because, always separated from my Empress by a mere screen, I have long ago made peace with my desire for the taste of flesh.

IT TAKES THREE days, but they come. I am ready; when Baozhai and Dongmei place their feet on the weighted panel, a whisper passes from cog to cog beneath it, magnifying until it triggers. Springs in the walls are released; metal struts snap down, and they are impaled.

I expand our culinary ability; I cannibalise plating from the walls, and redirect the steam vents such it bursts out against a flat metal sheet that heats until it is red hot. I bid Suyin and Liu to slice apart the bodies and place each strip of meat on the makeshift griddle until it is cooked.

Wenling refuses. She backs away, and vanishes beyond my sight.

This time they do not fall upon the body and devour it. It is rationed as long as they dare—seven days until there is nothing but bone. In all that time, there is neither sight nor sound of Wenling, though I bid them call for her to come and eat.

I have been keeping an eye on the window; the star is larger, though still distant, and without an ocean between us it shines clearer, highlighting the Empress's tomb bright white in the dark.

SUYIN AND LIU return to their vigil at the coffin; it is the only way they know how to stave off the hunger. I dare to climb down; I have grown spoilt

---

hidden up in my self-made nest, my body untaxed. Now, the simple exertion of moving through the ship again leaves me breathless, my chest aching. It fills me with fear: if Suyin or Liu (or Wenling, wherever she is) sense my weakness, even my ingenuity may not keep me alive. I cannot rely again on a right-placed foot, on weights and tricks.

Once, an engineer taught me to make a stork, more complex than my copper sparrows or brass mice. The stork could flap its wings, turn its head, walk in a circle. It had been intended as a gift, the engineer said, but then pressed a finger to his lips. "Watch." He stroked its beak, and the moment skin touched metal, the bird's neck snapped forward. The beak, serrated and sharp, bit at his hand as he pulled it away, laughing.

I marvelled, begged him to show me how the trick was done.

There are three skeletons on the deck. I can no longer tell them apart.

I HEAR SUYIN and Liu talking, and see them look towards me. It is a look I have grown to recognise. I wonder—on the days when the screens were drawn around my sisters and the Empress, and I was left to stand with the men listening to the panting of ecstasy from within—whether my face also betrayed such an uncontainable hunger.

I close my eyes. I am learning now, the time between desire and action. I have some hours before the hunger outweighs the guilt, before need outweighs fear. When it does, I am prepared.

It is Liu who ventures near first; I am surprised, for Liu was always reticent. Where I was subjected to the moans and cries of the others, she was always silent, and thus I was forced to imagine her pliable and unmoved by the Empress's attentions. She was never kind to me, but she was never cruel.

When she draws within striking distance, my creations move as one. Pistons lever their arms; the clanking workings within their ribcages jettison gouts of steam. They brandish what weaponry I could fashion—more struts pried from the walls.

Liu spreads her arms. "So be it, Qiaolian."

<hr/>

SUYIN REFUSES TO touch the body, so I order her to step far away and manoeuvre my creations between us. I have made alternative use of the plate, and so I sever a gas pipe and strike a spark. It leaves the meat blackened and tough and I laugh to myself that I can raise such a criticism in the circumstances.

Suyin does not look at me, nor see me laughing. I can only imagine how it would appear if she did. I offer her food, but she prays without response. I wonder what unspoken history of Suyin's sets apart the flesh of Liu from the flesh of the others.

I return to my nest. The star is nearer; somehow I have imagined that the simple act of continuing to survive every day will delay its arrival, but the truth is quite the reverse. I have lived only in order to meet my death.

The secret to changing the ship's course died with the engineers. The door behind which they lie would be easy to open, but I do not dare risk descending to the deck.

The full stomach lulls me; I fall to sleep and dream of the Empress.

<hr/>

I AM AWOKEN by the sound of death. I find Suyin prostrate below me, one hand reaching for a slab of meat, the other pinioned beneath the feet of one my creations. A strut enters and exits her head on either side of her blank eyes.

Tears well for the first time. Suyin had come for food, not for me. She had not earned this end.

I let myself down from the nest, and find that my legs can barely support my weight. I crawl to her. I kiss her on the forehead and whisper an apology. No doubt she would prefer a prayer, but my prayers are to the Empress and not a god, and I doubt Suyin would approve.

I inspect the door behind which the engineers are walled. Many weeks have passed—surely the engineers must all be dead by now; I can risk entering. It is a matter of disconnecting the right pieces of machine, re-connecting the wrong pieces in the right places, and it is soon achieved.

An army of statues is waiting for me in half-shadow. Between their legs lie the engineers, bloody and crumpled. The smell is putrid and tears at my stomach.

WENLING IS WAITING for me when I return. She rests against the coffin; her face is drawn, her body leeched of life like a dried flower. I do not know how she is still alive, and I do not ask.

"I felt it change," she says. Her hand rests on the floor. Does she feel the ship like I do, as viscera and sinew? "We've turned away from the star."

"Yes," I say.

Wenling's eyes close tight. If there are tears, I cannot see them in the gloom. "We were meant to burn with her," she says. I hear some of my own pain in her voice, and I realise that perhaps Wenling loves the Empress as I do. Perhaps you imagine this would soften my heart towards her, but instead I feel a hot jealousy that she was permitted to both love the Empress and partake of her body. And besides, my heart is already soft enough.

"I wish to burn," Wenling says.

There is a gas pipe, and a spark by which to make a flame.

"As you wish," I say. "May you live eternally in the embrace of the Empress."

She smiles. "May you, also," she says.

***

THE TOMB OF the Empress has breath, and bone, and muscle, and I can feel her turning beneath me, shifting width by width away from the star. A green-white-and-blue planet rises into view—it seems so beautiful compared to the crimson planet I have left behind.

I lie face down on the coffin lid, and close my eyes.

She places two fingertips on my chin and raises my face to hers. First I see her face; she is beautiful in a manner unparalleled (and though in my life I am permitted to see no women besides the Empress and my sisters, I hold this to be an unequivocal truth.)

My heart swells, and then I see black.

I think about stripping my creations of their mechanisms, levering open the coffin, reattaching them to the Empress. I could bring her alive, make her dance with me. Her touch would be as cool as I once imagined. I am sure that this time I would not faint.

But alas, I fear the exertion of opening the coffin would be too much. My Empress will remain separated from me by stone as she has always been, by a screen, and a treacherous heart.

ANTONIA AND CLEOPATRA

T HE PLACE: THE Sahara desert, endless, arid, parched. The time: a little after midday, the merciless sun directly overhead. Somewhere like this, water can be more precious than gold, a drop of moisture worth more than all the riches one can imagine. It was this biological imperative that propelled the mosquito to land on the perspiring forehead of one Corporal Frederick Algernon Hooch, and the very same imperative that drove it to sup eagerly at the rivulet of sweat that tracked down the peaks and troughs of his sunburnt face, past the flick of his moustache, and down to his chin. Corporal Hooch slapped distractedly at his face. Failing to dislodge the insect with brute force, he exhaled heavily in its direction, seeking to dislodge it from its perch. This proved equally ineffective; instead, his moustache simply shivered comically, and he was forced to slap again, with increased force. The mosquito departed unperturbed, buzzing away far from Hooch's reach, where it taunted him with a lazy loop around feet of the sphinxes followed by an unhurried barrel roll around the pillars and a gentle landing upon the weathered nose-stub of the Pharaoh.

"Corporal?"

Hooch scratched his forehead where the mosquito had been, sighed, and turned to squint at the approaching figure. The Lieutenant was barely more than a lad, his face burnt and peeling. He clutched his canteen as if it were the most precious object he'd ever touched. He executed a salute so lazy it bordered on mutinous.

"What is it, lad?" asked the Corporal, though the answer was perfectly clear.

"The men, sir... they were hoping that perhaps we could... stand down?"

"Stand down?" The Corporal huffed and puffed. If there had been enough moisture left in his body, his ears might have steamed. "Stand down! What pultroonery! Need I remind you, Lieutenant, that we are on the hunt for a vagabond at large! A master criminal, Lieutenant Smythe! Shameless scoundrel of the sands..."

"Yes, Corporal, sir," said Lieutenant Smythe wearily.

"We must be alert, and ready! Poised to intercept her unsalubrious exit...!"

The rest of the soldiers all studiously avoided looking in the direction of the conversation, standing rigid to attention with the exaggerated indifference of eavesdroppers. They stood ringed around what might have appeared, to an unstudied viewer, little more than a dip in the ground, punctured in its centre by a half-submerged sandstone block the size and height of a man. The soldiers' rifles pointed in its direction, the bayonets gleaming in the relentless sun.

"Understood, Corporal," said Lieutenant Smythe. "It just... it's been seven hours."

The soldiers continued to, very obviously, exhibit no reactions.

"Absolutely not," said Corporal Hooch firmly. "She could appear at any time!"

For a few moments, not a great deal happened. The sun continued to burn, the sand continued to be sand, the temple ruins continued to be temple ruins. Then, with the air of a man no longer able to contain a sneeze at a funeral, one of the soldiers slapped himself firmly on the cheek, and there was one less mosquito in the world.

The Corporal's shoulders sagged. "Very well, Lieutenant Smythe," he said. "At ease, company."

Amidst a chorus of relieved sighs, the platoon relaxed. The bristling ring of blades dipped, some even boldly laid aside. Lieutenant Smythe bobbed a hurried, thankful salute, and retreated to his men, who slapped him heartily on the back and proffered water tankards, which he declined with a saintly expression on his face.

Corporal Hooch shuffled a little away from the pack. Their youthful bonhomie always made him uncomfortable, made him aware of the creak in his bones, hear the Oxford pedigree in his syllables. "Scoundrel of the sands," he muttered to himself. "That's a good one. The desert desperado. The scallywag of the souks! The Nile—"

He paused.

Beneath his feet, he fancied he felt a faint trembling, as if a herd of animals were stampeding under the sand. He opened his mouth to call to Lieutenant Smythe and the rest of the men, but none of them seemed to have noticed the vibrations. They were all slumped now in the vestiges of shade they could find. Two were even playing cards. He shut his mouth again.

Seconds later, he could ignore the growing shaking no more. "Lieutenant!" he called out, but it was too late.

The sandstone slab they had been guarding so diligently not five minutes before exploded outwards in a rain of shale and billowing sand. The soldiers dived for their rifles, spluttering and half-blind. Triggers were fumbled. There was the sound of bullets ricocheting and panicked shouts.

From out of the maelstrom, a creature leapt. It emerged from the sand, bearing down on Corporal Hooch, who fell back, his hands raised against its onslaught. It's powerful, mechanical legs were a churn of pistons; its jaws champed, levers pumping in its burnished cheeks; its eyes burned with fire from within a bronze skull. On its back, two bronze mountains—no, *humps*—jettisoned steam.

Gadzooks, thought Corporal Hooch as he fell beneath its galloping metal hooves, *it's a bloody camel.*

The Corporal's men made a shambolic attempt at pursuit, but they were outstripped in seconds. Somewhere, Lieutenant Smythe was shouting: *Kneel! Fire!* The platoon fell to their knees in ragged formation, raising their rifles and taking aim, but the bullets merely pinged off the animal's metal exterior, rebounding into the desert wastelands.

Atop the mechanical creature, a small figure was perched between the humps. The figure was female, diminutive, and clad in a strange mix of colonial military jacket and corseted bustle. Against the barrage of bullets, she clutched a dented pith helmet to her head. A mass of wild black hair streamed from beneath it as she galloped away from them on her steed.

Faintly, she could be heard, in a smoky, joyful voice, shouting, "Geronim*whoooooaaaaa!*" as the mechanical camel bucked.

"After her!" screamed the Colonel, dragging himself up from his undignified position on the floor. "Post haste! Make chase! The fiendish floozy!" The soldiers continued to fire, and he stomped out in front. "I said *after* her! Don't you know who she is! Antonia Jones, plunderer of the pyramids, pilferer of the pharoahs! *Apprehend her at once!*"

"Pursue her, men!" ordered Lieutenant Smythe, and at his word, the soldiers made for the corral of horses, galloping after her.

"That woman!" Corporal Hooch muttered, dusting himself down. "I have never encountered such a *larcenous* woman! Such a..." He cast around for words.

Beneath Hooch and Smythe the ground was continuing to shake. "Corporal," Lieutenant Hooch said, shaking his superior by the arm. "Cor-poral!"

"Such a... *what* is the word?"

From the shadowed hole through which Miss Jones had torn free of the sands, there came a sound: a skittering, hopping sound, the sound of many things moving in the dark at once.

"Such a... a..." Corporal Hooch continued to stare at after the departed fugitive.

"*Corporal!*"

A single, lone figure emerged from the hole. A statue, cast from clay, the size of a short man. Its face was painted in the simple, Egyptian style that adorned a thousand artefacts in a thousand museums across the world. Its mouth opened, wider than seemed entirely human, splitting at its painted lips, and what lay within was most definitely not of clay: sharp, canine teeth chittered in the rotten, festered mouth of a corpse long-dead.

It hopped forward, bouncing on legs that had been formed together by some ancient artisan. Lieutenant Smythe raised his rifle in shaking hands, but the strange-statue creature didn't flinch. Instead, it opened its dead man's mouth, and emitted a high-pitched, keening scream.

Behind it, from deep beneath the Egyptian sands, called up from the catacombs and burial chambers that lay beneath the temple, more of them came, teeming from the gloom to stand rank behind their horrifying leader.

"...a *magnificent* woman," Corporal Hooch said, turning. "That's it. *Magnificent*—oh my sainted aunt!"

He was thrust aside by the first statue-creature, and then barged and flung out of the way by a succession of them as they streamed between Hooch and Smythe. Their mouths opened in unison, screeching their chilling cry to the empty skies, hopping implacably towards the horizon, the direction in which Miss Jones, perched gloriously atop her dromedary automaton, was dashing herself.

<p style="text-align:center">~~~</p>

THE PLACE: THE Wagh El-Birket district, Cairo. The time: the purpling dusk.

Night settled over the Nile, the darkness creeping up the warren of narrow streets into the district, swallowing up the dancing girls who turned and swayed, the lairy soldiers who drank and whistled, the pantalooned men who watched and scorned. In the gloom the streets came alive with a new energy, like a caged animal prowling behind bars. On the surface there was warmth and light: the lanterns of the brothels warm and tempting, the drunken babble in a myriad of languages, the mingled aroma of roasting meat and hashish. Underneath it, unspoken and menacing, an undercurrent of silk-wrapped, shadowy secrecy, held in the dark hollows of the alleyway girls' eyes, in the cudgelled, jealous glances between the locals and the uniformed British, in the rustle of robes pulled up in discrete doorways, the clink of exchanged coin. This, *this* was why people came to Wagh El-Birket.

Where the banks of the river and the city met was a rickety dockland, strung with red lanterns. The incline of the streets and the narrow jetty conspired to point the stumbling footsteps of the needy in the direction of what lay floating atop the waters: the Elysium Parlour. But of course, you've heard of the Elysium Parlour haven't you? The boat, in a ragtag collection of shapes and colours. You heard tell of its bizarre and long-forgotten origins:

beginning life as a Chinese junk, or a Spanish galleon perhaps, though who can tell anymore? It's a patchwork boat, built from the body parts of other boats, stitched together with lanterns and blind hope. You've heard about its cabins piled on top of galleys, walkways piled on top of gantries until it resembles a teetering castle, complete with spires and gambrel roofs. You've heard about the silks fluttering at its door, enticing.

At the edge of the dock, a figure, short but feminine in shape, shrouded in a cloak both too thick and too dark for the humid heat, lurked, watching. With an air of concealment, it looked once left, once right, then scurried to enter.

Inside, hookahs breathed sweet smoky clouds into the air; women bound in silks and little else lounged on fine throws and cushions. Men, of all shapes and sizes, were attending to the women: intimately entangled, subservient or looming dominant depending on the size of their evening's pay or their particular speciality. In one corner, a gimlet-eyed Turk juggled bottles, poured the contents into a row of silver glasses, and set their tops alight in one theatrical flourish. Facing him across the sea of sensuous bodies, a small stage was lit by rheumy footlights, upon which a woman, naked but for the layers of gold paint, clutched a live, writhing snake to her breasts and recited petrarchan sonnets.

And if you've heard about the rest of the Elysium Parlour, of course you already know what else lurks within: beneath all of this saturnalia, below the feet of the patrons and the girls, below the hookahs and the cushions, the floor was glass. The murky green of the Nile curdled underfoot and, under the ample buttocks of a lady spread beneath the ministrations of a turbanned Arab, a crocodile blinked bewildered at the strange scene above him.

The Madame of the house swept forward, statuesque, leatherclad, a whip coiled at her waist.

"*Welcome* to the Elysium Parlour," she said, well-rehearsed intimations of depravity flavouring each syllable. "The jewel of the Nile, the Sultan's spicy secret, the answer to your heart's wanton cry. *I* am the famous Madame Cleopatra Bonny." She traced a finger along the whip lazily. "You may have heard me referred to as the Iron Mistress. The *ashikret al-hadikh,* also."

"Really, my dear," said the cloaked figure, "you *must* get a real job." She pulled back her cloak, revealing her face.

"Ah," said the Iron Mistress. "Good evening, mother."

<hr>

THUS IT WAS that the two most infamous ladies in Egypt sat down to tea and cucumber sandwiches.

The first, the lady Antonia Jones, renowned relic-thief and intrepid defiler of tombs, pyramids and necropolises, wanted in sixteen countries of Africa (as well as Tibet, Japan and Wales.)

The second, her daughter Cleopatra Bonny, possessing of both her mother's bosom and beauty, but rising a foot in height above the maternal curls of Antonia. The Iron Mistress, the madame of the Elysium Parlour, purveyor of peoples of pecuniary persuadability into passionate pacts, who had sailed her glass-bottomed brothel around half the world or more, before fetching up here, on the shrouded banks of the Nile, in Cairo.

"What *is* it?" asked Cleopatra, tilting her head.

Between them, a clay pot sat on the table amongst the tea-things. Its head was carved into the shape of a pharaoh, outlined in faded, red paint. In the hollows of its eyes, something gleamed. It was, in Cleopatra's considered opinion, singularly unremarkable.

"It's rather less than impressive, isn't it?" Antonia said, sipping her tea daintily. Held in her callused hands and against her sand-blasted, filthy face, it looked like an absurd, fripperous trinket.

"All that way—risking all sorts of danger for... *this?*"

"I was given very specific instructions," Antonia said. "Drawings. Descriptions. It's not even made of gold, but apparently its very valuable. The client was quite firm on the matter."

Cleopatra unhooked her whip and laid it beside the teapot. "Who's the client?"

"I have no idea," said Antonia. "We never met face to face." She set down her teacup and looked around the anteroom. "You really must have a tidy up around here," she said, tartly. "It's all a bit... bohemian, wouldn't you say?"

"Mother," said Cleopatra, refilling her teacup firmly, "I'm a brothel madam. We're hardly in the market for stuffiness and starch. Why, for Cairo, we're the very *lap* of luxury. Stop avoiding my questions. Mysterious client. Elaborate."

Antonia wrinkled her nose. "Brothel madam," she sighed. "So common."

"Internationally wanted thief," Cleopatra rejoindered. "So *criminal.*"

"Perhaps," Antonia said, "but never *common.*"

There was a knock at the door, followed by the tousled head of a young boy. "Missus said you wanted me, ma'am?"

Cleopatra waved towards her mother. "Thank you, Aziz. This poor down-on-her-luck beggar from the street requires some errands to be run."

Antonia rummaged in her pack, producing a clutch of folded parchments and a handful of an odd, shiny material.

"Is that *steel wool?*" said Cleopatra.

"Yes," Antonia said. "Aziz, take this to wherever you've stabled Barnabus and feed this to him. He gets hungry about this time. This should do it. His furnace will need stoking, too."

"Yes'm," said Aziz.

Antonia handed him the letters and a handful of paistres. "Deliver these to their addresses," she told him. "The blank one goes to The Eyes of the Sky. I'm sure you'll know how to pass a message." Aziz retreated.

Cleopatra arched an eyebrow. "The Eyes of the Sky?" she said. "He's... not a man to be trifled with, shall we say. Is he your client? I thought you didn't know..."

"I don't," Antonia said. "But if anyone knows the competitive value of things in this city, it's him."

"Dangerous game, mother," Cleopatra said.

"Perhaps," Antonia said, "but so is running a house of ill repute in the heartland of syphilis."

"It'll probably turn out to be worthless," Cleopatra said. "Wild goose chase—I'd put money on it. The Eyes of the Sky won't give you a handful of coin, and your mysterious client will have vanished. If he was a client at all. He could have been sending you into a trap, trying to catch the ignominious Lady Thief of the Deserts."

Of course, if they packaged it up and sent it off to London it'd would probably still fetch a decent price, where the populace grew ever more giddy at the faintest whiff of Egyptian history, fuelled by penny-dreadfuls and the lurid tales of expats. Even the status of her mother, the elusive master thief who shamelessly robbed her homeland of its treasures, would likely add a frisson to such a sale. But Cleopatra kept quiet about that.

"There *were* a good deal of soldiers camped out waiting for me," Antonia mused. "I didn't pay much attention to them. I was too busy with more... *interesting* encounters."

"Spare me the details," Cleopatra said.

"Oh, my dear, not *that* kind of encounter. No—something darker and more monstrous I fear, lurking amidst the cobwebs of the tomb. But no matter—I evaded them. Thanks to good old Barnabus."

Cleopatra leaned closer to the curio. "Shall we... take a look inside?"

"Tamper with the goods?" Antonia said, aghast. Then, after a moment's consideration: "Oh, go on then."

They cleared the table, setting the delicate tea-things aside and removing the white lace cloth. Antonia produced a set of delicate instruments in a leather case from her seemingly bottomless bag; Cleopatra fetched a gaslamp from the cupboard and opened its flame. They had just bent to their task when they were interrupted by a knock at the door, and a stifled, nervous voice announced, "Madame Bonny! The donkey is in the stable."

"It's a camel," Antonia said. "And we know. We sent Aziz down not two—"

"That's not what she means," Cleopatra said, sweeping the statuette off the table and seizing her whip.

"Well, what in heaven's name does it mean, then?"

Cleopatra pursed her lips. "It means, oh miscreant-mother-mine, that the *law* is here."

⌇⌇⌇

CORPORAL HOOCH FIXED his eyes firmly on Cleopatra's nose. Her eyes burnt too fiercely for him to quite dare meet her eye to eye, and to look elsewhere—be it further south on her body, or in any direction about the Parlour—was altogether too dangerous to risk. Thus, he addressed her nostrils: "We are in search of a fugitive, ma'am. We have reason to believe you can help us with your enquiries."

Madame Bonny shifted, rolling her hips and tutting her lips theatrically.

"A fugitive, sir? Oh, how thrilling. But no, no, nothing of that sort here."

Hooch dared to swivel his eyes a hairsbreadth to the left. Undulating bosoms swung into view, and he quickly looked back. "We have... information," he said, the words tripping over his tongue, "that suggests we are likely to find her in your... establishment."

Madame Bonny's lips formed a little *O* of shock, which she held a fraction too long. "Oh my! Sir, you shock me. No—not hide nor hair of a woman, fugitive or otherwise. Pray tell, who exactly is this person you seek?"

"She's... well... I don't quite know how to describe her. She's— somewhat short. Although, not in the way of a, er, gremlin, or such. Really quite—um—handsome. She is—well—"

Clearing his throat, Lieutenant Smythe stepped forward, interrupting his superior. "Perhaps this will help," he said, and produced a parchment on which was sketched a charcoal likeness of Antonia. The word 'magnificent' went unheard, mumbled into Hooch's moustache.

"That woman?" Cleopatra spat on the floor; it pooled above a submerged lilypad. "That *qahbaa!*"

"You know her?"

"Know her?" Cleopatra was practically apoplectic, waving her whip around above her head. "She's a filthy beggar from the district. Used to daily entreat me to come work at my fine establishment. I would tell her *no* and throw her out immediately. Why, she's ancient enough to be someone's mother. We would never have one so *old* or *common* here!"

From somewhere distant to the chamber, there was the pointed sound of something smashing.

Lieutenant Smythe possessed none of Hooch's shyness, and boldly stared around the room; the girls quailed beneath his gaze, as did those men sober enough to fathom the situation. "Is that so?" he said. "Work here, is that it? And this establishment is of course a—"

"—temple of religious worship," Cleopatra supplied. "The men come to consult my gurus on the matters of spirituality. Quite legally."

"Gurus," said Lieutenant Smythe.

"I promise you," Cleopatra said, "a visit to the Elysium Parlour is a *heavenly* experience. Isn't it—Private Lopjollop?"

Behind Smythe and Hooch, a soldier did his best to become very small and inconspicuous.

"Well," Lieutenant Smythe said, smiling sweetly, "if this woman should appear again, seeking employment... as a guru... please do inform the authorities immediately."

Hooch piped up, feeling it was time to take control of the situation. "Yes, quite right, little lady," he said. "This terrible, nefarious, beautiful woman *must* be brought to justice at once. I must get my hands on her!"

Cleopatra bobbed a curtsey. "But of course," she said. "I will immediately inform yourselves, good sirs, have no fear! The very moment I see her, that common fishwife."

The sound of the soldiers shuffling awkwardly back down the gangplank covered the sound of a second something smashing on the other side of the wall.

"Of course they would have been watching," Cleopatra told her mother, as they wound their way through the night streets. Music and singing, and the stamp of hundreds of feet, could be heard a few streets away, but here in the warren, following the lines on the scrap of parchment in her hand, there was no-one to be seen—as if they knew to avoid these streets in particular.

"No doubt," said Antonia. "Though they would have to have been particularly dedicated to have observed our passing tonight. And much sharper than I believe our Colonel Hooch is capable of."

Cleopatra craned her neck. "Hooch? Is that his name?"

"I know," said Antonia. "Ridiculous name for a ridiculous man."

The soldiers posted along the dock hadn't been particularly subtle. Despite their best efforts at appearing undercover, a white face stood out a mile in Wagh El-Birket, no matter how assiduously it was draped in robes. Aziz had returned, bringing with him reports of the watchers on the dock, and a note for Antonia.

"The Eyes of the Sky wants to see us," she said. "He's left us a map to find him."

Aziz pointed out the window. "But—the men!"

Cleopatra ruffled his hair. "I suppose we'll have to go the wetter way," she said. And they had—over the edge of the deck at the rear of the boat, swimming silently along the darkened Nile until they could alight from the river downstream, away from the watchful gaze of the soldiers.

And now they were here, in an area of the city where even Cleopatra felt a tingle of nervousness, deep in her belly, warning her. No matter how hard she tried, she couldn't shake the feeling of being watched.

"I'm quite lost," she told her mother. "We're going to have to follow the map back, otherwise we might never make it out of this warren."

"Nonsense," Antonia said. She thrust the bag containing the statuette into Cleopatra's arms, and snatched the parchment. The map was leading them deeper, to a point marked with a round, black spot. The music and singing was fading. "Just a few more turns."

"I'm warning you, mother," Cleopatra said. "I've never met the Eyes of the Skies—but I've heard plenty about him."

"If you think this is the first slumlord ruffian I've ever encountered," Antonia said, "then it's high time I told you some bedtime stories, my dear."

The music and singing was gone from earshot—which was when Cleopatra realised that one sound had not faded. The stamp of feet.

"Mother—"

The wall to their left disintegrated into a hail of adobe chips and billowing stone dust. From out of the cloud marched—no, *hopped*—a creature the like of which Cleopatra had never seen, the size of a man, but made of clay or stone, it's mouth open and screaming.

It wasn't alone.

"Run!" Cleopatra and Antonia screeched to each other at the same time.

They hurtled away, the map and their destination forgotten, taking turns at random, with the legion stamp of the statue creatures in pursuit. The tight-knit twist of streets would have been easy to lose a human pursuer in—a quick turn down a forking alley, a duck into shadow—but misdirection or subterfuge was useless; the statue squadron tore through anything it its path. Awnings, trees, carts: all were shredded in their implacable hopping path, marching furiously with their festered mouths opening and closing in sinister shrieks.

"Ready!" called a man's voice from somewhere nearby. Then, more panicked: "Aim! *Fire!*"

A parade of bullets slewed into the front ranks of the statue creatures. Where they found their target, shards blossomed like fireworks, but it slowed their progress not a jot. They bounded onwards with jagged holes in their torsos, limbs hanging askew. A second round of bullets rallied against them—and it seemed as if their salvation was coming from nowhere until Cleopatra's brain caught up and she recognised the voice.

"Fire!" hollered Lieutenant Smythe, and quieter, a fraction behind, a

"Yes, fire!" from a flustered, red-faced Corporal Hooch.

The soldiers were emerging from the side alleys, rifles blasting in their hands against the charging army of monsters. It seemed to finally halt their progress—or at least divert their attention. As one, the statue creatures turned to advance upon the soldiers, the two forces ranged against each other across the the narrow street, the ground littering with rubble and bullet casings.

"Mother!" screeched Cleopatra. "Are these... things... what you 'encountered'?"

Antonia daintily adjusted her hat. "Yes, dear," she said.

"I'm thinking..."

"Run?"

"Run."

"Oi there!" shouted Colonel Hooch, lurking behind his men. "You're not going anywhere!" His words fell on deaf ears—or deaf backs; Cleopatra and Antonia were already madly dashing away from the melee. "Stop right there!" And with that, he abandoned his platoon and took off, huffing and puffing, in his own pursuit, calling after them almost pleadingly.

He caught up with his quarries in a blind alley.

"Hold up right there," he said, between breaths, brandishing his revolver. "You *fine* ladies are under arrest."

Antonia and Cleopatra caught each others eyes as they turned from the blank wall.

"Now really, Corporal," Antonia said, stepping closer. "Is that quite necessary? I'm sure you could turn a blind eye. Just for tonight. I could... *reward* you." She draped a hand around the Corporal's neck. His huffing and puffing redoubled. "My daughter here has a fine establishment where we can be alone. I mean... it's a bit bohemian for my tastes, but—nevermind, I'm sure you'd be *quite* comfortable..."

Corporal Hooch spluttered. "Well—that's a fine offer—and you're a fine woman—but—*duty*, you see—"

"I quite understand," Antonia said. "An upstanding man like you, that just *thrills* me. I wonder... are you quite as *up*standing... in the boudoir?" She leaned close.

"Well—I—er—I must confess, you've quite unmanned me, miss..."

"Indeed, it seems I have," Antonia said, stepping away, the Corporal's pistol twirling elegantly on one finger. "I suggest you turn around, Corporal, and forget you ever saw us."

"Oh," he whispered, almost to himself. "I could *never* do that."

"Put the gun down!"

Over Hooch's shoulder, Lieutenant Smythe advanced, his rifle aimed squarely at Antonia. She sighed, and let the pistol fall, stepping back towards Cleopatra. "Oh fine. What do they say in the penny dreadfuls? It's a fair cop, guv'nor."

More soldiers were assembling behind Smythe, uniforms ripped, some nursing bloodied faces. They too aimed their rifles.

The stamp could still be heard, drawing quickly nearer.

"I suspect," said Antonia, "you should arrest us with all due haste. I don't think you've held off our mutual friends for very long."

"Kneel down," Lieutenant Smythe ordered.

"Poor you, dear," Antonia said to Cleopatra. "Always a bus-man's holiday."

"Mother," said Cleopatra, enunciating carefully. "Hold my hand."

"Hold your hand? Don't be silly, my dear. They're not going to execute us. How mawkish of you. I raised you better than that."

"Mother," Cleopatra repeated. At the length of the street, the statue creatures had reappeared, bounding towards them with savage glee. "Hold. My. Hand."

And, with that, they were fifty feet above the city.

One second she was mired in their blind alley, the next Antonia was soaring upwards, into the warm night air, whipping up through the clouds. The city receded below, her feet scudding over the domed rooftops. She was above the battleground, a ranged fight as the soldiers and the statue widened, the chaos becoming bloodier.

For a moment, she thought that perhaps, at the most fortuitous of moments, she had sprouted wings and taken flight, but then she gathered her wits enough to look upwards. Cleopatra was splayed in mid-air, the arm pointing downwards clutching Antonia's wrist, the other upwards to a dangling rope. Following this lifeline, it vanished into the belly of an airship that loomed above them, though at this angle, and partially obscured by cloud, there was little more visible than a mossy keel and the suggestion of the huge balloon from which is hung.

The hull of the ship was carved and shaped into the visage of Horus, its round angry eyes glaring down at the rooftops of Cairo.

"Tremendous!" she hollered against the wind. "We found our destination! The Eyes of the Skies has found us!"

"*Ladies!* You—are—under—arrest!"

Antonia glanced back down, momentarily dizzied by the fast-receding skyline, then swore richly. Clutched to her ankle was an unexpected passenger.

"Under arrest, I tell you!" shouted Colonel Hooch.

Antonia waggled her foot, attempting to dislodge him, then—gauging the potentially fatal distance to the ground below—thought better of it. Instead, she opted for appealing to Hooch's better instincts.

"Oh, lay off, you buffoon," she shouted down.

"How dare you! I am a member of Her Majesty's finest!"

"Mother!" Cleopatra's call was frantic, drawing Antonia's attention—

but too late. Spreadeagled as she was, with both arms fully occupied, Cleopatra could do nothing to intervene. The bag strung over her shoulder—the unremarkable artifact at the heart of their current travails tucked neatly inside—was falling open.

The pharaoh head of the statuette emerged from the bag, like a curious cat, and then—painfully slowly, inevitably—it tumbled out.

Antonia snatched with her spare hand, but it bounced through her fingers, plummeting downwards towards the vanishing city.

"And I am certainly no buffoon!" Hooch cried upwards, which was all he managed before the statuette struck him squarely on the temple. It shattered, bathing him in a fine, diaphanous sand. His head lolled, unconscious and his fingers opened around Antonia's ankle. She swung wildly to grab him; the corpulent Corporal might be intent on arresting her, but letting him plummet to his death wasn't all that attractive a prospect either.

"Well," she shouted up to Cleopatra, "at least that's shut him up."

For a moment it looked as if the airship above them was descending, and then her brain realigned and as she realised that, no, *they* were being drawn up, wound into the belly of the ship, under the savage beak of the eagle.

—~~~—

"IT WERE," REMARKED the Eyes of the Sky, "tremendous valuable. I woulda been prepared to offer ye a deal more than yer client. If ye hadn't gone'n beaned this poor bloke on t'head and lost it."

He was sat cross-legged in what was most accurately described as a throne, swathed in purple velvet robes that would have seemed ostentatious—even ridiculous—in a person of less poise and threat. With each word he spoke, there was a glimpse of teeth, filed to points. The top half of his face was hidden by a silver mask, fashioned into the visage of Horus. A cruel beak overshadowed most of his lower face, and the eyes of the mask, unmoving and dead, pinned them unblinkingly.

"Perhaps," said Antonia. "It is a great loss to be sure, though one feels that if you had arranged a more traditional transit to your abode, we might not have been in the position to disperse the goods over *the whole of bloody Cairo.*"

The Eyes of the Sky chuckled, licking his teeth. "Ye talk pretty," he said. "And you talk clever." He ran a finger up the delicate carved inlay of his throne, rough yellow fingernails counting out the notches. "I like pretty," he said, each syllable as sharp as his teeth. "I don't like clever."

"Since we're here," Antonia said, "perhaps you could illuminate my daughter and I. We were curious you see—quite a few people seem to be have gone to some lengths to retrieve our poor deceased artefact. It was very well protected." She peeked over the boom to the city below. "Still is."

The Eyes of the Sky leaned forward; Horus, despite its fixed expression, looked affronted. "Ladies, what t'hell do you fink I am? Does this *look* like a library."

Alexandria had to admit that the poop deck of the airship did not, in point of fact, look like a library. It was a little heavy on armed pirates for that.

"I'm not a bloody curator," the Eyes of the Sky continued. "Do you know who I *am?*"

It was hard not to know who he was, not in Cairo. It was whispered that he owned most of the dignitaries in town—Egyptian, British, French, it didn't matter—and half the army majors too. And that was the tip of the iceberg. Stories abounded. Men scooped up from the street by the ghostly airship, found days later killed in horrific, though inventive, ways. The philandering sheik dissolved in a bathtub of leeches. The swindling oil trader, force-fed hunks of bread containing scorpions. The crooked consulate, left mummified alive in the baking sun on the steps of the Consulate.

"No," said Alexandria, "I can't say as I do really."

"But," said Cleopatra, "we know you were interested in what we were selling, which means you know *why* it's valuable. And since I've been attacked by statues and swung through the sky all for nothing—the least I'd like is an explanation."

The Eyes of the Sky rose, and walked to the edge of the deck, a king surveying his kingdom. "A *khat nejena*. A soul prison."

"A soul prison?" Cleopatra asked.

"It was only fer the greatest men of Egypt," the Eyes of the Sky said. "The Heka, they had t'power—to preserve the soul, in a vessel. Went against all the laws of the gods, but it could be done. So's it could be returned to 'em at a later time in history. To claim their glorious reward, presumably. Course, it meant they were kept out of the claws of Anubis. Suspended between life and death. Anubis wouldnae like things like that. They'd be damned when they finally made it to t'Underworld."

"But it's just a clay statue. One myth is as good as another. The ancient gods aren't real, they're just another paper pantheon. They died out."

The Eyes of the Skies' teeth glinted in the moonlight as he smiled. "Mayhap," he said.

"So what—drag these soul prisons out somewhere down the line, pop the soul back into another body, off they toddle?" Antonia asked. "Bit of a kerfuffle, given they'll end up with eternal damnation."

"That's why it was for only the greatest, bravest of pharaohs," the Eyes of the Sky said. "Or craziest. They were buried deep, protected by their *shabtis*—the statues built to defend them against harm and evil."

"The hoppy creatures," Cleopatra said.

"Yes. *Shabtis*. Implacable, inhuman, and unlikely to stop until they've recovered the *khat nejena* in their care. Or the soul is restored to a body."

"Well that's just spiffing," said Antonia. "Seeing as I don't have it."

Cleopatra peered over the rail. "They seem quiet enough now," she said.

"Yes," said the Eyes of the Sky. "Funny, that. Vanishes just at the convenient time, don't it, your precious cargo?"

"I can assure you it's most certainly *not* convenient," Antonia said.

The Eyes of the Sky stalked toward her. Around, the casually alert crew stiffened, and reached for their weapons. He cupped her cheek. "Perhaps, m'dear. Perhaps. You know—I'd pay a great deal to have a soul trap. 'N if I thought someone was hiding it from me—"

"I assure you," Cleopatra told him, seeking to distract him from her mother, "it's definitely gone. Smashed open on the good Colonel's head. Nowt but dust and shrapnel by now."

The teeth clacked together smartly. "Prove it," he said.

On the deck, the previously comatose body of Colonel Hooch sat bolt upright, as if awoken from a dream. "𓃂𓏏𓈖𓂧𓏤" he announced. "𓄿𓏏𓈖𓂧𓈖𓈖"

"That should do it," said Antonia.

"You don't understand, we need to see Sephiroth *right now*," Cleopatra said.

The girl squinted at her through the narrow crack in the door.

"Right now!" Cleopatra repeated.

"You will meet a dark and bloody death," the girl said.

"Bull!" Cleopatra retorted. "I know exactly who you are, Tawaret. You weren't a mouthpiece of the spirits last I checked. Though you were promising that you were the best in the Sahara at giving b——"

"But stranger, you will find many fortunes before your untimely demise at the hands of the cruel desert and the merciless sun!"

"Tawaret, you know exactly who I am. I'm the Iron——"

The door slammed, then reopened a second later. The girl curtseyed them inside. "I predict many mysteries and pleasures for you," she said.

"𓀀𓂋𓈖 𓀀𓈖," said Colonel Hooch.

"What on earth's he jabbering about now?" asked Antonia.

The Eyes of the Skies, his blade resting against the base of Hooch's spine, just above his bound hands, snickered coldly. "Not for your pretty ears to hear," he said.

"The language is old," Antonia said.

"Well 'course. It ain't tripped off t'tongue in centuries."

Cleopatra advanced on the girl. "Now—I know this operation. I am not looking for trinkets. I am not looking for fortunes. I do not need to know I will meet a tall handsome stranger, because I employ plenty of my own. I need the *real* service—understand?"

Tawaret cringed. "The spirits grant us many wisdoms."

"I *need*," Cleopatra said, "to see Sephiroth. Now"

"I see... I see... I see a man who was wandered many leagues from his home."

"Don't give me that!" Cleopatra said.

"A man who cannot linger long in his domain at the behest of his burning loins!"

Cleopatra sighed, and fingered her whip. "Tawaret, let me explain a few things to you. It's been a long night. I'm here with my dodgy mother, an even dodgier gangster, and what is—if things are really to be believed—the disembodied soul of Khufu I in the body of a rather hairy British officer. I'm in need of a Heka, and there aren't many around these parts any more. Show me to Sephiroth, or I'll show myself. Through you."

The face of Horus interjected itself over Cleopatra's shoulder. "I have a chest full of ravenous scarabs in the cart, if that helps?" it inquired helpfully.

Tawaret stamped her foot, glaring. "I see *a man who is not here*."

"Well then," Cleopatra demanded, "where is he?"

———✺———

"I'T'S A SMALL world," Antonia said.

"Not so much as you'd suppose," Cleopatra said. "He's here more nights than not. He's a big fan of Nyssa. She does things that—well—"

The Eyes of the Sky flourished his knife. "Can we get on," he said. "Things to do, people to exorcise."

"𓊝𓊝𓊝𓊝𓊖𓈖𓂝," spat Hooch.

"Not since I were a lad," the Eyes of the Sky said.

Blasting into the Parlour, Cleopatra lay about her with alacrity, puncturing the languid malaise of the late evening's work. "Fetch Nyssa and Sephiroth!" she demanded. The girls scattered, leaving a confused heap of addled men beached on the floors, blinking at their hookahs and squeezing their empty pockets. Cleopatra strode across the room, not bothering to step over the bodies where she encountered them, eliciting pained squeaks from those unlucky enough not to roll away quickly enough. In the doorway leading into the heart of the Parlour, she hollered after the scurrying feet: "And quickly!"

"Madame Bonny," Sephiroth said, when he had been fetched, half-clothed, red-faced and still tying his robe.

"Sephiroth," she said, snapping her fingers. "Time to unsaddle the powders and chantings. Unleash the unctions and bones. I've got a job for you."

"Uh—" he stumbled for words, and Cleopatra cracked her whip.

"Oh, for crying out loud, Sephiroth. I know Nyssa's good, but she can't have knocked your senses clean out." She pointed at Hooch. "Soul trap. Statue go boom, Hooch go pharaoh."

Sephiroth threw himself down at Hooch's feet, bowing and scraping.

"Oh for crying out loud," Cleopatra said, poking him with the toe of her boot.

"hhas'i" Hooch said, pleased.

"You need to get it out of him," Cleopatra said.

"No! No!" Sephiroth looked aghast, as if Cleopatra had desecrated his home in front of him. "Sacred!"

"Yes, probably," Cleopatra said. "Sacred pharaoh, I get it. But do you really want the sacred spirit of a pharaoh... in *that* body?"

───※───

"THEY'RE ON THE docks," Aziz said, peering into the door. Sephiroth was circling the room, chanting words Cleopatra had never heard spoken before, his eyes half-lidded, his concentration total. He had chalked hieroglyphics onto the floor in a circle, in the centre of which sat an engraved statuette of Anubis. (At first no-one had been quite sure how to get hold of that, but it was surprising what sort of trinkets could be found at short notice in Wagh El-Birket.)

"The *shabtis* or the soldiers?" Antonia asked. She was pacing by the door, turning her pith helmet over and over in her hands.

"Both," Aziz said. "On either side."

The Eyes of the Skies frowned. His knife was still held warningly against Hooch, who was now seated in an armchair, muttering happily to himself in an unintelligible language. "And they're not... doing anything?"

"No," said Aziz, peeking out of the window.

"Why are they not tearing each other apart?" said Cleopatra.

"They're waiting," Antonia said. "The *shabtis* for their pharaoh, the soldiers for them to make the first move."

"Be that as it may," Cleopatra said, "but they *will* move."

"Yes," said Antonia. "I imagine so."

"Right then," Cleopatra said, and stalked out.

In the main chamber of the Elysium Parlour, Cleopatra took the stage. "Ladies!" she called. "Attend!" and waited as the girls gathered from every twisted intestine of the boat. The threat of danger had spread through the Parlour quickly; they were restless and wild-eyed.

"Something is coming," Cleopatra said. "Thanks to the ministrations of my mother—a woman capable of getting into just as fine a mess as myself on occasion—we will shortly be called up on to fight for our lives against two forces. One, horrifying monsters from the margins of history. The other, British soldiers. I shall leave it up to your discretion to decide which to be more afraid of." She paused. "I'm fairly clear, myself."

She rested a boot on the footlight, spread her arms wide, a warrior princess addressing her tribe.

"Girls," she said, "we will take up arms, and we will fight them! We will not be alone. The Eyes of the Skies' minions shall rain down fiery tears upon our attackers. And here—in our home—we shall make our stand! Take up anything you can consider a weapon." Conspiratorially, she added: "I have discovered in my time that a hatpin in certain sensitive areas is quite effective."

Antonia bobbed her head in. "Not to interrupt the rousing speech," she said, "but Sephiroth is ready."

"Very well," Cleopatra said. "Ladies—do me proud."

They raised a cheer for her—a weak one, though perhaps in the circumstances it could be excused—and she stepped down amongst them, directing them towards the accoutrements of the Parlour that could be turned to violence.

From the anteroom, chanting began.

"He's started," said Antonia.

<hr />

IT WAS A bloodbath.

The second the chanting began, Hooch's eyes flew wide. He stood straight up and screamed, "𓏞𓏤𓂝𓃀𓈖𓏤"

Attack.

On the dock, *shabtis* took up an excited hopping and hurtled forward as one towards—not the boat—but the platoon. The soldiers raised their rifles, their shots proving as ineffective as in their last encounter. Lieutenant Smythe— gibbering in terror at the head of his troops—led a ragtag retreat to the doors of the Parlour, only to be met by a bristling array of makeshift weapons. Curling tongs, fire irons, flails and pleasure implements, all brandished with ferocity, trapping the soldiers between the women and the *shabtis*.

From above, a rain of fire—arrows poured down upon the *shabtis* from the airship that swept in above, the vast beak of Horus plummeting in from the thermals. Some of the *shabtis* shattered, some burst into flame, hurling themselves into the Nile where they extinguished with a potent sizzle.

The destruction of its front flanks did nothing to discourage the rest though: still the *shabtis* advanced up the jetty, towards the soldiers—only now they they had a new target, and rather than ripping into the remains of the platoon, they hurled themselves at the Elysium Parlour, bursting in through windows and ceilings, making short work of the matchstick walls.

No longer being ripped apart at the hands of stone teeth, the soldiers rallied, striking out to rescue their Colonel. The entry chamber of the Elysium Parlour descended into a maelstrom of fighting, the three forces meeting in a flurry of action: a trio of girls shattered a *shabti* between their flourished brands; the Eyes of the Sky leapt falcon-like through the air, his knife flashing, his teeth ripping at the throats of soldiers; Aziz vanished beneath the gnashing jaws of a *shabti;* Lieutenant Smythe grappled with a stone warrior, emptying his last round into its temple, wriggling free from the grip of its still-moving torso where it pinned him beneath its weight.

In the centre, Cleopatra wielded her whip like a conductor in the grip of an overture, sending soldiers flying back from the door to the anteroom with weals rising on their faces, shattering *shabtis* at the neck and stamping on their remains.

And then, beneath their feet, the glass floor cracked, and the Nile rose amongst them. For a moment, everyone was equalised, spluttering for purchase and breath, and then the fighting resumed, frantic amidst spumes of bloody spray.

Cleopatra retreated to the anteroom, bounding across the heads of sinking *shabtis* like stepping stones in a graceful one-two-three dash.

Hooch was thrashing in his chair, spitting obscenities in his ancient tongue. Sephiroth was still chanting, the words echoing with a depth and vibration the walls of the room could not have created, his eyes vacant and unseeing.

"Daughter!" Antonia proclaimed, hugging her tight.

"Mother," Cleopatra said, extricating herself.

"The battle rages?"

"The battle rages."

"Then I have a friend I must rescue. Attend to the ritual."

And with that, Antonia vanished through the door, into the rising river water.

"A friend?" Cleopatra mused to herself. "Surely she can't mean...?"

But that was precisely what Antonia meant.

And so it was that, as Sephiroth completed his ritual and slumped in a faint to the deck, and as Hooch's eyes reopened once more lit by the tea-stained soul of a British Colonel, the first sight to greet his rheumy eyes was Antonia Jones perched atop her dromedary automaton, pounding through the water towards him, swinging a cutlass at the enemy hordes around her and shrieking, at the top of her majestic lungs, "*Geronimooooooooooo!*"

"What a magnificent woman," he said to himself, and lapsed back into unconsciousness.

"Such a helpful man, The Eyes of the Skies," Cleopatra remarked.

"Quite so," Antonia said. "Remarkable really, how you've wrapped him around your little finger."

"Not so much," Cleopatra explained. "It was those teeth, you see— filed to points. Quite memorable. At least, that's what Fabian thought."

"And who," inquired Antonia, "is Fabian?"

Cleopatra smiled benignly. "Oh mother," she said. "You think the Parlour only has girls?"

"Ah," said Antonia, then, after a moment, "I see! A most potent secret, in these times."

"Indeed," said Cleopatra. "Of course, he's still got his soul trap. And you've got a very nice price. I'm not a cold-hearted blackmailer. Just—calling in a favour or so."

"Quite right," Antonia said.

"Mind you," Cleopatra said, leaning close to her mother, "it was quite a mess in there during that ritual. One couldn't be completely sure that bounder Khufu's soul ended up in the Anubis statuette. It could have been anything. Anything close to hand."

She produced a bottle from her pack—a dusty, battered whiskey bottle.

"A present. To your health, mother," said Cleopatra, passing it to her. "Until next time."

Antonia kissed her daughter on the cheek. "Until next time," she said. "I shall keep an eye out. Where are you planning on going?"

"Oh," said Cleopatra, "we'll see how far he'll fly me. I was thinking... Japan? I'll learn the dance of the seven veils, become the Silken Mistress."

Cleopatra Bonny rose up, borne away on the winds, proud at the entrance of her Elysium Parlour, the dilapidated boat festooned in ropes and strung below the Eyes of the Skies' airship. She raised a hand in farewell, soaring up and away from her mother, into the skies.

"Well, that's that," said Antonia. She tucked the flask away and turned to face the horizon.

"Are we ready?" said her companion, shuffling up to her, sweating and red-faced.

Antonia kissed him on his perspiring forehead. "We are, my lovely Colonel Hooch. Come along, Barnabus."

Into the desert sand they strode, the great relic thief Antonia Jones swaying aback her trusty steed, her companion following behind, clinging nervously to the back of his own. Into the sunset, towards tomorrow.

"Geronimo," she said.

BY CHANCE,
IN THE DARK

"*Isn't it queer,*" *says one boy,* "*how we've been in this place all this time and never met.*"

"*Isn't it,*" *says the other boy. He looks over at the one; their eyes meet, crease with conspiracy.*

"*Try it,*" *says the one, and so the other does, and coughs, sharp in his throat. The one laughs; he has assumed a position of knowledge that he does not in fact possess, and he is fully committed to the role.*

The other wipes his mouth on his sleeve, and licks his lips to ensure there is no trace remaining, but it proves ineffective; the taste remains.

"*Here,*" *says the one, taking back the bottle.* "*Let me show you.*" *And he does.* "*Now,*" *he says,* "*it's your turn again.*"

The dormitory is empty in a way that, even when unoccupied, it never is during term-time. It is just the two of them, the one and the other, cross-legged beside each other on the bed, passing back and forth the contraband alcohol. Through the arched windows, snow falls, at first aimless and furtive and then, as a wind picks up, decisive.

"*Oh,*" *says the one, and draws away.*

"Um—" says the other. "I'm sorry—I—"

The one says nothing; he leans back, stares at the other. There is something in what has transpired that has exposed him, disrupted the cloak of experience he had affected. The other wipes his mouth, but it seems that this too is a taste that cannot be obscured. He places the bottle on the floor, his bare feet on the boards, and walks away; it is not his dormitory, so he must be the one to leave, return to his own bed.

Beyond the window the snow has stopped abruptly, as if silenced by a celestial switch, and now there is nothing but a brilliant stretch of white, settling like a blanket shaken out over a bed.

"Wait," says the one, but the other has already gone.

IT IS AN old story, and so of course you know how it begins. So too does Ebenezer Scrooge, and thus when he awakes to the first ghost, he is quite adamant that he is having absolutely none of it.

"No," he says, "I am having absolutely none of it," and pulls the duvet over his head. He hides in the stifling gloom beneath the bedclothes, marinating in the hot, sour clouds of his own breath, and waits for the ghost to go away. He does much the same when those people—the charity-collectors, or the religious types—come uninvited on his front door, hanging on the doorbell; he waits behind the closed door until he hears their footsteps recede, the sound of the gate closing, watches them on the intercom screen until he knows their incursion has passed unvictorious.

But ghosts are not known (except in certain localised circumstances) for their footsteps, nor their shortness on time, and so when his shelter beneath the bedclothes grows too stuffy and breathless to stand the ghost is still waiting for him, black-and-white amidst the silver shadow of his bedroom.

"Hello pussycat," she says. "I am the ghost of—"

"Bollocks to *that*, lady," says Ebenezer. "It's the middle of the night, and I'm in *no* mood. Now will you kindly f—"

She looks taken aback at his language, her eyes welling briefly with tears. Her presence carries a sadness about it, sat primly at the bottom of his bed, half-absorbed by shadow, and though she is young there is a sense of the motherly about her. Another man might have been struck by guilt, though of course you know that Ebenezer Scrooge is not that kind of man.

"Oh boy, that's quite enough of that," she says. She stands up, smoothing down her dress, a white, silky number that shimmers with a quality more glamorous than ethereal. "If you could dress, that would be marvellous." When he doesn't move, she sighs, and turns around. "I'll look away, if that's what you're worried about."

He rubs his eyes; the doctors had warned him this might happen. "Carry on like you are…" they all said, but he waved them all away. "I saw worst in the sixties," he told them, and laughed, but he had misplaced the mirth somewhere in the off-license on the way home.

"Oh for heaven's sake, if you're going to be so stubborn," says the ghost. She looks faintly piqued. "I'll wait for you downstairs. Do hurry."

To her departing back, Ebenezer called out stubbornly, "I shan't!" and feels like a spoiled child.

Halfway down the stairs she stands on tip-toes and peeks between the stair-rails. "Now, darling, I really should warn you that it's not worth arguing."

And Ebenezer dresses, and they leave—although none of this seems to precisely *happen* in the way that Ebenezer is accustomed to things actually *happening*, so much as he find himself in the car remembering that these things have occurred: he remembers selecting the black suit from the back of the wardrobe, and he remembers locating his smart shoes from the rack by the stairs, and he remembers her holding out his thick wool coat for him to slip his arms into, and he remembers her draping the scarf around him, and he remembers her shaking out the little medicine bottle and offering him one of its contents *to steady his nerves*, and he remembers her tweaking his cheeks and leading him over the mountain of unopened cards behind the door, and into the street where the car waits, and he remembers all of these things as though none of them really happened and actually he is just here, with her opening the car door for him outside the church.

"Here we are," she says. "I told you it wasn't worth arguing."

If there is a time for mourning, it is winter. The church, crooked beneath a bruised sky, is rimed with a bitter frost; the grass between the graves is sharp and breaks beneath the feet. It would seem as if the colour has been drained from the world if it not for the people; the curious assemblage of mourners winds up the steep path, though it is difficult to imagine that these people attending a funeral. There are colours, and dresses, hats, gaudy makeup, like impressionistic smudges of colour daubed by artist across an empty canvas. The ghost puts her arm through his, and leads him in their colourful, frivolous wake.

At the door, he is handed an order of service by a six-foot woman in a thick veil and a scandalous basque (though, Ebenezer admits begrudgingly, both are at least black.)

He reads the name.

"Oh," he says.

The ghost smiles her sad, faded smile. "Yes darling," she says. "Now do you see why you're here?"

They take a seat on the right-hand side, half-hidden behind a pillar.

The ghost fishes out the medicine bottle again, opens the lid and tips two pills into the gloved palm of her hand. She offers one to Ebenezer, but he shakes his head. "Suit yourself," she says, and swallows them both. She shudders. "I never liked funerals."

There is a photograph, framed, at the front of the church on a table. Ebenezer examines it, tilting his head. He always finds something disconcerting about the photographs that are selected for funerals. They are always cheerful, luminous, and somehow disingenuous; he finds it impossible to forget that its corporeal counterpart lies only feet away in a wooden box.

He stares at the well-worn lines of the face he has looked at some many times before, the features he is so intimately familiar with, and feels an urge to dash up the aisle and hurl the picture from its place. But instead, he inspects the Order of Service. At the top is the name, in ornate script, and below that, the date—

"Hold on." He nudges the ghost. "You're doing it wrong," he tells her. But she isn't listening—she is staring off into the distance, glassy-eyed, and her lips are moving in an absent-minded, automatic way as if she's singing something he can't hear. He nudges her again.

"Hmm?" She blinks, watery-eyed, and looks surprised to find him there.

"If you're the Ghost of Christmas Past, you're really mucking it up," he says. "Because firstly, this is the future, and second, it isn't Christmas Day. It's the twenty-seventh."

She pats his leg. "Dramatic license, pussycat."

He sniffs; frankly, he thinks, if he is going to be subjected to this absurd pantomime of a hallucination then it could at the very least be accurate— and then he looks down and realises the Order of Service is crumpled in his hand, this thumb smudged across a phrase further down on the paper:

survived by his only son...

"As moral lessons go," he tells the ghost, "this is rather heavy-handed."

She dips her head against his shoulder, briefly, conciliatory, like a cat. "There's not really any other way," she says. "And besides, this *is* a Christmas story."

In moments when he has allowed himself to consider his own funeral, Ebenezer has conceived of nothing like this. He sneaks a furtive glance over the ghosts shoulder, at all the strange faces in the church. He wonders why some of them are here, though they are here to mourn irrespective of his incomprehension. Few are immediately familiar, and he experiences a sudden horror that perhaps he has looked right past the face he should recognise but has not, but then he rejects the feeling as another false fear of this night's fever dream. "Of course, he won't be here," he says to the ghost. "The absent son, so I will learn an object lesson in the consequences of a father's action."

She looks away. "Wouldn't that be simple," she says, and then he sees them, entering at the back of the church, the coffin hoisted on their shoulders. Ebenezer's son, red-eyed, dressed in a suit that is a pleasingly appropriate black, and behind him—

"His partner," says the ghost. "You can say it, you know. Or think it, it's all the same to me. His partner."

"That," says Ebenezer firmly, "is his *friend* Robert."

She leans her head against his shoulder. "Oh, pussycat."

Their appearance is the signal; a sussuration runs through those gathered as they turn to observe. From speakers concealed somewhere in the vaulted ceiling above, music begins.

"I don't understand," says Ebenezer, sotto voce to the ghost, and he finds it echoing—*I don't understand I don't understand I don't understand*—

as the procession, bracing against the coffin's weight, begin their careful journey down the aisle. His reaches for the ghost's hand, clutching her freezing fingers tight in his own.

"Shhhh," she says, as the first line of 'Somewhere Over The Rainbow' comes over the speakers. "They're playing my song."

—and then, he is awake, and in his bed that smells of stale beer and fresh piss, and is cold and wet beneath him. Sweat is soaked through his shirt and he gasps for breath. There is no ghost at the end of his bed, just the squat, rectangular silhouette of the television he has dragged into the bedroom. The screen is on, the volume down low. On the screen a black-and-white woman sings about happy little bluebirds flying, and Ebenezer Scrooge wearily swings his feet onto the cold floor, stumbling on the empty cans, and trudges to the airing cupboard to fetch fresh sheets as a brittle dawn breaks on Christmas Day.

THE OTHER BOY meets the one in the quadrangle; at first he is frightened, the one appearing like an apparition out of the shadow of the archway from sickbay, but he is reassured when he sees that the boy is as startled as he is, stuffing something hastily beneath his jacket.

"Hullo," says the one boy.

"Uh—hello," says the other. He doesn't recognise this boy, though he is new and the school is big, so perhaps that is not surprising. The one boy is a little older, perhaps, by a few years.

They both stand for moment, saying nothing, until the one boy dips his head and waggles it in the other boy's direction, as if he is trying to get the attention of a puppy. "So..."

"So?"

The one boy gestures around at the empty quad; snow is falling, and the air is freezing. The school, shorn of light and sound, is sepulchral, and it has been easy to convince themselves that each was totally alone. "So—why didn't you go home then?"

The other boy bites his lip, hugs himself tight; and then, he tells him, all about his parents, and the mission abroad, and being called to the headmaster's office to be read the letter that wished him a merry Christmas and promised to see him in the spring. The one boy listens, and smiles, and then he tells his own story, his own personal tragedy that has left him beached amongst the stones of the school like so much driftwood.

This is how two people meet sometimes, by chance, in the dark, and tell stories.

YOU KNOW, OF course, that this isn't the end of the story. Christmas is a time for ghosts, and there are always more to come.

At first he thinks the second ghost is a woman, but when he has rubbed the sleep from his eyes, he realises his mistake: she is tall, slim, dark-skinned, and unlike her predecessor she is defiantly in colour: a garish, purple that shimmers and undulates.

"Hello hello hello!" she crows.

"Which one are you?" he asks, though at first the words come out as more of a retch. He coughs, holding on to his chest, and repeats the words a little more clearly.

"*I* am the Ghost of Christmas Present." And then she cackles until the light fittings vibrate.

"Well," says Ebenezer, "bollocks to *this*!" and dives back beneath the safety of his blanket, where the sheets turn traitor and sucks him struggling down a spiral, depositing him in an undignified heap somewhere cold and hard. He rolls on his back and find himself staring in confusion at a slate-grey sky.

A mountain of golden, bouffant hair interjects itself into his field of vision. "Oh queen, we play don't like that." She extends a hand. Ebenezer defiantly ignores it, and hauls himself upright; the sudden change of altitude makes his head swim, and somewhere in his stomach half a litre of vodka—still swirling from the bedclothes tornado—makes itself known. He clutches an icy drainpipe, swallows back the urge to vomit in the snow.

When he finally straightens, he sees he is beside a window, and through that window Ebenezer sees a family, of a sort.

"Oh," he says, resigned.

The ghost lays a comforting hand on his back. "Yes," she says.

Picture the scene then: the sofas dragged to the side, and two tables—slightly different heights, but disguised by a voluminous tablecloth—pushed together in the centre of the room, and laid with a dizzying assortment of food. Around the table a disjointed assortment of chairs have been placed, and they are filled by a disjointed assortment of people. Their faces are familiar—some of them have been at last night's funeral—but one he knows well: Aoife, a childhood friend of his son Tim's. This year it appears she has shaved her entire head save for a waving, livid-blue quiff at the front; it also appears—judging by the way she tangles her fingers below the table with a neat, bookish girl beside her—that she has found her self a new girlfriend. Her previous girlfriend—a wide, heavily-mascaraed girl whose name Ebenezer can't recall—sits opposite them, chomping on sprouts. There are others he doesn't know: an enormous bearded hulk of a man in a red check shirt who laughs boomingly at little provocation, and who studiously ignores the gaze of the slight, wispy-looking blonde gentleman who sits across from him.

And presiding over this small gathering, Tim and his—

"Partner," says the ghost. "Say it with me, girl."

Tim and *Robert*.

Ebenezer stalks pointedly away. The ghost sashays after him, hoiking up her dress. "There's not escape that way!" she calls after him, and she's right, because the next window is the kitchen, and Ebenezer's flight has coincided with Tim's own. Ebenezer sees him through the window, plucking glasses from the cupboard, running them under the tap.

The door behind him opens, and Robert enters. He sidles up behind Tim and wraps his arms around him, plucks him from his preparations. "Are you okay?" Robert asks, mouth pressed against Tim's ear.

"Yes," says Tim, wriggling free. He looks out of the window; Ebenezer feels a chill pass down his spine as his son locks eyes with him, but Tim doesn't react—he looks right through Ebenezer as if he isn't there. Robert raises his eyebrows, and Tim repeats himself; it's a taut *yes* that brooks no argument, but in the manner of couples who have been together a long time, Robert required no actual words to counter him. "Yes," Tim says for a third time, ducking below Robert's gaze and bending to open the fridge, but this time it is a *yes* that admits it is a *no*.

"You invited him—you sent a card. Not sure what else you could have done...?"

Tim plucks a bottle from the shelf and thumps it down on the side. "Yes. I know. I just thought this year, what with... y'know. Felt like the right time..."

"Don't see why anything should have changed him. He's the same man he's always been."

Tim is peeling the foil fastidiously from the cork. "I'm fine, honestly. And anyway—today really isn't the day for *you* to be worrying about *my* father."

Robert backs away, hands raised. "Of course it is." He grins. "It's what a *friend* would do."

Tim chases him back into the living room with a tea-towel.

The ghost has backed away, and is peering into the living room window, inspecting her reflection. She beckons Ebenezer over and wearily he obeys. Tim and Robert are filling everyone's glasses, proposing a toast; there is a clinking of glass, a chorus of 'Merry Christmas!'

"Sickening," says Ebenezer, and spits on the ground.

The ghost glares at him. "You're not using that word right."

The revolting display of Christmas cheer isn't done, it seems. Tim is standing, raising his glass again, proposing another toast—"to my wonderful Robert," he declares to the table. "It's Christmas, but it's also our anniversary—did you know?" They all groan and smile, though it is good-natured; clearly everyone *does* know, in great detail, though this won't prevent the story being told again. "The two of us the only ones left for the holidays, complete strangers, and—well, we found each other. Although—" he laughs, "—when I made my move would you believe he said *no?*"

Robert shakes his head, scowling. "Well—I'd never kissed a boy, and..."

Ebenezer turns away. "I can't watch this," he says. "Take me home."

"It's just a love story, like any other," the ghost says.

"Not like any other," says Ebenezer. "Not at all."

"That's your *son*." She approaches him; there is something threatening about her when she is no longer smiling, something uncanny about that male face hidden behind a female's. "Does it make you uncomfortable?"

Ebenezer coughs; his throat is burning, and his tongue tastes bitter in his mouth. "It's just—my son and *him*. It's... it's wrong."

The ghost grips him by the shoulders. "Have you ever looked deep inside yourself and wondered why you think that, Ebenezer Scrooge?"

He wrenches himself free of her grip and retreats down the driveway, along the lane. His feet skitter uncertainly on the ice; he is going far too fast, but he doesn't care. He isn't the one in heels.

"If you can't love yourself, Ebenezer Scrooge," she calls after him, "how in the hell—"

A stretch of black ice proves perilous and he finds himself facedown on the ground, blood pearling on scuffed palms, and unbidden from inside his chest words have come spilling out: "I want to go home, I want to go home, I want to go home," until his throat can no longer make sound and the ground beneath him is the smooth stone of his own front doorstep. Here it is raining and he finds he is soaked immediately to the skin as if he has been subjected to its onslaught for hours.

A couple pass by, sheltering beneath an umbrella. They look down at him slumped in his own gutter, shake their heads sadly, and hurry on.

The ghost kneels down in front of him, seemingly heedless now to the fate of her dress. She cups his face tenderly. "You know it isn't done, don't you?" she says. "You know there's one more to come."

He closes his eyes against the rain and the cold, and nods weakly.

"You'd best be ready," she says. "And don't fuck it up."

And then she is gone.

———

Before the love story, before the one boy, there is only the other—though we cannot yet call him that for there is only him, alone. He spends the days of the holiday raiding the library, reading in his bed, disconsolately beating a path

*through the teasel patch by the school pond. He sees no sign of anybody—master
or pupil—and thinks nothing of it.*

*He is tremendously alone, the other boy, though he isn't to know it until he
first catches sight of another out in the quad. But that's yet to come. For now he
is just... the boy, slowly freezing to death of loneliness beneath the endless snows
of winter.*

———

You know what comes next.

It is a hand and a sleeve—a boy's hand, and a boy's sleeve, the sleeve of
a school uniform, and it is impatient. When Ebenezer does not immediately
leap from his bed, it clicks its fingers and beckons him. The message is clear
but, deep in a whiskey fugue, Ebenezer is argumentative. "No," he shouts
in its direction, and hurls a bottle at it. It smashes against the wall, brown
remnants dribbling down the wallpaper. "I get it—my son, I've hurt him.
I'm a terrible father. I'm a monster. I *understand*. We don't have to carry on
this nonsense..."

The hand continues to point at him as he vomits his bile, a thick torrent
of questions, of invectives, of accusations, until Ebenezer has no more left
in him and his cheeks ache from tears. He sinks back into his sallow pillows,
the resistance sucked out of him, unable to summon even the defiance to pull
the bedclothes over his head.

The ghostly hand slips into his, like a son's into a father's—

—and he's here. Of course he's here.

"The Ghost of Christmas Past," Ebenezer says; his breath opens up
white in front of him, wreaths above him like an anointment.

The school is a slumbering animal, restful but alert for intrusion; the emptiness of its halls feel uncanny, as if without the stamp of boy's feet and the ring of chatter they have become something misshapen and ill-purposed. The quad is bitterly cold; Ebenezer shivers. The ghostly hand seems to feel nothing; it does not even tremble.

"I wasn't really alone, of course," Ebenezer tells the ghost. He is surprised to find his diction clear; his shivering, he realises, is not only the temperature, but also the first flush of sobriety. He runs his fingers along the bricks, breaks off a frosty section of moss. "I mean—it felt like were were, but some of the masters were still here. Somewhere. I imagine they didn't want to see us either, really. We never saw them—they were distant, like—" Ebenezer laughs humourlessly. "Like *ghosts*."

The hand points across the courtyard; a boy enters from the direction of the library.

"Look at him," Ebenezer breathes. He can barely recognise the boy before him, crossing the yard, wrapped tight in his coat; he seems as alien as the school itself, as if in the strange absence of the school's usual occupants the boy has in turn become someone else too.

Ebenezer looks about. "And that means—"

The boy in the courtyard startles; he has seen something, and for a second he seizes in fear. And the someone steps out of the bushes—a second boy—and they both smile uneasily.

"Hullo," says the one boy.

Ebenezer looks around the quad—he knows every stone, every crevice, every arch of this place. And he knows too, every word that is about to be uttered.

He cannot help but listen, though he does not want to.

After a while, the boys depart the courtyard, and the ghostly hand follows after them, reluctantly drawing Ebenezer behind them. They follow them into the hallway, up the grand staircase, and—where the other boy would ordinarily turn right, instead they both turn left, towards the dormitory in the east wing.

At the door, the boys pause. One wishes to invite the other inside, the other waits for him to do so.

"Can you keep a secret?" says the one boy, and the other nods eagerly. The one bounces on the balls of his feet in the doorway. "Good!" he says. He fishes inside his coat, and produces a bottle of port. "Look what I... found." He grins devilishly; found is clearly not the word for how the came by the bottle. "Do you want to—I dunno—do you want to come drink it with me?"

The other boy looks up and down the corridor; he is nervous, imagining that someone might be watching him, that trouble might be just around the corner. But he can see nobody, and the one boy's eyes are alight with mischief, the kind of infectious mischief that sweeps away any argument.

The other smiles shyly. "Okay," he says. He extends a hand, as he has been taught. "I'm Ebenezer Scrooge," he says.

The one grasps it firmly. "Jacob Marley," he says, and pulls his new friend into the dormitory.

And later, when the snow stops, when the other boy—always the *other* boy, for all the years of his life to follow—comes hurrying from the dormitory, Ebenezer Scrooge falls to his knees in the wake of his younger self's shamed flight and weeps.

———

HE AWAKES TO the sound of chains clanking, and the face of Jacob Marley.

"No," he says. "No no no no no no." He clamps his eyes shut again.

After a moment, he says: "Let me guess. It's Christmas Day. I've not missed a thing, and I've got plenty of time to mend my ways."

"No to the first. It's the twenty-seventh. As for the second—well, I couldn't say."

Cautiously, Ebenezer opens one eye. Jacob looks back.

—*I don't understand I don't understand I don't understand I don't understand*—until he does.

"Robert."

The man in front of him nods gravely; the clanking, Ebenezer realises, is not chains but cell doors.

"Where's Tim?"

"He's in the car. He didn't—" Robert swallows. He is debating whether to be kind. "He didn't want to come in."

Ebenezer sits up cautiously. His head is burning, and his stomach roils at even this briefest of movements. He reaches out to steady himself, finds himself gripping Robert's wrist.

"You were picked up the police, comatose in a ditch. Drunk." There is an unspoken word here that Robert does not say, though they both hear it anyway: *again*. "Miles from anywhere, god knows how you got there. Out by—"

"The Fezziwig Academy for Boys."

"As was, yes." Robert separates himself gently from Ebenezer's grip. "Hold on." He stands up. "Thank you officer, I'll take him. Have you got his—just these? And—no, I think we can bin those. Thank you." He stoops down, and wraps an arm around Ebenezer's shoulders. "Come on—up we come."

In the corridor, Ebenezer has to stop to heave over a bin, though nothing comes out. He clutches onto the metal ring, watches a yellow trickle of spittle trickle away over the crisp packets and cans at the bottom of the bin. He wipes his mouth, and clutches his forehead, dizzy.

"Robert," says Ebenezer. "I've not been very good to you."

Robert looks surprised; his mouth flaps for a moment, unsure of how to respond, and then he settles for a simple: "No."

"And I've hurt—"

"Your son."

"Tim. Yes."

"Yes," says Robert, though he softens it by once again reaching to help Ebenezer move.

They have to stop again in the car park for Ebenezer to take deep breaths of cold air, his stomach turning over and over. Ebenezer clings to Robert's coat, bends over. Across the way, the door of a land rover has opened and Tim is climbing out, looking concerned.

"It's just," says Ebenezer, "you always looked *so* like your father."

"I wasn't aware you knew him," Robert says. Ebenezer's words seem to have driven home in a way that none of his others have, tears pricking at the corner of Robert's eyes. He looks pleadingly across at Tim, who is waiting for a taxi to pass so he can cross to help them.

Ebenezer wheezes. "We were at school together. Years ago. But I kept up with his life—you know how it... goes." He trails off, noticing for the first time Robert's clothes: the dark suit, the shiny shoes, the tie. He has never seen him in anything other than paint-flecked artists' clothes before. "Oh," he says. "Oh, I'm so sorry." And then, as Tim dodges between cars to dash to them, Ebenezer feels the floor tip, suck him down towards it. "You're dressed wrong," he manages to say. "He wanted colours at his funeral." And then his legs buckle; his body, purged of food and alcohol, can no longer hold him and he plunges towards the snow-covered ground, into the arms of his son and his partner.

THE LAST DRAG
SHOW ON EARTH

T HEY COME OUT of the dark to Tallulah's. Alone and in groups, they make
their way along the street, follow-the-yellow-brick-road amongst the
cracked and rancid cobbles. The fairy lights are lit in the trees, just like they
used to once-upon-a-time, in flagrant disregard for the regulations—not
that they need telltale lights as targets to drop the bomb these days, or like
any of them believe the regulations really have anything to do with safety.
Regardless, it doesn't matter tonight: tomorrow this street will be gone,
sealed away for decontamination by the machines from the South. This is
the final hurrah, the swan song of the last speakeasy in Manchester.

And of course it's here, on Canal Street. Of *course* it is.

One by one—far more orderly than a Friday night crowd has any right
to be—they present themselves to the bouncer. There's all manner slinking
through the wreckage to join the queue tonight: a kaleidoscope of hairstyles;
a barrage of outfits—they've outdone themselves for the occasion. There's
representatives of all the genders, in every configuration of grouping
imaginable—although it's so hard to tell these days, when you can never be
sure what's really written on the skin underneath.

The bouncer shines her torch where they indicate—a neck, a hip, one smart-alec who bends over and points at his podgy left buttock. In the incandescent beam the glamour-tech ripples and shorts, and you can see clear through to the pink lipstick triangle on the skin—tonight's secret sign, passed in whispers around the city.

The tiny bar is nearly full to capacity. Tallulah has outdone herself. She's stripped out all the threadbare old tech and taken the bar right back to how it was at the turn of the century—this is beyond retro and into historical. Behind the bar, men in old-fashioned tank-tops are handing out drinks—no charge tonight—bottles of the kind too obscure for even the hipsters to get their hands on these days. WKD, Bacardi, VKs—even honest-to-god Coca Cola. How she's procured them is anyone's guess.

The crowd jostles and press against each other impatiently—looks are exchanged and assets are assessed, but there isn't the usual frisson of sex in the air that any other night at Tallulah's might have carried with it. Not that Tallulah's on a regular night was all about cruising for sex, because there were better places for that; anyhow, it was so difficult these days. Half the time if you pulled a cute guy into the cubicle for a quick fumble, they'd drop the glamour and you'd find yourself with an entirely unexpected set of genitalia on your hands.

You can screw with the glamours still on, of course. But that's only for the real perverts with no regard for health and safety.

In the tiny cupboard she calls a dressing room, Tallulah finishes strapping on the ninth layer of quick-change dresses, and sits to apply her makeup in the ancient mirror surrounded by a rectangle of doddery lightbulbs.

"The place is full, hunty darling," Shiva tells her from the door. Tallulah presses her face close to the mirror, inspecting her make-up, turning it side to side to check the contouring.

Spectacular. Even if she does say so herself.

Tallulah raises a lumpish hand, points a single lacquered nail into the air decisively. "Play something to get them in the mood. Let's get a little nostalgia flowing, shall we?"

There's an encouraging cheer from outside—they can glimpse her through the open door. They're waiting.

"Play something old," she says. She touches up her lipstick. "They're not ready for me yet."

THEY COME OUT of the dark to Tallulah's. The dark waters of the canal awaken, and releases those who sleep in its eddies to walk the street. Brackish water trails their footsteps. They say no words to each other—it is not clear if they even see each other. Perhaps they do not even see the street as it is now; perhaps instead they see it as they remember it.

Aloysius Coal was an officer in the war—but probably not the war you're thinking of. He wrote poetry while he served, page after page in a notebook he was given by his spinster aunt the night before he set sail. She had kissed him on the cheek, and reminded him that he should remember who he was at war, because men often forgot. And she, better than anyone knew who he was, after she'd caught him with—well, it didn't need to be said out loud, did it?

The book was lost—not dramatically in a bomb, or a fire, or anything like that. Just sometime in the last few days before victory was declared—gone. He didn't miss it too badly. Instead, he returned home to his wife who, with trembling lip, showed him the child in the crib that could plainly not be his. He kissed her on the forehead, and then did the same to his new son.

Some months later, on the way home to his wife and children he took a detour down a street he had heard of, but never visited. There weren't many bars then—although of course there was Tallulah's decades before it was called Tallulah's. Sipping whiskey in a quiet corner, he was approached by a man. Older, and gentle, they fell to talking. The man told him he was a poet. Aloysius did not tell him about the lost notebook.

Under the bridge by the canal, the poet turned Aloysius around and yanked his trousers down around his thighs. A little while later, when Aloysius turned to try and kiss him, he startled and lashed out. The cold stone received Aloysius' temple with a wet finality. The poet ran, and so did Aloysius' blood.

Tonight, the bouncer doesn't even give him a second glance.

<center>~~~</center>

THE CROWD ARE getting impatient, albeit in a jovial, benevolent way. They're stomping for Tallulah, despite the best efforts of Shiva MaTimbers doing her routine bit on stage with the torch.

Ezekiel Hodge is a boy tonight, and he's caught the eye of a silver-haired gentleman by the bar. Ezekiel likes the distinguished type, although he's not quite as sold on the man's husbands lolling on either side of him. They look rather gauche, and Ezekiel can't help feeling that they're unlikely to appreciate the true significance of tonight's entertainments. They wouldn't know drag if it popped an inflatable breast in front of them—no sense of *heritage*.

Still—if it's a package deal. He approaches the man and introduces himself. The man shakes his hand. "My name is Magnus," he says. A good name, thinks Ezekiel. Rich, like something from a storybook.

They talk a little, of this and that: of how the bar isn't what it was when Magnus was young, and how youths like Ezekiel couldn't begin to imagine it, no matter how many photographs or movies they've watched. Ezekiel smiles politely.

On-stage, Shiva gyrates the torch, issuing gargantuan chortles whenever the beam ripples the façade of her outfit enough for the punters to glimpse that, just maybe just maybe, underneath it all, she's a man. Ezekiel bites his lip. Glamour-tech, however expensive, isn't *real* drag.

Shiva's torch-beam rakes suggestively across the audience, and Ezekiel catches a glimpse of the flesh beneath Magnus' glamour. It is youthful, in first flush. For all his talk, he can be barely twenty. "You young'uns wouldn't remember, would you?" Magnus says to Ezekiel, and the words ring as false as his glamour.

Ezekiel backs away, recedes to the shadows, sets his sights on someone else. There by the door: in a war uniform—though probably not the war you're thinking of—with impeccable attention to historical accuracy. A long way from the reaches of Shiva's torch, where the beam could not possibly catch him, and there is no chance of the man in the ancient uniform catching sight of the sag of ten decades that hangs beneath Ezekiel's own glamour.

Failing singularly to appease the thickening crowd, Shiva ducks into the cupboard-cum-dressing room. "Tallulah, they're waiting."

Tallulah shakes her head. "Not yet," she says. "They're not ready for me yet."

<hr />

ELIZABETH BENNETT, FULLY cognizant of the absurdity of her name, had never read a book to the end. Instead, she painted—from the day a paintbrush was first thrust into her chubby infant hand to the day she died, although it has not a straight line in between.

When she was ten, she painted pictures of her back garden. Sometimes, the girl from next door leaned over the fence to watch her. Sometimes she did not. Nevertheless, the girl appeared in all of her pictures.

When she was fifteen, she plumped up her breasts, and conned her way into Coyotes. At nearly 1am, after sipping three sweet cocktails that were better named than they were flavoured, she was surprised to find herself sat opposite the girl from her back garden, grown up but unmistakable. She was deep in conversation with another girl—a woman, really—but she caught Elizabeth's eye and smiled. The woman asked Elizabeth's neighbor how old she was, and her neighbor answered 'eighteen', and gave Elizabeth a conspiratorial wink.

When she was twenty-five, the national newspapers declared Elizabeth the foremost painter in the UK. After she conducted a couple of interviews, they started to call her the foremost *lesbian* painter in the UK, and the extra word never disappeared.

When she was twenty-seven she put on her second exhibition. She hung paintings in pairs next to each other: one from the awkward childhood drawings she had rescued from her mother's attic, hung beside a new, re-painted version. 'Improved', she thought. In a breathless gap at the opening, she looked at the collection and thought to herself, *when I have a daughter I'll give her all my paintings and she can copy them, and we can hang this exhibition again, in reverse. It'll be a sensation.*

And then there was the girl from her back garden, stood with her head cocked, looking at the twin visions of herself in watercolour. Elizabeth drew breathlessly near. "Excuse me," she said. "I couldn't help notice you looking—" The girl turns and smiles, and introduces herself—an Elizabeth too, though she goes by Lizzie. Elizabeth is smitten.

When they were thirty, giddy with the novelty of a change in the law, Elizabeth and Lizzie were married in celebration. Elizabeth's mother was not present, but Lizzie's was. A world-famous photographer took the pictures.

When she was forty-seven, Lizzie died, and at eighty-six, Elizabeth followed her. She was found after a month, in her studio above Canal Street, surrounded by hundreds of paintings, a platoon of portraits of Lizzie at aged fifty, sixty, seventy, a hundred, and at aged ten in a quiet back garden in Manchester.

The bouncer is stooping to inspect the pink triangle on the ankle of a stilettoed biker bear, and doesn't notice her slipping quietly into Tallulah's.

EMMELINE PANIC—FOR such is her chosen, if not god-given name—is a rock-chick of the most subtle variety. She eschews the obvious choices that glamour-tech place before those of the sartorially rebellious nature: no plastic androgyne, no physics-defying piercings, no choreographed tattoos.

Instead, she cleaves tight to the old mother's saying: 'we are all born naked, and the rest is drag.' Every breath from our very first is a performance, and Emmeline Panic's more than most.

Straight out of university she had conned her way into a contract with a major publisher, and since then her whole life has been a performance, each year sub-divided neatly into the chapter of the eventual book. At first she'd started impersonating the obvious ones—she'd been Marilyn for a year, and Gaga. Easy, and ostentatious. When, in her tenth year, she'd essayed the Mona Lisa, she knew she'd found her groove: the elusive women of great art.

Tonight is a first outing, a test-run in the dead days between Christmas and New Year when the publisher's dictadrones are off duty. Time to smooth out the rough edges in the performance. And it was fitting anyhow, to appear here tonight on Canal Street, as *her*.

On stage, the drag queen is failing for the second time that evening to amuse the crowd. Poor woman, thinks Emmeline. An average performer, quite frankly. Despite the towering wig and wafer-thin heels, she just doesn't *commit* to the role.

Then she notices the woman watching her—an old woman, haggard in the way that old women aren't any more. Like she's from the history channel. She has white hair, shoulder-length. She's wearing a nightie, of all things. Still, Emmeline thinks, who am I to judge?

The woman approaches her, and Emmeline shifts uncomfortably. Looking closely, she wonders if maybe the woman isn't all-natural, without a trace of glamour-tech. There's a few like that going around at the minute— if they weren't careful it'd become a fully-fledged movement.

"Excuse me…" says the woman. Her voice is barely there, as if it has been swept away the second it leaves her mouth. "I couldn't help notice you looking—"

Emmeline simpers sweetly. "Hello, dear," she says, unsure what else to say.

The old woman cups her cheek. Her touch is cold, which it shouldn't be, not at the amount Emmeline's glamour cost.

"Lizzie…"

Emmeline's face lights up. "Yes!" she says. "I'm so glad you recognized me! I've been so worried! I thought she might be a little too obscure, you know…?"

She might be mistaken, but there are tears in the old woman's eyes.

In the dressing room, Tallulah silences Shiva before she can even speak. "Nearly, darling, nearly." She casts a scarlet smile back over her shoulder.

"Do your three-legged can-can routine, that always goes down a treat."

The door closes, and Tallulah stands, smoothing her skirts in front of the mirror, adjusting her bosom. "They're nearly ready for me," she whispers to herself.

〰

AT 5.30AM, ALEX Dale threw hirself from the bridge into the cold waters of the canal. Although the coroner later placed the time of death anywhere between 5am and 6am, the time could be stated exactly: zie jumped the moment that the notification symbol popped up on on hir wrist, and she knew *it* had been published. No backing out now.

Then zie was gone.

On hir desk at home, a screen was left awake, and beside it the glamour-tech strap, with its shattered stinger. Four months saving—this stuff is new, and expensive if you want the ones that support the hacked outfits—and gone in one swing of an angry fist.

At 5.30am the screen pings.

It doesn't bear repeating the contents here. The majority of it was for hir father. Some of it was for the world at large, although, in the swell of history, it would turn out that the whole thing would be for the world, in a way.

There are phrases that jump out. There's the ones the campaigners use: *Not a choice. Neither one nor the other. Not a phase.* Then there's the ones that no-one seems to notice: *Sorry. Love. Daddy.*

That last one especially.

Daddy, they're not ready for me yet.

They call it Alex's Law, but it doesn't make any difference to the canal.

You're not ready for me yet.

So they come out of the dark to Tallulah's—not just these three, but all the other ghosts: the mollies in their frock coats, the happy drunks who slid into the water instead of another man's bed, the old and the young, the men blackened by lesions with the skin loose on their bones, the women who loved loudly, and the women who loved secretly. The bouncer doesn't see them—or perhaps just pretends not to.

And anyway, the show's about to start.

———

SHIVA IS PANTING. She's never had to work so hard for so little applause. It's Tallulah they want—and, it seems, it's Tallulah they're going to get.

She pats her hair. "I'm ready," she says. "They're ready."

Shiva crosses to her, embraces her like a mother. "There's more ghosts than bloods out there," she says. "I've never seen it like this. Not that most will even notice..."

Tallulah breaks the hug. "Once the morning comes, it'll make no difference," she says. "We're all ghosts now, really."

Shiva licks a finger and dabs a spot of errant make-up on Tallulah's face. "Knock 'em dead, bitch. The last true drag queen on earth."

Tallulah fingers her corset. "And don't I just feel it."

There's an impatient cheer from outside. *I Am What I Am* has started, and most of them know that's Tallulah's song, the one she comes out to every night.

"I'll do the honours," says Shiva. She turns to the door, primps herself.

"Is zie out there?" asks Tallulah quietly.

Shiva doesn't look back at her. "I don't know," she says. "You'll have to go out there and find out."

Then she flings it open and prances out. The crowd roars appreciatively. Her voice booms, barely muffled by the thin walls. "Right then, you horrible lot… are you ready? I said *are you ready*? Yes? Then it's time to introduce her… the one, the only, the incontinent… Tallulah Trout!"

───※───

WHEN IT'S ALL over, and they've all gone home—even Shiva, whose battery runs low in the last ten minutes, reverting her to a portly thirty-year-old in ill-fitting underwear—Tallulah returns to the dressing room and locks the door tightly behind her. She sits in front of the mirror, and begins to meticulously remove her make-up.

It doesn't take long, stripping back layer-by-layer, lipstick swiped away to reveal the thin, cracked lips beneath, the removal of contours transforming the rounded full cheeks into sharper, masculine forms. Then the eyebrows, and the eye-lashes and she's left with her ordinary face. A pedestrian, unremarkable face: a brother, or a father, perhaps, but one easily forgotten.

When the light-bulbs switch off—accompanied by the sound of all the electricity in the bar shutting down—she knows the machines are near.

The last dress of the quick change is dark blue with military insignia, like a naval captain. There's a bit that goes with it—sweeping up the most bearish man she can find in the audience to do a gender-swapped *Officer and a Gentleman*. A good captain always goes down with their ship.

And so they come out of the dark to Tallulah's—for these days, even the mornings are dark. The machines, and the men in the masks, with their seals and their fire. The flames reflect from the black waters of the canal where Aloysius, Elizabeth, Alex and all the others silently watch as Tallulah's vanishes in smoke. The men with the machines don't see them—

or perhaps pretend not to.

When she closes her eyes, Tallulah can't feel the blistering heat anymore. Instead, she imagines she's sinking into black waters, swimming free towards the others up ahead of her, the last true drag queen on earth.

NO SLEEP IN
BETHLEHEM

I HAVE A story to tell, about the winter we lived with ghosts in the house that shook at night. It begins with a telegram delivered in the early hours of the morning, and ends with letters interred in dirt at sundown—that is if it can honestly be said that anything *ends*. Even from the vantage point of decades in which I've watched the jackboot of history crush so many delicate flowers, even then I find it harder and harder to believe that anything truly constitutes an unequivocal ending.

Even—or perhaps especially—including those things that are dead, gone and buried.

Perhaps that is hope, or perhaps it's dread.

Germany, December 1936

LET'S BEGIN WITH the arrival.

The train surged through a wilderness thick and heavy with pine and fur, half-buried in drifts so deep that the trunks and lower branches were swallowed whole. Whenever we passed close enough, I saw spindly fingers grasping up through the white ground for air. The tracks wound and detoured as if intimidated by the blackwoods, afraid to press straight through and disturb the natural geography, but despite this the engines strained, eager to deliver us from out of the land of sunlight and terraces we came from, and into the wild winter in which our destination lay. It was a landscape so perfectly fitting to our journey and its ill mix of gloom and anticipation that I might as well have conjured it myself with paint and brushes.

Opposite, Hans ignored me, as he had ever since we boarded at the connection in Mannheim. Until then he'd been capable of mustering a patina of good spirits, but as the landscape darkened, so had his mood. I couldn't blame him, but it still set me feeling like a useless accessory to our journey ('neither use nor ornament', as my mother would have described it). Brow furrowed, he stared out of the window into his own pale reflection in the glass. Having foolishly packed my drawing things away in my trunk where I couldn't easily reach them, I had little to occupy me besides obverving him, though I tried to do it lightly, concealed in absent-minded changes of position or the stretch of my neck. Hans always wore attention heavily, especially mine. The only time he would readily submit to my undisguised gaze without discomfort was when he sat for me to draw.

He caught me looking, and shifted. (In another time and place: a wry "He spends his days staring at drawings, and his nights staring at the real thing; what do I have to do quench the thirst?" to gently shrug me away, but not today.) I quickly averted my gaze, into his glass-twin, the exhausted imitation of my love, trapped in the flurries of snow and steam fleeing past the window.

Grim, yes—but can you imagine the sun shining on a son returning home to bury his mother?

<hr />

BACK HOME (WHEN did I start calling it home? Around the time I met Hans, I think) in my cosy little sun-soaked Montmartre attic, Hans always left before dawn. The first few times it was under the full cover of darkness, but little by little his departures crept closer to daylight, a contest of nerve with the morning, until we both became accustomed to the first fingers of light on the horizon as an urgent signal for him to arise from my bed, dress and leave. It never occurred to me to challenge it, though I would happily have kept him there with me; we dressed it up in a need for secrecy, though given the louche company we both kept, there was little need for that had we applied a few moments thought to the matter.

I knew each sound of his departure with the same intimacy as his body. I knew the quiet click of my door closing behind him; I knew the creak of the loose floorboard in the corridor; I knew the the groan of the banisters in the stairwell; I knew the faint but audible sound of the front door closing; I knew the sound of his footsteps dancing across the cobbles; I knew the sound of his own door, the mirror of mine and yet subtly different in timbre.

The routine is inviolable; I stand at the window and wait for him to appear. The street is narrow, close enough that you could leap the gap, could maybe even stretch across to clasp hands with someone opposite if you had a will, but the drop is vertiginously deep.

He would sweep open the drapes—satin, a lone extravagance in a room otherwise self-consciously devoid of clutter—and face me across the way. A gift to be unwrapped with exaggerated care; he sheds his clothes, item by tantalising item. In the morning, his attic gets all the light, and in it he displays himself, pink and naked and clean, and smiling roguishly across the gulf. Then the curtain would fall, and that would be it, until the next night's performance when his knock would arrive in the midnight hours—a diffident *rap*, a swift *rapraprap*, and a final confident *rap*.

"Rest your bones," I say, every time he crawls beneath the sheets to nestle against me. The phrase is a ritual, almost devoid of meaning when uttered here in my bedroom, but imbued with potent, conspiratorial magic if either of us utters it in company.

And just once: "I love you." Whispered in the last minutes before dawn, before daylight robbed me of another chance to say it.

He said nothing then, only curled in tighter beneath my arm and nuzzled against my side, until the window grew pale. Then: door, floorboard, banister, door, dancing. His shoes struck sparks on the cobbles as he danced away, away, away from me and I pulled the bedclothes over my head and sought to bury my embarrassment in the stuffy gloom.

No second door. The routine had been broken, and even this minor deviation made my stomach twist in a nervous knot. I crawled to the window and peered down. Hans was paused on the front step, speaking to a apologetic youth in a messenger's uniform. I pulled back, crassly aware of my nakedness, and dragged the thin sheet from the bed to wrap around my waist. When I returned to the window, the step was empty, the messenger pedalling rapidly away around the corner.

I leaned against the dormer frame, waiting for the curtain to rise on this morning's performance. The gambrel roofs of Paris lit up like the embers of a cigarette as you suck in the first lungful, smoke rising. It was the last sight of warmth I was to see for some time; the curtain did not rise. Instead: banister, floorboard, *rap-rapraprap-rap. RAP.*

It wasn't a Hans I recognised on the other side of the door; it was a strange imitation of him, a broken, sobbing one. He pressed a crumpled piece of paper into my hand—a telegram, I realised, smoothing it out. I clumsily deciphered the German. FRAU SCHAUS VERSTORBENE STOP KOMM SOFORT STOP.

There is almost certainly no good way to be made an orphan (and heavens knows in the years since we've grown practised in new and horrifying ways), but a telegram is perhaps one of the most abrupt; a bereavement charged by the word.

Hans fell into my arm, and I cradled him until daylight filled every last corner of the attic.

A WEEK LATER, here we were.

A thin crack ran across the carriage window; I hadn't noticed it at first, but now that I had, I could see nothing else. Frost gathered along its rim, silvery and glinting. It ran at the level of our chests, from me to Hans, like a fragile thread connecting us.

The woodland dropped away suddenly, giving way to a narrow, huddled station that seemed to appear from nowhere, approaching all in a rush and then hardly at all as the train slowed. A sign manifested from within the blizzard: Zuabarnasshalt. Though the sign slid conspicuously past his vision, Hans didn't so much as stir, just continuing to stare out of the window lost in thought while I gathered our things. I nudged him, and he blinked around in confusion as if he had woken from a long sleep and was surprised to discover himself in a carriage. I pressed his overcoat and scarf into his hands and chivied him out of the compartment and down onto the platform. The train strained to be away, engine growling, and its sentiment seemed to be shared; a square of yellow light burst amongst the flurries at the opposite end of the station, and a guard expelled our trunks onto the platform, slammed the door without a backwards glance, and then off and away hurtled the train without delay, eagerly abandoning Zuabarnasshalt and us behind it.

"Well then!" I said, as cheerfully as I could muster. It was a tone that irritated even myself, but ever since the morning of the messenger boy and his telegram I had found myself powerless to keep from adopting it. "What now?" Hans stared vacantly down the empty line, his coat hanging open, apparently ignorant to the abject weather. A sense of motherliness stung me; I resisted the urge to button him up and wrap the scarf tight. "*Hans*."

He stirred. "König will be here," he said dimly.

His words were a summoning spell—the wind snatched them away, and in their place presented us with the man himself. He materialised at my elbow, the largest person I had ever seen in my life, in every direction you can imagine. His sudden arrival startled me; he had all the massive permanence of an ancient oak, and he loomed so still and immoveable that it was almost impossible to fit the idea of him *moving* alongside the very physical reality of his presence. Just as I thought this, he swept past me so fast and gracefully that I was left with nothing more than an impression of a dark bulk, gathering up our trunks as if they were nothing, and then we were being herded wordlessly out of the station. A car waited outside, parked carelessly half-on and half-off the kerb. It was an old thing, similar to my father's back in England but older and in considerably more disrepair. My father had kept his immaculate and gleaming at all costs; this was quite the opposite. Once grand, it was now dilapidated and in severe need of attention. The door was dented, one wing-mirror trembling loose in the wind, and the running board visibly sagging. I found it oddly incongruous and realised I had been expecting something more like a horse and cart (— *perhaps driven by a hooded figure, pursued by wild wolves?* I chided myself for my own ludicrous fantasies.)

König heaved the trunks onto the roof with one hand, and lashed them with ropes. Despite this they wobbled alarmingly and I found myself thankful I hadn't packed anything valuable in the case. Satisfied they were secure—to his standards if not mine—König opened the rear door and gestured for us to climb in.

Hans was standing away, almost lost in the storm despite being only a dozen paces away. I called to him but it was ripped away by the wind and Hans didn't stir. His coat still hung open, arms dangling like a puppet's with its strings cut. He stared off into the distance, in the direction the train had departed.

Hans had a trick I had grown accustomed to back in Paris; a habit of switching personas with the ease of a man shuffling cards, deftly flipping cards between his fingers. One moment this person, another moment that. It was something I had initially admired and sought to make a part of my own work, this nimble juggling of disguises. I thought I had seen the full deck, though since the morning of the telegram I'd realised there were cards at the bottom of the deck that rarely reached the top. But right now, half-swallowed my snow, he wasn't any of these: he was the empty box.

I moved to him, and touched his elbow. "Hans," I said quietly, "come on. Let's go home."

"Yes," he said hollowly. "Home."

I led him to the car and bundled him into the back seat, wedging him into the tight space behind the driver's seat where he sank back, vanishing beneath his lapels. I climbed in behind him. "Thank you," I said to König, who minutely inclined his head then slammed the door behind me so quickly that it nearly took off my fingers. "*You're welcome,*" I muttered under my breath, and looked over to Hans. The huge shadow of König crossed the windscreen as circled the car. "Did I say something wrong?" I had intended it as sarcasm, but instead it came out obsequious and needy. I shuddered at myself.

A flicker of a frown before Hans caught my meaning. "Oh," he said, "no, not at all. König's a mute." He made a hand motion, rigid fingers slicing across his mouth. "No tongue. Can't speak. Hasn't for years."

"Oh," I say, adding churlishness to my catalogue of mis-steps. "Well... you've never mentioned that! A sinister train station, a gothic pile out in the black country, and now I find you have a mute butler!"

"Wait until you meet the banshee in the attic," Hans said, and for a moment a familiar card flashed into view: Hans the Jester.

The journey from the station was long and excruciating. We inched along narrow roads with the snow driving in at the windscreen relentlessly. Several times the wheels failed to grip, and we were left spinning fruitlessly. Each time Konig would heave himself out of the car, lumber around to the back, get us off to a start again with a tremendous heave. I was starting to think that the car journey was going to last as long as the train when finally the headlamps illuminated something new amidst the blizzard: enormous gates, a heavy wrought-iron affair rising to an arch over a turning in the road. They were a design of intertwining roots and thorns, and suspended amidst this metal thicket thick letters spelling out (at last) our destination: BETHLEHEM.

We had arrived.

OUR ROOMS WERE next to each other, up two staircases, along several corridors, none of which I could distinguish—König didn't light any of the lamps, not even so much as a candle, and so our arrival at the house was profoundly inauspicious. We were led to our respective bedrooms without even a backward glance to check if we were following, and I could garner nothing about the house besides a vague sense of a huge, dormant blackness.

"I shall be right on the other side of the wall," I said to Hans, half-observation, half-invitation.

Looming above us, König shuffled, and Hans darted me a swift, warning glance. "I shall see you in the morning," he said stiffly.

"Of course," I said. "Go - rest your bones!"

He smiled stiffly. "Sleep well."

Sleep well; was that a warning? No room even for private jokes, here. Were we to be two friends in separate rooms then; I of course hadn't imagined that we would be sharing a bed, not here in his family home even if he was the only one left in it, but stil I felt wrong-footed, unsure of whether I should expect a clandestine *rap-raprapraprap-rap* in the middle of the night, or whether it would be my lot to sleep alone.

Behind the closed door, I told myself I should follow his instruction. *Sleep. You've had a long day. You're exhausted.*

I undressed by the window, thinking fleetingly about hauling back the heavy drapes to display myself—but of course, it would be to no-one. We were side by side and I would be invisible, to Hans or anyone. My window would look onto nothing but dark tonight, the kind of complete darkness that is never possible in a city. I crawled beneath the heavy covers, trembling in the chill, and rested my fingertips above my head, tracing the lines of the beaded wallpaper. Perhaps, on the other side, Hans did the same, our hands separated by nothing more than a slim divide of bricks and mortar.

Or perhaps he was already asleep, turned on his side away from the door.

I fell asleep half-waiting for a knock that never came, and dreamed vividly of faces in the snow and bones resting amongst black tree-roots.

I do not recall if the house shook that night as it did all the nights after. Perhaps it did, and I slept through it. Or perhaps the house wanted to give it's returning son that one night of peace.

———

I AWOKE COLD and shivering, able to see my breath in the air. Darkness filled most of the room, but around the thick curtains a watery daylight seeped, and I was able to better make out my room. It was like many of the rooms in Bethlehem, I was to discover: by which I mean, it was huge, beset by drafts that rattled up through its shrivelled floorboards, and eerily empty. Like the car, it was once-grand but now dilapidated; the decoration was what might have once been rococo but had long since lapsed into decrepitude, dark ghosts on the wallpaper betrayed where furniture had once stood but had been removed. I wondered why—though perhaps, given the cold, they had been chopped into firewood? I could not imagine how a house like this could ever be warm.

At the foot of my bed, the contents of my luggage were stacked neatly on the linen box in two piles. The sight sent a queer tremble through me; they hadn't been there last night, which meant that *someone* (not König, surely? I couldn't imagine his bulk moving around my room without rousing me, but I had no idea if there were other servants at Bethlehem) had delivered them to my room while I slept. The idea of being intruded upon in the night, even without my knowledge, unnerved me but then again the simple presence of others in the house was something I found alien. Back at home in Shropshire, though the farmhouse sat amongst vaste acres of land, they hadn't yielded enough for our household to keep servants since long before I was born.

I thought about saying something about it to Hans when I found him that morning but cautioned myself against it. I was in a foreign country, I reminded myself—figuratively and literally. I had come here to support Hans, to be whatever he needed me to be. I couldn't start that by looking like a country rube unaccustomed to being waited on.

There was a crack in the window here, too. I saw it when I opened the curtains. It ran horizontal across one square pane of the window, and I had a momentary sensation that the crack had followed me here from the train. But then I saw what had caused it: on one side of the frame the thick branch of a vine had pushed its way through a seam and into the room, expanding until the frame warped, exerting pressure. Physics, not an omen.

I followed the vine with my fingers; it snaked along the inside of the wall and down into the corner of the room where it vanished behind the skirting board. Along its length it sent off little tendrils to burrow into the wallpaper. The wall felt spongy and moist where I touched it.

I plucked my fingers away and dressed quickly.

"Is that your mother?" I asked Hans.

We had taken up residence in the breakfast room. He was hunched in an armchair by the tall glass doors that opened onto the terrace and I was stood by the door, peering back into the hall from which I had entered. A huge portrait hung there, where the first flight of stairs divided. It depicted a woman, perhaps in her late thirties, with long dark hair, painted wearing a simple but regal blue evening gown. She sat in a garden blooming with a multitude of colours, the train of the dress flowing like water off into the undergrowth. It was a curious painting; a formal pose, but set amongst this detailed array of sprawling flora. My masters back at the college could no doubt have given me volumes on its influences and references but all I saw when I looked at it was a sense of both propriety and wildness held in balance, like a princess sleeping in an enchanted forest.

"Yes," Hans said, without looking up. The breakfast table was laid with freshly polished silver, gleaming so brightly they were at odds with the shabbiness of the rest of the room. A quick glance at the room betrayed where a sideboard and armoire had once stood, their imprint still visible on the figured wallpaper, but now there was only the breakfast table thrust by the window, so off-centre that it seemed like an afterthought to furnishing the room. But for all that, the breakfast itself certainly didn't follow suit— the table was stuffed with enough to feed ten; eggs (boiled and scrambled), kippers, brötchen, sausage and cheeses. Hans was applying himself with excessive vigour to a boiled egg.

"She looks very beautiful," I remarked. This was the first window I had been offered into Hans' past before Paris; I was lapping it up, studying every clue for what it might tell me about him.

"She was." He wielded a spoon with military vigour.

"And kind."

Hans said nothing to this, only assaulted the top of his boiled egg with his spoon and fastidiously picked away the shards.

I joined him at the table, brushing a thin layer of dust from the worn velvet cushion before I sat. "I'm sorry if you knocked last night," I said casually. "I was dead to the world."

"Oh," said Hans, eyes darting under clenched brows. "No matter." I could tell from the way he said it that he hadn't knocked; I smirked, and he caught it, and blushed.

"I'll try not to take offence at that," I said. "Pass the kippers."

He handed over the plate. The powerful scent made my stomach growl, and I realised I was ravenous. "Did you sleep well?" Hans asked.

"Yes," I said, then added piquishly, "Perhaps it was the novelty of being alone in the bed."

If Hans picked up the mild reproach, he didn't show it—instead he concentrated on the efficient disembowelment of his breakfast, scooping out the violently orange innards and chewing on them slowly. So slowly, in fact, that by the time he had reached his third spoonful I had devoured my whole plate and was ready to heartily have at a second. There was a domesticity about our breakfasting together that I stealthily relished, though I would never have admitted it to Hans.

"So," I remarked at length, by way of changing the subject, "exactly what does it fall to you to do, now you're back? I presume you will need to organise the funeral?"

Hans set aside his spoon, and swivelled in his chair to stare out of the glass doors. Outside was half-lost in a thin fog; there was little to be seen at all. "I believe so," he said. "We do have family undertakers in town— Hartmann and Sons, though I think they're down to just the one son these days, and possibly a daughter they keep hidden in a cupboard in case the sight of a gainfully employed woman alarms the yokels. I understand they've been informed of... of the passing, but haven't been able to make it out here through the snow yet. Not everyone has a car like us."

It was an odd sort of undertakers without a car in this day and age, I thought, but then reminded myself—for the umpteenth time since setting out from Paris, it seemed—that we were no longer in the big city. And then

I heard again what Hans had said. "Does that mean…" I struggled to form the sentence delicately. "I mean—where is the—"

I was going to say *the body*, but it felt unwieldy and obscene in my mouth.

"—your mother," I finished lamely.

"In the ice house," Hans said. "In this weather it's colder than any morgue the undertakers have, anyhow."

I followed his gaze out of the window, realising what preoccupied him. There was an indistinct block, somewhere near the treeline, barely visible in the mist. Between it and us were clues to what lay hidden—gateposts peeking up, the tips of stone angel wings, the backs of topiary animals cresting the fog—but the icehouse, bilt on an incline, lay above those like a ship marooned on an albescent sea. It looked unbearably lonely all the way out there, on the very border of the estate before wilderness took hold. I imagined the woman from the portrait, laid out in the ice-house, eyes sightless and staring, frost-rimed skin solidifying.#Once as a child, in the midst of the bitterest winter I can remember, my mother took me out in in the garden to see the flowers. I forget which ones they were but they were unseasonably bright and delicate and they had no right to have outlived the cattle that December had already taken; nut here they were nonetheless, blooming rebelliously. My mother knelt down and showed me one, encased in a glistening crystal. She took my hand and wrapped it around the head— and it snapped off, frozen right through, turning to icy fragments between my fingers.

I imagined that happening to Hans' mother—skin so cold that when the undertakers finally made it to the house to take her away she would splinter into pieces in their hands.

～～～

"I SHALL SEND König with the car to fetch the undertakers," Hans said, "and we shall see what instructions were left. In the meantime, the study—there are numerous papers. Despite her iron rule elsewhere, she did not keep her records tidy, apparently."

I clutched at this crumb of insight into Hans' childhood; the woman in the portrait I had thought looked kind but now I refigured her as a strict matriarch ordering around a recalcitrant young Hans. Had he had his trick even then, I wondered? Had he been able to switch so nimble between masks even then? From Hans the Rogue to Hans the Penitent, and back again.

WIth breakfast over, he had become another version I was entirely new to: Hans the Baron, decisive and efficient. The vacantness of the night before seemed to have been banished.

"Best to keep busy!" I agreed. "How can I help?"

He dissembled awkwardly, claiming first that he would rather sort through the study alone, and when he caught the disappointment that must have been far too obvious on my face, claimed that all the papers would be in German, so I would hardly be of any use anyhow. "Explore!" he suggested. "Draw! You'll find plenty of diversion."

It was a second small chip away at the vision I had of our trip—the vision I had of myself as the unwavering rock upon which he could lean in his difficult time of need. If I was a rock, it was a crumbling one. Hans this morning seemed barely in need of anything kind of shoring up, emotionally or otherwise. I remonstrated with myself not to feel uncharitably about this; he was in a peculiar limbo, I told myself—arrived home, but with nothing to do until the undertakers had been summoned. If sorting through his mother's papers—alone—gave him a sense of control, farbeit from me to interpose myself, and so I made a dutiful show of doing as he had asked, pottering about the house making my explorations seen (though he seemed hardly to register it; all I saw of him for the rest of the morning was the occasional passing of a shadow through the crack of the study door standing ajar).

The house was a curious beast. At first glance it seemed merely ramshackle and grubby, but the longer I spent roaming from one too-empty room to another, the stranger and more unwelcoming it felt. In my wanderings I uncovered numerous rooms that had, at some point, clearly held purpose: a dining room, a music room, a drawing room, a library. But each room was depleted so much as to be of little purpose any longer: the dining room contained only a long table set on either side with heavy narrow chairs, but the room was deathly cold and in its grand fireplace was such a mess of ash and debris that lighting it would have achieved nothing but choking diners on smoke; the music room contained nothing but a grand piano, painfully out of tune, and no seat at which to sit and play; in the drawing room stuffing poked through the seams of the armchair, and bottles filled only with sedimentary remains clinked in the globe cabinet when I opened it; in the library, the books were filmed in dust, and when I tried to pull some from the shelves, the books stuck to each other as if reluctant to give up their siblings for perusal.

And everywhere: the vines, the same that had caused me such revulsion to touch in my bedroom. They had invaded the entire house, creeping through cracks in the plaster, under loose sills, between floorboards, and with the vines came damp wallpaper, uneven floors, and unexpected hazards determined to trip you at every turn. At first I saw them as an infiltrating force, pulling apart the house from the inside out, but the more I explored the more I began to think of them as the only thing holding the house together.

Despite all this, the house still had a faded kind of allure; like one of our favourite showgirls from back home, the kind who drank absinthe like water and smoked cigarettes without a holder, tired and world-weary but dab on a bit of paint and slap a little glamour on to paper over the cracks and she could still dance you in circles. Bethlehem was our sort of woman, I decided.

I found my way (frankly; by accident—there were at least three staircases and so many corridors I easily lost track) back to the portrait of Hans' mother hanging in the hall. She was, as I had remarked earlier, beautiful—but that was such an inexpressive word. Mssr Carcassone would have withered me with a look for using it to describe a painting. "She is not merely beautiful," he would say. "What else is she?" *Powerful. Imperious.* "Good. And?" *Pliable.* "Pliable?" *Yes. Bending, but unbreaking. A willow tree among pines.* "Good. And now…" *And now?* "And now, draw."

I was without my drawing things however, and so I returned to my room to fetch them, only to discover with surprise that they were not amongst the pile of things that had been unpacked for me. I went in search of Hans, but instead caught König on his way out of the front door. Judging by his thick overcoat and clunking hobnail boots, he was about to brave the snow, and by the keys and snow chains he carried I surmised he was en route to Hartmann and his indeterminate number of sons. "König!" I called down to him, hurrying down the stairs. "Before you go—could I trouble you a moment?"

He heaved an expressive sigh and shuffled a hundred-and-eighty degrees to face me.

I explained about my missing drawing things. "They were in an inside pocket of my trunk," I said, annoyed that I sounded apologetic despite still being irritated that the contents had been manhandled without my permission in the first place. "Easy to miss, I'm sure!"

He deposited the chains by the door, and trudged to the stairwell, lifting aside a heavy embroidered tapestry that hung there. It revealed a small doorway behind it, the mirror of the door on the opposite side, though that one open to the passageway that lead to the kitchen and servants quarters.

(Though *what* servants, I had no idea—I had seen nobody but König, and even he had been elusive.) The door was small, perhaps only three-quarters the height of myself and almost comically small in comparison to König. He rummaged in his coat and produced a huge ring of clanking keys, rifled through them until he found a slender, silvery one, and inserted it into the lock. The door squealed appallingly as if under protest, and König had to set his shoulder against it to open it fully. I felt it vibrate right up through the stairs and through me; I craned over the banisters to look. König blocked much of the entrance as he stooped to enter but I glimpsed a floor caked in dust through which footprints and the tracks left presumably by the dragging of our cases were visible. My trunk was just inside the door, Hans' behind it—but as König knelt to open mine, I saw they were not the only trunks in the room. In fact, the little room below the stairs seemed to be dedicated solely to the storage of luggage and I couldn't have put a quick number of how many were there, lined up neatly in a row. ANd then König re-emerged, my drawing book and bag of supplies clutched in his hand.

"Thank you," I said, plucking them from his outstretched hand. König grumbled some indistinct sound far back in his throat, locked the door behind him, and vanished out of the front door, the snow chains clanking behind him like Marley's ghost.

I arranged myself cross-legged on the scratchy carpet on the half-landing directly below the painting, opened my sketch-book to the first blank page, and sketched out my own version of the portrait. I tried out a couple of mediums: pencils too soft, charcoals too diffuse, paints too delicate. ("Keep drawing. Keep drawing until it breathes.") I flipped a page and switched to ink, outlining a sharp, dark rendition of Hans' mother. ("Take no time—throw the shape onto the page, finesse later.") Of course, with ink it was harder to finesse later; the rushed, jagged shape was always visible beneath, but that was exactly why it was my favourite.

And there she was. The edges of her body dissolved into thin, striking lines that whipped across the paper. Her eyes were two dark, swelling dots of glistening ink; I had been too hasty in my attack and they beaded and burst. The white space of her face turned black. Frustrated, I pulled the sheet from the pad and cast it aside.

Absent-mindedly, I sang aloud to myself, "*A boy, a boy, a boy so blue…*"

A sharp gust blew through the hall, disturbing by pencils. The front door was open, I realised—and when I turned I was confronted by the sight of two unfamiliar men. By their age and dress, I gathered them to be Hartmann and Son.

"Good afternoon," I said in English.

The son looked up at his father, a smile passing momentarily across his lips. It was, I decided, not a very pleasant smile. The father's eyes crinkled in that barely noticeable manner of two people sharing a private joke—that particular way which is always imagined to be invisible but is so keenly felt by anyone accustomed to being the object of the joke.

"Spreche kein englisch," the older said, and they both turned away from me. Was it, I wondered, a snigger I could read between them? Or perhaps I was letting my imagination run away with me.

Hans appeared in the sitting room doorway. "Herr Hartmann," he said. "I'm pleased to see you made it through the snow. Please, follow me." He led them into the drawing room, and I clambered to my feet to follow, only to find the door already closed and myself left, useless again.

I sat down on the steps, idly considering attempting a second portrait in ink but found myself suddenly restless and out of joint. I hurled away the pen and paper in frustration and then, embarrassed, thought to myself bitterly that perhaps this was what the Hartmanns had shared their smile about—no doubt I looked every inch the ridiculous caricature of a Parisian artist: flustered, tempestuous, and covered in ink-spots.

Or perhaps (the thought occurred to me more soberly) they were unsurprised to discover the master of the house had brought a young man home with him.

Some twenty minutes later, the Hartmann's made a rapid exit, pursued by Hans. They dithered in the hall and Hans overtook them, flinging open the front door and shouting for König, who materialised as if he had been waiting the entire time. "Kindly see the gentlemen safely to the town," Hans said. "You will be returning to collect them again tomorrow." He pivoted on his heel and addressed the senior Hartmann with ire. "I trust you will have everything in order by then."

The undertakers shuffled out, touching their caps respectfully. The younger caught my eye as he passed—no trace of laughter this time.

"Ridiculous," said Hans, slamming the door behind them. "Backwater imbeciles."

Another new card shuffling to the top of the deck: Hans the Tyrant.

"What on earth's the matter?" I asked, descending the stairs.

He ignored the question. Instead he crouched and gathered up my discarded drawings. He held up the last ink drawing with its shadowed face. "This!" he said.

"Oh—that was a mistake. The ink ran. You know how I get with—"

"You've captured her extraordinarily," he said. He ran his fingertips lightly over the picture, staring into the black well in the centre of the page.

I approached him cautiously like one approaches a wounded animal, rested a hand on his forearm and pulled him closer. "Hans," I said, "is everything well? What about the undertakers? Did they—?"

"They're idiots," he snapped. He dropped the picture and it floated to rest on the floorboards face down.

"How so?"

"They've lost the bloody will, for a start," he said. "It's nowhere to be found in the office and I'm sure Mother would have left it with them, along with her instructions."

I frowned. "I'm confused—they're undertakers, not solicitors—why would they have the will?"

He disentangled from my grip. "This is the country," he said. "Nobody can survive doing just one thing. The undertakers is also the solicitors. The vets is also the doctors. The butchers is also a mechanics. The greengrocers is also a brothel."

He looked so impotently furious—like a child about to throw a strop—that I found myself beginning to laugh. He glared at me. "What's so funny?"

"Please tell me," I said, "that Bethlehem grows its own vegetables."

Sun burst gloriously through clouds; he grinned. Hans the Rogue.

"Most of them. But some we have to order in. Carrots. Parsnips. Leeks. Cucumbers."

"Marrows?"

He winced. "Marrows. Ambitious."

He flopped down on the stairs and I sat myself gingerly next to him.

"Are you certain it's not in the study?"

He nodded wearily. "I've been through every paper in that damn room."

"Perhaps I can help? A second pair of eyes, or—"

"Hartmann and his useless son will look again, and no doubt they shall find it."

"I'm sure they will," I said. "In the meantime, perhaps—"

"In the meantime, nothing." He looked at me, and softened. "I'm sorry—I know you're trying to be helpful."

"I am," I said, "but it's more than that. In Paris we're just—we're... you know. And so now we're here, I'm trying to be more... *you know*. For you."

He rested his shoulder lightly against mine; a minute gesture speaking volumes. "Yes, I know," he said.

———

IN THE LAST moments of night, in my bed, in my attic, in Montmartre, in Paris, between saying "I love you" and the arrival of the telegram, in the enormous sound of him saying nothing in return, Hans sang absently.

"*A boy, a boy, a boy so blue...*"

"If you sing the next line," I said flatly, "I will send you home straight out the window," and rolled away from him.

———

I POOTLED AROUND the house for the remainder of the afternoon, until my hunger rose and the hour for dinner approached. I ventured downstairs, The door to the study stood open, a loud rustling coming from within. I poked in my head, expecting to see Hans buried in papers, but the room was empty. Two heavy doors hung open, opening onto the terrace at the opposite end to the breakfast room. The sound I had taken for Hans moving was in fact papers blowing across the cluttered floor.

I made to close the doors, but something caught my eye and brought me up still. Evening was drawing swiftly in, black clouds beetling above the pines in the purpling dusk, but I could still make out the shape of the grounds stretching out to the dark square of the ice house far out on the edge—and somewhere near it, a flicker of movement. I peered, hoping to catch it again. It could only be Hans, of course—I had heard König busy in the kitchen when I passed—and I decided there and then that I'd had quite enough of exploring and idling, and it was high time I went and found him and gave him my very capable support, whether he liked it or not.

I tramped purposefully into the grounds. The mist had lifted a little since the morning, and the pathways through the gardens were clearer, though now I had stepped outside there was a curious lack of wind despite the evidence of the upturned study. An ornamental hedge fringed the immediate bounds of the house, trimmed at intervals into the shapes of animals—bears, foxes, badgers. If I had been more fanciful, I might have found them unnerving, these beastly shapes in the flog, but I was determined at that very moment to not be anything of the sort; I was a *rock*.

A gate blocked my path; it was in the same style as those we had entered through the previous night, thick stylised roots interweaving. A hedge-corridor, higher than my head and shrouded in gloom, led from the gate—and, I realised several turns later, directly into the maze and not towards the ice house at all. The house, apparently, had other plans for me.

Or perhaps not; after turning this way and that, just as I neared the point where I feared I was due to spend my next hours circling fruitlessly around the maze's labyrinthine guts, it spat me out through another root-gate at the bottom of a sharp incline of tussocky, jewelled grass. It led up steeply to the treeline, where the ice house sat.

It was apparent that I was quite alone. No Hans. Not a single sign of movement to be seen, not even the trees. All was still and silent.

I pressed upwards, regretting not putting on a coat. The cold was insidious this far from the house; I could barely feel my fingers. I ran them over the wall of the ice house, and so desensitised were they that it felt as if I was watching another's hand trace it's way over the uneven rough-cut stones. My fingers dipped into the deep valleys between each and found brittle, frosted lichen between the cracks.

Don't think about her in there, I told myself. *Don't think about the ice on her skin, or her lips cracking, or—*

My hand caught in a snarl of vines (yes, they had reached even here too) but I experienced them as a hand suddenly gripping mine. I swallowed a yelp and a primal urge to *run, run, run* shot through me. I snatched away my hand, trying to convince my racing heart that I had touched nothing but branches.

A freezing hand plucked at my wrist. I am not ashamed to say, I screamed.

Hans threw up his arms and backed away. "Sorry! I'm sorry!"

"*Hans*. For christsake!"

"I *thought* it was you coming." He looked sheepish. Hans the Contrite.

"Well, I bloody didn't think it was *you* coming!" I said. "I was having visions of allsorts after me just then! Demons and ghosts and I don't know what. You can't go grabbing a man like that without warning!"

He held up his hands, palm-first, placating. "Sorry, sorry, bärchen."

The last word had more effect than any apology could have. It had never been uttered outside of my bed before. *Bärchen. Little bear.* I glanced at the sky; still some light there. Not quite night. I would take that.

Nonetheless, my heart was still racing and I was unprepared to let him know I had forgiven him so easily. "What on *earth* are you doing out here all by yourself?" I said. "And where *were* you? I thought I saw you from the window but when I got here you were nowhere to be seen."

He looked rather pleased with himself. (it was the smug face he wore when he regaled me of tales of intellectual victories over the Sorbonne philosophy gang—he could spend whole night knocking back spirits with them in back alley ginhouses, arguing the night away, and then in the small hours come knock-knock-knocking at my door.) "Come look!" he said, and grabbed me by the hand. He lead me up the incline, past the ice house, to where the trees began.

Between two thick-trunked pines there was a dell, deep and capacious, carpeted thick with green needles and beechmast husks. Somehow it was sheltered from the elements; everything around it lay thick and swallowed in snow, but within this hollow it was green and soft. Stood on its edge and looking back I could still see everything—the ice house roof, the maze, Bethlehem skirted in mist beyond—but the dell had been completely invisible from the gate, lost entirely in shadow.

"What is this?" I asked. "Your secret hideaway. Let me guess—your love nest." It did resemble, literally, a nest.

"*Perhaps*," he said, mischievous. "Or perhaps you could think of it as a battleground."

I looked back into the hollow. "A battleground?"

"Yes." He smirked. "The site of many a conquest, you could say."

"Oh I *see*." I crossed my arms. "Of course. Where better, I mean— really? Many a battle, was there?"

"More skirmishes than battles," he said. "Young Hans was an enthusiastic soldier but not very schooled in strategy."

"I'm glad he's learned some more tactics."

"You've been an excellent General."

We were *flirting*, I realised, obtusely slow. It felt rather daring, the act of exchanging such words made outré purely by virtue of being spoken in *fresh air*. Yet below this there was a nagging current that tugged at me: the idea of Hans in that dell, bedding men before me. Somehow it didn't seem to tally up, to fit the diffident, tacitly ashamed figure I knew him as in Paris.

Perhaps it was a different Hans, I thought dryly. *Hans the Libertine.*

Perhaps it's always been this way. Perhaps he leaves them all *at dawn.*

Hans looked childishly excited. "Wait, though!" he said. "This isn't all. Watch this." He leaped into the hollow, sinking up go his ankles into the bed of needles. He scrabbled around at the base of the tree-trunk.

A clear, high bell sounded.

"What the devil?"

"It's a bell!" he proclaimed.

"Well—yes. Thank you. I'd gathered that much."

"They're all over the grounds," Hans said. "A very modern invention— mother was extremely excited when they were installed. We had all sorts put in—the electric lights, the telephone. But we also had these bells put all over, so you could ring through to other parts of the grounds. Back when we had servants, of course.

"And I was a curious boy, you see—with a knack of persuading people to do things for me. So the workmen installed one of the pipes for me. It runs right around the field, buried a foot or so down."

"I don't understand," I said. "For what purpose? Why would you want someone to be able to ring for you all the way out here?"

"The catch isn't in the house," he said. "It's by the gate out of the maze. If anybody comes through it, the bell rings up here."

I understood all at once. "So you could—"

"—avoid any unplanned ambushes and strategically withdraw, yes."

"Ingenious," I said, and meant it, though I didn't know if it pleased me. I reached down to help him up. I was amused by the bell's inventiveness, but the undertow plucked harder at me now. The pathological need for concealment back in Paris no longer seemed quite the daft affectation I had imagined it; now it seemed more like a pattern.

I hauled him out of the dell, but he impishly resisted and so instead I toppled in on top of him. We sank into the pungent bed of pine, entangled.

Have you ever kissed someone tenderly, only to realise they have their eyes open? It jars; the illusion of intimacy punctures, and you may as well be nothing more than two dolls pressed together by a little girl playing at romance with her toys. When I kissed Hans, he did not kiss me back.

As soon as I realised I pulled away. His eyes were wide open, fixed over my shoulder.

I realised a moment too late that of course he was looking at the ice house; down here in the dell, it was the only part of Bethlehem still visible, sat reproachful in the mouth of the hollow. In a rush I felt the presence of… of the *body* there (*skin, lips, hair*) in uncomfortable proximity to us. I felt immediately clumsy and improper; if *I* could scarcely manage to push the image of his mother lying so close out of my mind, how much harder must it be for Hans?

I opened my mouth to apologise, but the words died on my tongue, interrupted by the single, clear chime of a bell.

<hr>

WE SPRANG APART like scalded cats, hauling ourselves out onto the clear ground, smoothing down our clothes like naughty schoolboys. No one emerged up the hill—no-one and nothing stirred. The night remained as still as it had been on my approach.

"Must have been the wind," I said, in hopeful defiance of all evidence.

He jittered, saying nothing. Hans the Flighty.

"We should go back," I said carefully. "You look half-frozen. What were you doing out here without a coat, anyhow?"

"Says you."

"I was coming gallantly to the rescue, it doesn't count." I tried to smile at him but he refused to meet my eyes. "We'll both catch our death if we don't get back inside. That's if I can even find the way back through that damn maze."

He perked up. "Oh, we won't get lost in there. I know it better than the streets back home." (*Home*, I thought. When we were in Paris he referred to Bethlehem as *home*. Now we were here, he meant Paris.) He was right though: he *did* know the maze well. He led me surefootedly, calling out the turns as we took them—*left, right, right, left, right, left, left*. "Here we are," he said, but we had arrived not at the root-gate to the gardens but in the centre of the maze. A tall ring of hedge circled it, high enough to be left with the feeling of existing in a solitary, slumbrous bubble away from everything else. A low stone pond was in the centre, though it had largely been claimed by the vines that plagued everything—they snaked around it, consuming the masonry, spilling over the lip. It surface was frozen, gripping the vines where they broke the surface, but below you could see the tendrils, wavering.

"Hans," I said, "this is *lovely*, but it really is getting too cold to be—"

"I want to show you something else," he said. "My other secret."

I couldn't feel my fingers, I was shivering uncontrollably now, and that discomfiting current still plucked at me but despite all that the prospect of a *secret* was intoxicating. A secret is something that can only be *shared*.

He craned his neck to see the the chimneys of the house, as if to orient himself, then turned and stalked purposefully around the pond, head down, lips moving silently. He was counting as if the pond was a clock; at seven o'clock (assuming the house to be noon) he stopped and knelt down. He pulled away the vines and began to jab his fingers sharply into the earth where the pond met the ground, breaking up frozen clods of dirt and pulling them out in lumpish handfuls.

"What are you doing?"

He ignored me, scrabbling away like a dog single-mindedly digging after something it scents buried deep. He had broken the top ground and now the mud was wetter, warmer. I watched with a morbid fascination; this was yet another Hans, one I didn't have a word for. Hans the the lover, the provocateur, the playboy, the wit, the orphan, the baron, and now this, this unnameable, animalistic thing consumed with intent.

Down nearly a foot now, his sleeves soaked and filthy, the knees of his trousers no better. "Just wait," he muttered. "Just wait."

I knelt beside him and tried to help, though I had no idea what I was assisting with. Our hands collided, and he pushed them away. "Just wait," he said, "I'll show you." He dug, ever more furious. "I'll show you, I'll show you, I'll..."

He sank back suddenly on his haunches and wiped a dirty hand across his forehead. I thought perhaps he might cry; I had never seen him shed even a single tear before. Another seldom-seen card in the pack.

"Hans," I said, taking his hand in mine. "It's okay. Don't fret."

He sank his head on my shoulder. I heard a muffled sob, felt it soak through my collarbone right to my heart. I cradled his head against mine, tangled my finger in his hair. I was caking dirt into the blonde curls, but that ship was long sailed. "What were you trying to show me?"

"It's..." He sniffed loudly, and raised a hand, blinking away tears. "It's a box."

"A... box?" I said cautiously.

"A biscuit tin."

"*A biscuit tin.*"

I twisted a limp curl of his hair tight around my finger, not sure what to say, waiting for him to say whatever needed to be said instead.

Muffled; "It had things in it. Things from when I was a boy. I just wanted to show you, that's all."

I let my hand wander down to stroke the short hairs at the nape of his neck. "It's okay," I soothed. "I'm sure it'll turn up."

He shrugged exaggeratedly, sucked in a shuddering breath and exhaled long and slow. "Perhaps," he said, sounding not for one second convinced.

"What was in the tin?"

"Oh. Nothing much. Not really."

The devastated earth beggared the lie. "It doesn't look like nothing much," I said with care.

He shrugged again—sulky child embarrassed at his show of emotion now. "Doesn't matter, anyway. It's gone."

"Why did you bury it in the first place?"

He looked away, up towards where the ice house lay, now lost in the dark. "To keep them all safe," he said, and that was all he would say on the matter for the rest of the evening.

I AWOKE IN the middle of the night, shaking.

I was cold (because when was I anything but in this damn house?) and in the first befuddled moments this was all that was amiss; I had been dreaming of icy ponds and snowy dells, and to wake shivering felt entirely natural. But as my faculties reclaimed a footing, I realised that it was not I that was shaking, but everything else. The house itself quaked, and everything in it. It was a deep, rhythmic tremor, not violent but certainly emphatic, like the growl in the throat of an angry animal. It came from somewhere deep, though I could not tell you how I knew that; it presented itself to me as an inarguable truth, that somewhere deep in its heart Bethlehem was convulsing, and I inside it.

I kicked away the covers and tottered to the window, thinking perhaps that I would be able to see something outside that would explain the phenomenon. The boards thrummed beneath my bare feet. I threw open the drapes to reveal... nothing. What I had expected I did not know—a light, or a fire? *Something*. But there was nothing besides an impenetrable dark as black as the ink I drew with. Nevertheless I pressed my face close to the glass and peered this way and that, as if a few inches closer might make something materialise. The panes themselves vibrated too—and as I watched, the crack began to creep further, spreading across a third pane towards the wall between that separated Hans and I.

It might perhaps have occurred to another man to wonder if this was a dream, or a hallucination, but the thought never crossed my mind. If anything, after the dreadful stillness of Bethlehem in the light, this felt more real than anything I'd experienced since stepping off the train.

What time was it? I crossed to the dressing table and fumbled for my watch. My grasping fingers had just settled on metal when I was interrupted by a knock at the door.

It was a short resolute knock—not Hans' surreptitious *rap-rapraprap-rap* but a single decisive rap. It was the kind that expected an answer. *König?* My brain was tripping over itself trying to get a grip on events, and even as I thought it, I simultaneously knew that the knock was not how König's knock would sound (his would sound like a Viking beating on the gates of Valhalla) and scuttling along behind these thoughts, the realisation that the knock was not on *my* door.

It was next door, I realised. Hans' room.

I tiptoed to my own door, cautiously cracked it open, and peered out.

The air in the corridor smelt metallic, like pennies. On a sideboard, a picture frame was slowly rotating on the spot as it shook.

Again, the knock. A decisive *thunk* against Hans door.

And yet—*and yet,* my panicked brain screeched inside my skull—*the corridor is empty.*

A moment after, it was empty no longer. Hans' door creaked open and out he stepped, dressed in his pyjamas and robe.

"Hans!" i hissed at him—but it fell on deaf ears. I caught a glimpse of his face, unseeing eyes looking straight past me—the empty Hans once more. *Sleepwalking*—though I had never known him to do it before.

Thunk. The knock again, further down the corridor, towards the stairs. Hans followed in its wake, and I in his. I caught up in time to catch him descending the stairs, eyes still blank and fixed on a point a little above his own head, a disconcerting manner to witness someone walking down steps; I half-expected him to miss his footing and tumble down. The *thunk* sounded again—several in quick succession, as if they came from each stair, a hidden hand knocking on each in turn, though the only thing I could see touching each was the pale skin of Hans' bare feet.

Now too the shaking had increased, as if something was building in the heart of the house from where it emanated. The portrait on the half-landing bounced on its hangings, swinging left and right as Hans passed it unseeing. The boards beneath me shuddered to the queer rhythm that gripped the house; I half expected to see planks burst their fixings and jut up through the threadbare carpet.

Thunk, thunk thunk, descending. The knocks stopped seven or eight steps before Hans reached the bottom, as if the origin of the sound preceded him.

I stole down the stairs behind him, careful not to catch up for fear of startling Hans awake (my mother's warning to not wake a sleepwalker jostling for position amongst a few choice other of her choice superstitious proclamations right then) but keeping him in sight. A *thunk* by the low door to the servant's quarters led Hans across the hall. *Thunk* down the corridor to the skullery. *Thunk* by the door to the kitchen as it swung silently opened by itself. *Thunk* from somewhere beyond as Hans vanished in the caliginous gloom within.

I tiptoed to the door.

Here in the kitchen the shaking had crescendoed; the pans that hung on hooks from the ceiling rack leaped and crashed against each other; ladles, spoons and knives on the side juddered along the worktop. The stools around the table inched along the flags. The floor shook violently—down here, it felt as if the whole house was an engine straining to rip the house up out of the ground and race away into the dark, Hans and I trapped inside its belly.

In the corner of the room stood a door the green colour of pondscum, three-quarters the height of a man. Hans stood against it, head bowed, like a classroom dunce.

Thunk—and Hans' hand is rising, reaching for—

—"Hans," I called out, my mother's warnings be damned—

—the door handle and as his fingers touched the metal—

—everything fell still.

The spoons were silent.

The pans slowed to a gentle rocking.

The floor quietened, solid and dependable once more.

As if in reaction, keeping a balance somehow, I myself began to shake-- with cold and delayed shock. I panted, and white clouds of breath ballooned in the air.

And somewhere just on the edge of hearing, through the open window, I heard the sound of a bell ring.

"Hans?"

I thought for a moment he had vanished, but he was instead curled in a ball in the corner at the foot of the green door, his arms wrapped protectively above his head. He rocked back and forth. I rushed to him, wrapping my arms tight around, coaxing him gently to life his head. "Hans," I whispered. "It's me. You're okay. You were just sleepwalking, you were just—"

Just what? I couldn't have told you. Just hallucinating? Just imagining a house that vibrated with agitation like a living thing, imagined an invisible visitor that knocked on your door? Perhaps. But the morning was the time to think of those madnesses; in that moment all I saw was my Hans, frightened and small, and I wanted to scoop him up and hold him until he was safe.

"Come to bed," I said. "Come on—let me help you up. There you go, that's it." I led him by the hand back down the passage, up the stairs, along the corridor. "You were just sleepwalking. It's all fine now." Both our bedroom doors stood open. I paused, not wanting the decision to be mine, but Hans just merely hovered uncertainly until at last I closed his door quietly and led him into my bedroom.

Beneath the sheets, he curled against me. I kissed his forehead, and whispered, "Rest your bones."

He mumbled something, just beyond my hearing. It sounded like: "I'm sorry. I won't do it again."

I shifted against him. "What was that?"

He looked up at me, bleary-eyed and confused, like I was a complete stranger. As if, I thought later, when his breathing had slowed to sleep and I was left alone with my own thoughts, his words had been addressed to someone else entirely.

THE FIRST TIME Hans slept in my bed it had been a warm summer's night, and it was this very thing itself that had led us there; the lengthening shadows as the cooling sun passed across my attic (his was the light of morning, mine the light of sunset) had stretched us closer to intimacy with each passing hour as the socially proper time to have left wafted away through the open window.

"The Knight of Cups," he said. "I approve of him. Keep him." It was a joke, of course—he proclaimed it as he lifted up his own cup, swirling it's contents (bright green, like a witch's potion, I remember).

I lay on my front below the open window, drawing. "I'm sure the Knight is deeply grateful, but I'm afraid it's still not enough to save him from the chop."

"Is there none you'll save?"

"None."

That evening I had explained to him my plan—a new tarot. Gone the Fool, the Magician and the Hierophant, and gone the centuries of weight they carried with them. I had been in Paris for six months, free of the farmyard yoke of my adolescence, and I was entranced by the idea of creating something entirely neoteric and pioneering. It was to be the portfolio I presented in two years time to the college, I had decided—a collection of paintings as a new tarot.

And in my class, the curly-haired boy by turns shy and bold, who had captured my attention from the first class we had shared. Somehow, despite our rooms in such dazzlingly close proximity, our paths never crossed—until that morning when we had run into each other on the steps. I had never had the nerve to strike up a conversation in class where I was just another student among many, but alone on the street our mutual recognition bridged the gap.

And here he is as the sun sinks, and still not left.

"Will you sit for me?" I had asked. "I'd love you to be a study for one the cards."

"Which one?"

I mused theatrically. "The Artist."

He sucked his teeth. "Too obvious."

"The Quill."

"Better."

Even then, I knew he would be the study for more than one of the cards. I knew the second he stepped through the door he would be the study for all of them.

The sun is gone, and still he's here.

"There is one card I could keep," I said, drunk on my own daring even as the words swelled on my tongue.

He rolled over on his front and stared along the lines of the floorboards at me. "Oh? And which is that."

I took a deep breath and leaped. "The Lovers," I said.

And now here he is in my bed, miles from Paris, miles from the sun. If I studied him now, what card would he be now?

When I eventually fell asleep, it was into such a deep, dreamless slumber that I failed to notice neither the arrival of dawn, nor the departure of Hans.

———

I HAD PLANNED to address the night's events with Hans over breakfast, but was foiled by his complete non-appearance. On the table by the window I found just one egg waiting for me, and a round of toast cooling and limp in the rack—apparently König had been aware before I was that Hans would not be joining me and adjusted his preparations accordingly (rather meanly in fact, I thought, remembering the previous morning's generous spread.)

The day passed in an anaemic crawl. Hans emerged from upstairs at midday but he responded to my cheery greeting with only a stiff nod and immediately withdrew himself to the study, and so I loitered around the house making desultory attempts to draw. I swung nauseously between trying to put the night's events out of my mind and examining them from all angles to try to make sense of them, my mood changing capriciously like a rapidly swinging pendulum. At the apex of the swing I would pace back and forth along the route I had travelled the night before, knocking on each stair and chilling to recognise the *thunk*, telling myself that there was no possible way it had been a figment of my imagination; at its nadir, I would remember how I had begun to shake when the spell had broken, thought how much a fever can feel like cold when one is in its grip, and ascribed the whole thing to febrile hallucination.

Stress, I told myself. *Hans may be the bereaved party here, but it's me that is in a foreign land, in tow of a man whose demeanour is impossible to predict from one moment to the next, with no idea of what is expected of me.* I was, I realised, exhausted.

But nagging at me was my own mother's voice, whispering warnings. She had come from romani stock, and though she laughingly claimed to have left it all behind when she kissed my father by the oak trees in the garden, she would still spill salt to prevent bad luck, still nail a horseshoe above the door, still leave out supplicatory gifts for the faerie folk on the moor. And of course, it was she whose soft nimble fingers I had first watched shuffle a tarot deck and unfold the top three one by one across the crushed velvet tabletop for the amusement of the town women. Always a wry amusement at her own absurdities, a silk glove slipped over the calloused, hard belief below.

Far out here, in this grand house crumbling to dereliction amidst an eldritch forest, it was so much easier to believe in phantoms and shadows.

Midway through the afternoon I caught König in the hallway, dressed again for travel, presumably setting off for a second day running to the town to hold Hartmann the undertaker-cum-solicitor to his ultimatum to produce the will within the day. He closed the front door behind him with such force that the whole hallway shook. A little over an hour later, he reappeared, his enormous puffy overcoat layered so thick with snow he appeared almost entirely white. He shook himself like a great big dog, spattering slush across the hallway.

"Did they find the will?" I asked. He looked up at me and seemed to debate about answering before finally he shook his head curtly and then vanished off into the servants quarters without a word.

Hans belatedly emerged from the study just shy of our evening meal. He looked drawn and pale and scurried off to the kitchen, returning some time later with the fringe of his hair damp and his face and forearms scrubbed and tender. We took our meal in the breakfast room (another sumptuous spread of game meats, delicious thick breads, and pickled cabbage—though when König had had time to prepare all this I couldn't have guessed) and Hans presented himself with a forced cheer, asking me about my day. I answered sparingly, not honestly having much of interest to tell and finding the subject inane in the face of the other topics that loomed undiscussed.

"So," I said, "has the will been found?"

"I have no idea," he said. "König was unable to make it to the town—the snow had gotten worse, the roads are impassable, even with the chains."

"Can't we just telephone them?"

Hans scraped his knife along the grouse-bone, stripping off the last of the meat. "Oh, I have," he said. "Nobody answered. Cowards."

"I'm not surprised," I said. "You did go rather Bloody Red Baron on them. They'll be quaking in their boots."

Hans chewed thoughtfully for a moment, and then he smiled wearily. "Yes, I suppose I did," he said. "I don't know where that came from, to tell you the truth. I gather Father had quite the expansive temper running the estate, but I was too young when he passed away to remember that. Perhaps it's just in the blood."

"I'm sure the will shall turn up," I said, as if it was a missing sock.

"No doubt."

Hans' fingernails, I noticed, were rimmed with dirt beneath, despite how violently clean the skin way.

"Hans," I said carefully, "have you been out in the grounds this afternoon?"

He withdrew his hands beneath the table. "No," he said. "I've been in the study sorting papers." And that was the end of that.

Now that he was sat in front of me in the flesh, I wasn't quite sure how to go about the conversation I wanted to have, and so I went at it sideways. "This must have been quite a place to grow up," I remarked. "So huge and wild."

Hans shrugged. "It was fine."

"I can't imagine it, though. Everything here is so different to Paris. So heavy, so dark. So permanent. I don't know how to describe it, but in Paris you seem so—I don't know." I fished around for a word. "So light." *So impermanent*, I added silently, thinking of him dancing across the street away from me every night. "This was not what I would have imagined, if you'd asked me to where I thought of you growing up. But you've never talked about it…"

He shrugged. "It was a good place to have left," he said with a wry smile.

"Tell me about it," I said. "You've never said a thing. Was it awful?

Was it wonderful? Were you happy? Were you desperate to leave?"

He considered for a moment. "Yes," he said, "to all of the above."

I sighed theatrically. "*Hans.*"

He smirked. "Well what do you want to know?"

"Well what about your father, for a start?"

"He died when I was six." Hans sat back and frowned. "As far as I know, he owned mines--at least, I think that's what it was. After he died we never really talked about it very much, but I remember picking up odds and ends. I don't think I entirely understood what mines were, I used to picture something like the craters in the moon and lots of people trundling around with carts picking up stones. Like ants--I had an ant farm, I think I mixed up the two. I suppose it's not all that from the mark when you think about it. But anyhow--after he died they still kept us in money, at least for a while."

"What was he like?"

"Angry alot, but kind as well. He used to scare me when I was young, from what I can remember, but when I think back now it was bluster more than anything."

"What about your mother?"

His face clouded. "She married young," he said. "Younger than us. Daughter of a vicar, though I never met him--he died the same year as Father. I imagine they were delighted that she'd married so above herself though--snared a wealthy landowner."

I pictured the woman from the painting, tried to imagine her young, younger than I was now. How would she feel, setting off across country to her new husband, finding him holed up amidst the gloomy bulwarks of a place like Bethlehem? "What was she like?"

Hans steepled his fingers together. "Unbending," he said, after some thought. "She had her ways, and that was how things were. I think it was

Father's death that did that--no husband to overrule her, and a son too young yet to do the same." His gaze had drifted far away. "But I do remember--she loved hedgehogs. If anything made her go soft, it was them. One summer we had ten of them roaming the drawing room that she'd rescued."

Nothing about the willowy woman in the painting chimed with his description, and I wondered how much license the artist had taken; it was artistic tradition of course, just ask Anne of Cleves. "That's sweet," I said.

He frowned. "Only hedgehogs, though," he said. "She couldn't abide any other animals. They were safe inside being fed drops of milk, but that same winter she had the ratting cats poisoned because they kept leaving a mess in the vegetable patch. One of them crawled away to die, and we didn't discover it til months later, nothing but bones. It was me who found it--I screamed the whole place down."

I wasn't quite sure what to say to that; feebly, I managed; "Well... at least she loved the hedgehogs."

"Love doesn't preclude cruelty," said Hans, and in that moment he looked so deeply disquieted that I couldn't bring myself to discuss anything serious further with him that night, and so I turned the conversation to trivialities in a futile endeavour to lift his gloom until finally he made his excuses and we both departed for bed.

I hovered by my door. "Hans," I said. "I--I'll be listening for your knock."

His face twisted into a look of such pure distaste he might as well have stepped in the picked-clean bones of the cat right that very second. "No," he said, "not here," and without another word he was gone, the door closing with a heavy finality behind him.

That's that, then, I told myself wearily; the look on his face had been the final chip away at my imagined purpose here. I was to be a companion and nothing more. I would not see Hans that night.

As it turned out, this was not to be the case.

———

THE KNOCK WOKE me up. Not the sharp, decisive knock I had dreaded, but the familiar Hans knock: *rap-rapraprap-rap*.

I sat up in bed, disoriented, thinking for a second I was back in Montmartre, but instead of comforting warmth I faced a bitter wintry chill and instead of the sounds of the city there was just that louring Bethlehem indolence.

The knock again, more insistent. *Rap-rapraprap-RAP*.

I threw open the door. "Hans, I don't—"

But I froze as soon as I saw him. At first he was that blank, expressionless Hans of the previous night, but then like the paint washing off a canvas to reveal another picture below, his face creased into one of terror. He oscillated on the spot, arms crossed tight over his chest, fingernails digging into biceps like he was wearing an invisible straitjacket. "Please," was all he said.

"Hans, what—?"

"*Please.*"

Without question, I pulled him to me, cradling his shivering body against me. "Of course, bärchen, of course. Come in." I lead him to the bed, pushing back the covers so we could climb in beside each other. He curled up, knees drawn to his chest, and let me enfold him. "Shhh," I whispered, lips pressed against the spiral of his ear. The trembling wasn't subsiding; if anything it grew more violent. "Shhhh. You're safe. Rest your bones."

Me nuzzled himself below my chin but said nothing. His breath was hot and fast against my throat. His whole body was a sweating, panicky furnace.

I held him tighter.

After a while, I realised the shaking was not only coming from Hans. As the night before, it grumbled up from deep in the house.

He muttered something inaudible. "What was that?" I leaned in closer. "I can't hear you, Hans."

"*I don't want to go*," he hissed.

"Go? Go where?"

No answer, just the same thing repeated. "*I don't want to go.*"

I pressed my lips against his ear, kissed him. "You don't have to go anywhere," I soothed. Wherever 'anywhere' might be.

Thunk.

And then I knew.

The knock sounded against his door, once, then twice. Sharp fingers dug between my ribs; Hans clutched desperately at me. His breath burst torrid and fearful on my chest. The bed shuddered, and us in it.

Thunk, a third and then a fourth time, more insistent. *Thunk.*

"You don't have to go, you don't have to go," I whispered over and over into his ear. "You don't have to go, you don't have to go." Repeated until it was a mantra that lost meaning, just sounds, one after the other to calm him. Soft words, the best I could offer, and though I barely understood their meaning or their significance they did at least seem to have some kind of calming effect on Hans.

The knocking abated. The shaking of the house did not.

Hans mumbled something else; I craned to hear. He whimpered, and then began speaking rapidly in German, words I couldn't decipher properly. "Estut mirlaird mudder," it sounded like.

When the knock came again, it was on my own door.

Hans' body seized within my encircling arms; he curled yet tighter, head stuffed between his knees. His trembling ceased, as if every muscle was held tight in awful anticipation. My own reassuring words shrivelled, useless.

We lay there, him curled inside the protective harbour of me, the both of us suspended in this pregnant moment of anticipation after the knock, the moment in which a response is invited, a moment that stretched, stretched, stretched so far that eventually it burst and I realised that the house had fallen quiet and still. Realisation dawning on us simultaneously, both Hans and I began to shiver in unison—not a fearful shivering any longer but one of profound cold. I pulled the bedclothes up and over both our heads and held him in the amniotic darkness until we both drifted away into sleep.

When I awoke it to light once again seeping around the curtains and the sensation of Hans' head still resting against my chest. The combination of the sensations was jarring, a juxtaposition that seemed somehow illicit. My movement stirred Hans. "It's morning," I whispered. "You should go back to your room, before König notices."

Hans chuckled sleepily. "Oh, don't worry about *König*," he said, wriggled back into the crook of my arm, and closed his eyes.

"So…" I said.

"So?"

"So. Last night?"

A boiled egg, decapitated. "I'm sorry about what I said."

"I mean… in the night."

"Oh, I see." He considered his breakfast with elaborate interest. "Thank you."

"*...thank you?*"

"Yes. It was good to finally get some sleep. I haven't slept well since we got here."

"I think there's probably more to talk than whether you got some decent shuteye, don't you?"

A spoon, stabbing.

"*Fine*," I said.

"Salt," he said, and I thought for a moment it was some particularly germanic retort lost in translation, until I realised he simply wanted me to pass the shaker. I did so, trying not to make it look like relenting.

"Where does the green door in the kitchen lead to?"

He froze, salt cascading.

"The green one," I pressed. "Short. You'd have to stoop. It's locked."

"Why?"

"You damn well know why."

"I have no idea at all."

"About why I'm asking, or where the door goes?"

"Oh, I know where the door goes."

"Well—where?"

The thumped down the shaker. "To the cellar. It's empty. We never used it. I imagine by now the vines will have overrun it, judging by how far they've made it into the rest of the house. It will be unnavigable, I presume."

"I'd like to take a look inside. I've explored everywhere else."

"No."

"Why not?"

There was a fraction of a paused before he replied. "We've lost the key."

I nodded to myself, not believing him for a second. "I see. Well, I have another question."

He pushed his plate away, saying nothing.

"My question is: *who knocks?*"

He stared down at the table for long enough that I had to prompt him. "Hans, did you—?"

"Yes, I heard you."

"And?"

"And I have work to do. Hartmann telephoned and left a message with König. They're coming for her in two days; the weather is predicted to clear enough to get the cart through."

"What work do you have to do? Have they found the will?"

"They didn't say."

"So presumably not. What work do you have to do, then? More holes to dig?"

He removed his blazer from the back of his chair and pulled it on slowly and deliberately. "I shall see you at dinner time," he said.

"Hans, you can't turn up in the middle of the night shaking with fear, and then refuse to talk to me about it the next day."

He sighed deeply, and sat back down. "I know," he said. "I'm sorry." He reached over the table and took hold of my hand, a gesture I found so suddenly intimate it startled me. "I was trying to show you—that's why I was digging. I wanted to find—well, it doesn't matter. It's nowhere to be found. I've forgotten where it is. And I know you want to *help* me."

"I want to do more than *help* you, Hans, you know that." Sleeplessness and frustration had stoked a sudden fiery anger over something I hadn't even know I was angry about. "Christ, Hans, I just want you to let me l—"

He hung his head. "Can we just…leave this? For now."

I looked him up and down. He looked exhausted, and I felt a surge of affection. This was yet one more Hans—Hans the Weary. Perhaps I had been churlish in my estimation of him, in finding reason to feel cast aside when he flipped to yet another unfamiliar card; after all, it was I who had put him on a pedestal as a whole host of different people. Perhaps I should be taking the opportunity to get to know the new faces he was allowing me to see.

"Can we please agree to talk about this at dinner?" I asked.

"Talk about what?"

"About green doors, phantom knocks, and shaking walls."

He released my hands, exasperated, and stood back up. "I shall be in the study," he said and withdrew, stalking off into the hall.

"How does König even answer a telephone, anyway?" I called petulantly after his receding back.

<center>~~~</center>

YOU MAY HAVE been under the impression so far that my only part in this story was to stand on the sidelines and pout miserably as I was batted this way and that by Bethlehem's shifting tides. But my mother had raised me better than that; she was a woman of a different tribe trying to fit in amongst families who had lived in the same spot for so many generations they might as well have grown roots. If you didn't like what you had, you went out and changed things. (Sometimes this would be by leaving out a saucer of milk for the pixies, but it was the spirit of the thing I cleaved to more than the specifics.) If Hans wouldn't give me any answers, I would find them myself, starting by getting the green door in the kitchen open.

The prime target was König's ring of keys. In pursuit of my objective, I spent the day stuck to him like a shadow under the pretense of drawing practise. I showed up wherever he was with a drawing pad. He began in the kitchens scrubbing and peeling potatoes and I contrived to appear there also, mapping out a series of small sketches of his thick hands submerged in the sink. "Capturing movement," I told him, though he merely shrugged and carried on his work unconcerned. After that I just *happened* to be out on the terrace when he emerged to shovel snow and hammer at the icy layer that had formed below with the sharp end of a pickaxe. I ended up with three pages of charcoal sketches, pronouncing it a study of "figure and form" when he glanced briefly over my shoulder in passing.

I was realising, as I drew, that König was actually quite handsome, in a gargantuan, arboreal kind of way, in the same way a centuries-old mountain chiselled by wind and rain into a form of natural beauty could be appreciated. It was the attention to detail that fuelled this—the breaking down of the body into individual parts, all beautiful in their own way—that caused this sway. I wasn't unaccustomed to it; I frequently found myself swooning for the life models that posed for us as the college, even those for whom I had been unstirred when they first entered the studio.

In some way, I realised, Bethlehem was the same. As a whole it loomed and lurked and other grubby things I wasn't too fond of, but when I paid attention to its eccentricities—the patterns and shapes that lay below its layer of grime and vines—it was quite possible to love it.

With this new reconfiguration of König as a male body upon my page, I remembered anew Hans' words this morning: *you don't need to worry about König* with all the implications of knowledge that carried. Could König have been one of the men invited to the dell beyond the ice house? I held this thought up to the light and examined it from every angle, eventually dismissing it—I wasn't sure how old König was, but as far as I knew he had been the family's servant since Hans' childhood. I couldn't imagine a liaison. Though perhaps König had known about the others—had known about the warning bell?

At some point in the day, König ventured out further into the garden, where it was less easy to inconspicuously accompany him. I took up position at a distance, seated on a low stone wall that trapped a forlorn topiary gryphon within its sphere. I watched König venture back and forth from a coal house I had hitherto failed to notice, concealed behind trees. He wheeled a barrow filled with clinkers to the house and returned with it empty. By now I had forgotten my pretence of drawing and he furrowed his brow as he passed me and my empty page; swiftly I began to etch out a landscape of the garden, the untidily trimmed menagerie in the foreground, the maze lost in mist behind.

Having established my cover, and in some part motivated by how cold I had grown sat on the stone, I tucked away my pad and wandered deeper into the garden. It was only then that I noticed what had previously been hidden: holes. Holes everywhere. At a conservative estimate, I counted perhaps thirty. They were deep, rough holes, like an animal's, dotted through the garden with no immediate logic or pattern. Some were in corners, some at the feet of topiary beasts, some untethered from any conjoining landmark.

I thought of the dirt beneath Hans' fingernails, and understood.

"What is he looking for?" I asked König. If he was not someone from whom we needed to keep a secret, I reasoned that perhaps he knew something that would shed some light for me. But König only shrugged and lumbered away in the direction of the coalshed. "Will *nobody* answer a questions around here?" I remarked in his wake, though not loud enough for him to hear me.

Dejected, I abandoned my quest. I had not seen the slightest opportunity to slip away with the keys, and I felt sodden and miserable. I trudged back to the kitchen, thinking to inspect the green door one last time (I had some vague idea of picking the lock, though I had no knowledge of how to do such a thing) and there, beside the sink where the potatoes sat, denuded and submerged in a pan of water, lay König's keys where they had presumably lain the entire day I had been trailing around after him.

They were lighter than I'd imagined; I'd expected them to be weighty and portentous, like a medieval jailor's keys, but found myself disappointed. I flipped through, searching for a likely candidate. The first that looked like it might fit—a thick, ornate piece made of the same dark metal as the keyhole—refused to even slide all the way in, let alone turn. I flipped to a second, then a third, unsuccessful at each try until I'd worked my way around the full set. Nothing. Not one turned.

I flung the keys back where they had come from in. It was, I'll admit, nothing more than petulance. They clanged down onto the stone like church bells, louder than seemed natural, and I froze involuntarily like a naughty child; I imagined König bursting in, and then remembered that, guest or not, I did still have every right to be here, and every right to open any door I liked.

No König presented itself—nor indeed any Hans, presumably buried in the study still. Either that or he was out on the front lawn, digging up holes like a rabbit.

A stray memory sweeping by in the current of my frustration snagged at me. I picked up the keys again. If I couldn't satisfy one curiosity, at least I could satisfy another.

The green door's twin, in the hall. I pulled aside the tapestry—this at least did have the good grace to be as heavy and resistant as befitted the atmosphere—and found the slender, silver key I remembered seeing Hans use. It slid right in, and turned with a sharp click that passed right up my arm.

The room was thick with dust. I'd seen that the first time, but it was quite another thing to be breathing the dry, geriatric air. I coughed, and it sent eddies and whorls dashing through the clouded air. I wafted my arms in front of my face and peered in. My trunk was sat neatly just inside, Hans' behind it, a little larger. Behind that, in varying shapes and sizes, was a procession of others. That word—*procession*—specifically sprang to my mind; they were perfectly aligned with each other, a phalanx of luggage standing to attention all the way back into the stuffy darkness below the stairs, even though there would have been plenty of room to stack them more efficiently. It was unsettling in a way I couldn't quite put my finger on; perhaps it was that they didn't look like they were stored, like someone had put them here. It looked instead like they were *waiting*.

Waiting to what? To sprout legs, stand up and march out one by one? This house was starting to addle me, with its nighttime queernesses leeching every ounce of peace from my sleep, and now here I was imagining all sorts of nonsense, even in the daylight.

Knees bent—the room was low, and though I could just about stand upright, it felt awkward—I shuffled to the first trunk I didn't recognise. A tag tied around the handle was lettered in neat copperplate handwriting— *Oskar Muller*. Below it was an address, a street in Berlin I didn't recognise the name of. I tried the catch on the trunk, discovering it locked. Beside the catch was a small keyhole, but there was no sign of a key anywhere. I shook the case, delicately as if it was a finely-wrapped Christmas present and I a curious child in mid-December; it wasn't full, but it wasn't quite empty either. Something inside rattled back and forth.

I worked my way along the row, inspecting the tags. This army had names, all male: Felix Bauer. Moritz Wolf. Anton Fischer. And more-there were, I counted, thirteen in total besides those that belonged to Hans and I. All locked, and all empty apart from a few loose items that knocked against each other when I disturbed the cases.

I backed out of the room, pulling the stiff door closed behind me.

"Have you seen König?"

I jumped guiltily. It was Hans, clutching a sheaf of papers, looking distressed.

"I was just looking for my case," I told him, hiding the ring of keys behind my back, clutched in sweating palms.

He titled his head like a confused puppy. "Right," he said, "but have you seen König?"

"He was outside near the maze somewhere last time I check. Had a shovel with him."

"Ah, of course." Hans bit his lip. "I asked him to go make sure the path was clear from the terrace to the ice house, I remember now. It needs to be clear when Hartmann comes to collect...her." That miniscule pause again, before the last word, that same pause I had felt slip into my own speech a few time when the word about to come out felt inexplicably unnatural to the situation it was meant to be describing.

"That'll be it!" I said. "That's where he is."

"Right," Hans said vaguely. We stared at each other, him searching my face for some conversational clue, me tongue-tied, the keys now exactly as heavy as the jailor's ring I had yearned for. I hoped Hans didn't make the leap from me breaching one green door to the idea of me breaching the other.

Eventually I broke the impasse. "What did you need him for anyway?"

"Oh—nothing really. I just came across some stationary with the letterhead of a solicitor in Mannheim—Fisscher and Sons. I wondered if perhaps it might be with them the will had been left, and not Hartmann. I was wondering if Mother had ever mentioned their name to him."

"Fisscher and Sons? Would that be Anton Fisscher?" I asked, remembering the luggage tucked away below the stairs.

I might as well have slapped him. His mouth fell open and he sucked in a breath. "*No*," he said, with some emphasis I was taken aback. A moment later he too seemed to have realised how undue his own response would be and he promptly clamped his mouth shut, and arranged his face into an unconvincing expression of calm. "I shall go search out König. Thank you."

He disappeared off in the direction of the kitchen. I followed him, waiting for him to vanish out onto the terrace, dropped the keys back beside the sink, and stole away to dress for dinner.

WE ATE COMPANIONABLY enough for our evening meal; the crumb of a clue as to the location of the missing will seemed to have cheered up Hans somewhat, and for my own part my search for some answers during the day (no matter how ineffective they had been) had taken the sting out of Hans' customary evasiveness, and I was willing to let conversation drift from the topics that had preoccupied the last few days. We discussed mutual acquaintances back in Paris, this person or that person's late night high-jinks, which bars they had been thrown out of, in which dancing dens they had successfully found someone to take home, who was stealing out of who's bed in the small hours. From there to art, to Mssr Carcassonne who was no doubt still terrorising our classmates in our absence, Christmas spirit be damned. (And it *was* Christmas Day soon, we realised, counting up the days—in five days time.) The talk of drawing brought us to the portrait in the hallway, and Hans revealed to me who had painted it. A travelling artist, by the name of Remy Martinette, passing through the district, and who had insisted Hans' mother sat for him in payment for room and board. (He was handsome, Hans told me with a lascivious arched eyebrow, so of course she said yes.) It was Remy who had regaled Hans—just about to turn fifteen and starting to wistfully dream of horizons beyond the pines—with glittering tales of Paris, had laid out a vision of the city as a city perpetually soaked in sunset and wine and captured Hans' imagination, and in a rush I understood so much of Hans' life now, realised how so many of the things he chased after were in service of the gilded *belle epoque* dream that the artist had spun so spellbindingly for him.

The artist had been the same summer as the modernisation of Bethlehem, a summer of comings and going, men over-running the house. I arched my own eyebrow at that. "Just people," Hans said. "People overrunning the house. Mother hated it." He shook his head. "Not like *you* are suggesting." He trailed off, wistful. "Not that summer. Not quite.."

"It's a shame the modernisation was let go to seed," I said, though Hans was far away, lost in some memory that was furrowed his brow. "But it could be fine—the house, I mean. It's a beautiful old thing, underneath everything. Clear away those bloody vines that are getting everywhere, rip up the carpets and scrub up the floors, fresh wallpaper. It could be grand again."

Hans stared down at the picked-clean bones on his plate; I should have seen the thunder that was about to erupt, but I didn't—I didn't catch the scent of danger in time. "Is that what you'd do?"

I looked around at the shabby breakfast room. "Perhaps," I said. "But it's your house."

"It's my mother's house," he said, scraping back his chair suddenly. "Not mine. And *certainly* not yours."

Too late, I understood I had waded too far into uncertain waters. "Of course, I know—I'm sorry, I didn't mean to—"

He stood over me, burning with an incandescent fury like nothing I had ever seen from him—Hans the Inferno. "My mother's not even—

she's not—she still *out there*, for god's sake. I didn't bring you here to start planning how to tear the house apart around me."

I should have demurred. I should have remembered I was speaking to someone in the grip of grief, and who knew what else. I should have been kind. To my shame, I was not.

"Well why *did* you bring me here?" I threw down my knife in frustration. It bounced across the table, splattering the cloth. "To slope around the house all day drawing things? Because I can't see what else you want me here for! Christ, I thought I had it bad in Paris when you skulk off dawn but at least I got to *see* you there. Here apparently I'm—what? "Friend of the family"? Trust me, judging by the smirk of the face on the undertaker's lad, no-one in this town is under *any* illusion what *that* means, so this ridiculous characade is fooling nobody except *you*."

At the mention of the undertaker, fear chased anger out of Hans' expression. He stepped back. "I brought you here because—because—"

"Because what? Because I was the nearest person when the telegram arrived? Because you needed someone to traipse around the grounds after you? Because you needed someone to come rescue you when you're sleepwalking and tuck you up in bed?"

"When I'm... what?" Hans had flushed a livid red. He gripped the edge of the tables, knuckles white. "When I'm *what*?"

"Wandering around the house at all bloody hours of the night," I said.

Hans was wobbling, the fury all gone, replaced my something I couldn't read. He was turning rapidly pale now, fading in front of me from red to white. I thought for a moment he was going to fall. All at once, it sapped the righteous anger right out of me. "Hans... are you...?"

"I will be retiring now," he said, sharp as shears pruning away dead branches. "I shall see you in the morning." And he tottered out of the room, closing the door firmly behind him.

I sat back sulkily. "And not before, I imagine," I remarked, to nobody but the cutlery.

BACK IN PARIS, there are a hundred Hans' in the attic.

Well, an exaggeration perhaps—at last count, there were thirty-six, my burgeoning collection of alternative tarots, each a version of him, drawn from life. He had taken to the roles with gusto, enormously enjoying the performance; for my part, I had found my pleasure in the permission to study him at length.

I wearily ascended to bed, picturing my attic filled waist-deep with pine needles, through which I would have to wade to turn the army of faces to the wall.

I FOUND MYSELF avoiding the bed. I was wary of sleep, reasoning (unsoundly, I'll admit) that if I did not sleep, I could not then be roused from it later. Whether I meant by the shaking of the house again or by a *rap-rapraprap-rap* offered in apology I couldn't have told you with any certainty; I welcomed neither. Instead, I sloped listlessly back and forth from the dressing table to the window and back again until the bilious anger had cooled to an ashy lump in my stomach. I was sick with myself.

The crack in the window, I noticed, had spread further.

There was a light outside in the grounds. I polished the glass with my cuff and squinted. It was indistinct but as I deciphered its components it coalesced into the shape of a person, some way out, near where I was dimly aware the maze must be. The figure was on hands and knees digging in the ground. I couldn't see a face at this distance, but (fresh-scrubbed arms, dirt under fingernails) it could only be Hans.

What was it he was so desperately searching for? A 'biscuit tin containing nothing' didn't have you out at all hours, scrabbling in the mud like a madman.

It was time to leave, I decided in that very moment. Not right then in the middle of the night of course, but in the morning. I would request my case back, pack it up—with my *own* hands—and ask König to drive me to the station. ("He couldn't get through—the roads are impassable.")

I unbuttoned my collar, number fingers clumsily prying loose each button down my shirt front, and stripped slowly. Trousers, socks, undershorts pooled at my feet. It was not the tantalising burlesque that Hans enacted—I was the opposite: a defiant soliloquy, the last night before closing. Then I jerked shut the curtains. Whether Hans looked up from the ground even once, I had no idea.

IN THE MIDDLE of the night I was roused by the sensation of covers lifting, a body slipping in beside me. There had been no knock—no *rap-rapraprap-rap* and no sound of the door opening, just the feeling of warmth and movement. I rolled over, half-asleep, and was unsurprised to find Hans curled tight and trembling. He laid his hands on my chest, so cold that it propelled me up, breaking the surface of sleep and thrusting me blinking into wakefulness with adrenaline pumping. I was strung between two simultaneous but opposing desires: to eject him summarily from the bed, still angry as I was from our argument, and to wrap my arms around him and shush him until he slept.

I was unsurprised when, moments later, the house began to shake, and unsurprised that when Hans' fingers dug into my chest in panic, he left streaks of mud across the skin.

"*IdontwanttogoIdontwanttogoIdontwanttogo…*"

Thunk. The first knock, on his door. *Thunk*, the second.

And then:

Thunk. On my own.

"Don't," Hans whimpered, his eyes squeezed close. "Don't answer it. Please. Don't answer it. *Please*."

I rose from the bed. He scrabbled pathetically to hold me back but I brushed his hands away. I crossed the room in a rush, before I could let fear turn my feet to flee, and answered the knock.

———

THE CORRIDOR WAS deserted, exactly as I had known it would be and yet somehow no less shocking in its emptiness. No-one stood on the other side of the threshold, though it had been only the briefest of moments since the knock had sounded.

I looked both ways, just to be sure, as if I might catch someone hiding, as if this was all an elaborate game of knock-a-door run played by children. There was nothing—except for another knock, some way down the corridor. It was too sharp for flesh—a stick, perhaps, rapping on boards. As soon as I thought this, the picture came to me clear: a figure knocking sharply on the door with the head of a cane then leading the way down the corridor, point sharply marking out each stride.

Had the house been shaking this much the previous night? The sensation tonight was consuming, as if the whole house was a machine and I nothing more than a tiny creature running loose within it's complications. No—not even a creature. Nothing more consequential than a grain of sand, a dust mote. *This is what it would feel like to be swallowed whole* a breathless, primal part of me thought, the deep animal part of the brain that still remembered fleeing in terror from the jaws of predators.

"Don't," pleaded Hans. He had pulled the bedclothes up over his face. I could see nothing but a single eye peeking above, a terrified, babbling child. "*Please.*"

I shot him a look—defiance, yes; apology, perhaps—and slipped out into the corridor. In acknowledgement, the *thunk* came from further down the corridor. *I am being led,* I thought a absolute certainty. *I am being led, and I know to where.*

Around the corner. Top of the stairs. The cane, marking out each stair—I was certain now, though I could see nobody. Something moving invisibly moving through this shuddering, rackety hurricane of a house, me the tethered to it and powerless to stop myself following in obeisance.

Looking back, I suppose I must have been frightened, but I do not remember it. The only feeling I can recall is one of being *compelled.*

To the bottom of the stairs, and again, across the hall. Towards the door, the corridor, the kitchen, towards—

Don't!

A blast of freezing air arrested me in the middle of the floor. It rushed past me as if it was moving of its own volition, another invisible beast. There was snow now too, falling fast, hard and flurrying, though we were still indoors. I turned, bewildered, certain I had heard a voice calling out, expecting to find Hans pleading fearfully to me from the staircase or to see König standing at the open front door, but there was neither. The stairs were empty. The door was closed.

The phantom wind whipped up stronger now, snatching at my hair. Stinging snow battered my face, though I still could not see its provenance. The house shook so hard that that the portrait on the landing was swinging left to right, so forcibly I feared it would fly from the wall at any moment. A vase on the mantel tumbled over, spilling the shrivelled husks of a long-dead bunch of flowers across the boards. The window panes rattled in their frames like frightened horses trying to escape the cart. The tapestry that hung in the corner came loose at one side and began to flap like an enormous, ungainly bird.

Behind it, the door stood open—the small green door from which snow flew and where *something* stood amid this bizarre, unnatural storm, a *something* that stepped towards me, reaching out a hand.

A boy, a boy, a boy so blue.

———

HE WAS YOUNG, perhaps seventeen, pale and thin—or not precisely thin, but narrow, as if he had grown too tall too quickly, the overall impression being of someone who had been stretched. He looked like the kind of boy who huddled in indoor corners by fires, who read books by the stolen light of the landing long after his light was lamp was extinguished, who shunned the outdoors at every opportunity. And he was blue—or appeared to me to be so, like a photograph submerged below a watercolour wash, flesh and clothing swimming through a mauvish haze.

Don't, I heard, though his lips did not move. The words seemed to exist by themselves, more intention than sound.

Down the passage, the kitchen door hung open. The stone floor caught the moonlight, reflecting back glossily. The snow had floated in but had evaporated at the threshold, the stones wet where it had melted. The house had ceased its shaking the moment the boy had stepped from the door. Nothing moved. The snow had slowed to a lethargic swirl.

Here, again, I know I must have been scared but still recall nothing of that feeling. The house was still; I equated that with safety, and the blue boy did not frighten me. Quite the opposite: the sight of him filled my chest with a desperate, churning melancholia.

I tiptoed gingerly down the corridor to the kitchen, the stones chill and slushy below my bare feet. The boy glided behind me.

Was it pure fancy to sense the invisible figure that had led me here still in the kitchen, standing sentinel by the green door? (Fingers on the handle; cane tip on the floor.) Would the door open for them though it had failed to open for me? I crossed to it.

Don't.

Plaintive, like Hans.

I took a deep breath and reached for the handle, turned and pushed. The door remained as resolutely locked as it had done in the day.

Though I hadn't seen him move, the boy was suddenly in front of me. He reached for my hand; his fingers gripped mine in a way I could not entirely describe as a touch, but as something akin to submerging your hand in the oily water left behind after cleaning paintbrushes. I jerked my hand back as if I had touched a hot stove, though the sensation was the opposite: an intense cold that travelled up my arm.

He stepped back, his hand held up in apology—a considerate phantom, apparently. The door to the terrace that had hitherto stood ajar swung open on a gust of wind.

Let me show you.

THE PRACTICALITIES OF the matter perhaps don't serve the atmosphere I've conjured for you. If this were a novel, I would have followed this ghostly boy out into the snow in my bare feet. I would not have felt the cold, perhaps, or would have been unheeding to its bite in the face of the supernatural. But sometimes the prosaic must intrude: a few seconds outside onto the terrace, and I was hopping in pain and dashing back inside to thrust on boots and pull my thick coat and scarf on over my thin pyjamas. When I returned appropriately armed against the winter night, the boy was nowhere to be seen. I peered about, frantically searching for him. It was a clear night for the first time since our arrival, a constellation of bright stars and a bloated moon casting the grounds in an eerie wintry subfusc. I caught a glimpse at some distance, shifting in the shadow of the topiary garden, and hurried after it.

Through the garden—through the rootgate—through the maze (as surefooted as Hans had been)—through the final gate. Above and ahead, the bell rang out. Past the ice house, to the dell, that deep, dusky, supple pine bed where Hans' lovers had lain outstretched in furtive pleasure, where now the boy led me with his slender outstretched arm to show me them, waiting there.

Boys, all of them. None older than eighteen, the youngest perhaps fifteen, and yet so brashly, heartbreakingly young in the way they look at me—lost, searching, forlorn. Just like the boy who had led me here, there was a sense that they were not quite here, not quite a part of the world, and yet in the strange luminescence of tonight's moon, in that shivering, tenebrous moment, to me they were keenly present, and I was compelled to look.

More came. The bell rang as they passed through. They surrounded me, though I felt no sense of threat. They did nothing more than watch me with pleading, doleful eyes. They were soundless and yet as they clustered a susurration sprang up—perhaps nothing more than wind, but then again perhaps voices. If these were the soldiers with whom Hans had made battle, they were a dismal army now.

"Who are you?" I asked, turning in a circle, looking at each of them in turn. When none answered, I tried again. "What do you want?"

Toseeeeeeeeeeeeeeeeeeeeeeeeeeeeeus whispered the wind.

My hands, thrust deep in my pockets to stave off the cold, closed around my drawing pad. I pulled it out, and flipped to an empty leaf. "I can do that," I said. I crawled into the dell, bedded myself down amongst the fragrant needles, submerged myself in the scent of wild forestry and wild sex and wild secrecy, and looked up at the boys arranged on the lip of the dell, luminous against the night sky.

("Draw! Draw! Draw until they breathe!")

For the next hour I drew, sketching each boy out in pencil until I had filled every page of the book on both sides. *Draw until they breathe*, I told myself, and that was what I did. All thirteen of them.

———

"SIT DOWN," I told Hans. "We're going to talk today."

Hans looked haggard. Dressed—just about—but unwashed, and clearly the victim of an awful night's sleep, though given my own circumstances I was not particularly in the mood to sympathise. I didn't know whether he had stayed in my bed alone, or slipped off back to his own when I failed to return. For my own part, I had snatched sleep in fits and starts at the breakfast table, waking up as the sun rose over a newly gathering mist, face down on my drawing pad.

He sat wearily opposite and covered his face with his hands in defeat. "Can I at least drink coffee first?"

"Let's start with the cupboard in the hall."

"Which one?" he asked, muffled but resigned.

"Green door. Filled with empty luggage."

He peeked through his fingers, confused. "It's… where we… keep the luggage?"

I glared at him. He peeked through his fingers at me. "Hans," I said, practically growling, "if you don't give me a straight answer, I will pack up my things and I will go home."

"Honestly, barchen, I'm giving you a straight answer. It's where we keep the luggage. It's never been used for anything more as far as I know."

He looked beleaguered enough that I was inclined to believe him, and so I switched tack while I had him on the ropes. "*Right*," I said, wielding it like a cudgel, "next question. What makes the house shake at night?"

Hans' stiffened. "You felt that too?"

I had been expecting another evasion, and so his confusion threw me off guard. I reach across the table to him and endeavoured to take his hands in mine. He allowed me, though mechanically. "Hans! Of *course* I do! For three nights now! I thought that was why you came to my room?"

He flinched away from my gaze. "I thought—I thought it was just—never mind."

"*Yes* mind!"

Before he could say anything else, the door opened to admit König bearing a teapot and cups on a tray. Hans withdrew his hands from mine, and settled back, looking grateful for the intrusion. He put on a show of enthusiasm, thanking König as he set set down the tray and meticulously dispensed its contents onto the table.

"Hans," I said, ignoring the warning glance he shot me; if this was the push it took, I would do it. "Who knocks on your door in the night?"

A loud crash made us both jump. A china cup smashed across the table, fallen from König's hand. He reared up like a startled horse, whipping his head back and from Hans to I and back again, eyes wide and fearful.

"Well," I said, "clearly *somebody* knows."

From König emitted a sound then that I had never before heard and still struggle to put description to. It was something akin to a howl, though more guttural, wordless but communicating with a pure depth of fear and sadness that required no words at all to express itself vividly. His mouth was agape, and as this gut-wrenching sound ullulated out of him I saw for the first time the cause of his muteness: the red and inflamed stump was plainly visible, wriggling but incapable of shaping syllables.

Hans sprang up, arms out as if to embrace König, though once he was on his feet some vestige of propriety halted him and all he did was lay his hands on König's enormous shoulders. He was saying something I couldn't make out in German, rapid and apologetic, and eventually König relapsed into deep, juddery breaths. Hans and he shared a look—a secretive look I recognised it as, the look of two people with a private knowledge that by its definition excluded all spectators.

"Hans," I said, quietly and deliberately. I refused to sacrifice my advantage. "Who knocks in the night?"

König took breath as if to begin his howling again anew, but Hans shook his head slowly at him. He ignored me, not so much as a twitch acknowledging my presence in the room completely, focusing all his attention on König.

I had one more card to play.

"If you won't tell me," I said, "perhaps you'll tell me who *these* are?"

I unwound the catch of my sketchpad and let the papers spill out, the thirteen boys of the hollow, sketching out in ink. They fell across the table amongst the broken china, fanning out.

A slap rocked me back in the chair, so sudden that I was sat back with my face smarting before I was even aware of Han's movement. My vision blackened for a second, and then everything in the room seemed to jump and now Hans was standing over me, his face a picture of pure, unadulterated rage, gripping me by the lapels. "*Where?*" he screamed, right into my face.

I had never before found his physical presence intimidating, but this was a different person entirely; another card turned up in the deck unexpectedly. Hans the Berserker, incandescent with anger, so detached from any iteration of Hans I understood that my entire body flushed hot with panic, a perspiring craquelure of fear springing up through my pores.

"*Where* did you find them?" He shook me, clutching at me so tight that he must have been able to feel the frantic tattoo my heart beat against its protective cage throbbing between his fingers.

"I—I didn't find them *anywhere*—I—I *drew* them…"

If he heard me answer, he didn't show it. "How fucking dare you? How fucking *dare* you?" He thrust against me so hard my chair overturned and I tumbled to the ground in an ungainly heap. He towered (Hans the Fortress, implacable and impregnable below threatening clouds) and I backed away. "You *saw* me—searching out in the dirt and the cold and—and the—and you *let* me. Even though *you* had them the whole—the whole—"

His anger was burning out in front of me; the Tower crumbled, battlements to dust, ramparts to sand, tumbled down to bare foundations, Hans to his knees, sobbing. Tears flooded down his cheeks. "Where did you find them? Just tell me where you found them? Where did I bury them?"

At last a semblance of understanding pieced itself together.

"It that what was in the tin you buried, Hans? Drawings?"

"*Where?*"

"Nowhere, Hans," I said, sitting up. "Nowhere. These aren't your drawings, Hans. They're mine."

He shook his head, wiping tears clumsily from his cheeks. "I think—I think—"

I bent low to crane and look him in the eyes. "Think what, Hans?"

His shoulders slumped. "I think you should go home. This afternoon."

"You don't want me here?"

He shook his head. "It's not that—"

"There *aren't* your drawings, Hans. I don't know where *they* are. *I* drew these—they're *my* drawings." He clambered to his feet, backed away from me. I pursued him out into the hall. "Hans! I drew them from life."

He frozen on the half-landing, beneath the portrait. He looked up at his mother's face, expression inscrutable.

"I answered the knock," I continued, "and I came downstairs, and there was a boy—and he led out out to the hollow, Hans. They were all there. But they weren't—they weren't exactly *there*. They were..."

(Dear reader, I'm sure you have already arrived at the word long before I have. Reading events set out in the manner I have done so it is much easier to put together the pieces than when one is knee-deep in the story oneself. So you'll have to forgive me that as I spoke the word it assaulted me as a revelation, though to you it will be barely anything of the kind.)

"*...they were dead.*"

Hans said something I couldn't distinguish in German, directed at the painting, and then he looked back at me. "All the more reason," he said. "Home. This afternoon." And then he stalked away up the second flight without another word; the last card in the pack—Hans the Executioner, pronouncing an ending without so much as a tremor.

In the breakfast room, I found König wearily picking up after us, setting the chair back on its legs, and sweeping the broken china into a pile. "König," I announced bitterly, "I shall be requiring the car this afternoon. Perhaps you'd be so kind as to check the times of the train for me?"

In response he gaped his mouth again and once more made that awful howling noise. He gestured at the drawings, trying to communicate something I had no hope of understanding.

"I don't know what you're trying to say to me," I said, too tired even to feel guilty about it.

He grimaced and made the sound again; this time it formed a semblance of syllables, something a little like *sorrrrrrrrrrrrrrrrrrreeeeeeeee*. Then he backed away, ducking his head below the lintel, vanishing into the house to who-knew-where.

So that was that then, I thought. The house had swallowed Hans and König and I was no longer required, no longer had any purpose here. If I ever even had in the first place—my fantasy of Hans and I as partners, me the supportive lover in time of great need, was in as fine a state as the poor done-for cup. I swept the pink-and-white shards carefully off the papers and gathered them together, each ink and line boy, and slid them back into my sketchbook.

It was only *then* that I saw it.

On the first page of my sketchbook was one of the copies I had made of the portrait of Hans' mother. Not my best (there were several others after that one) but it was not the realism of the portrait that struck me then. It was a single small detail that, whilst I must have seen it, I had obviously never *seen*.

At her throat was a necklace, and on that necklace hung a key.

(I'LL ADMIT: THIS was when I should have gone home. Perhaps *you* might have, dear reader. Perhaps you would have done the sensible thing and packed up your things, let König drive you back to the station, fought your way through the snowdrifts and packed yourself onto a train bound for the city, let it race you away from Bethlehem never to return.

(But I did not.)

THE DOOR FELL open with a remarkable ease, practically springing open at the slightest pressure of my fingertip, precipitating an immediate feeling of discomfort (as if my stomach wasn't *already* in enough turmoil just from approaching the building with tentative, nervous steps!) It felt wrong for access to be this easy, as if I should somehow have been had to work harder to earn this audience, that there should have been trials or at the very least a small amount of exertion involved to be brought into the presence of...

...of *the body*. I determined to call it that. The body—clinical. We studied 'the body' in our classes all the time, were taught to see the blood and bones and flesh and their shapes. Mechanisms, nothing more. Nothing to fear.

There was only one window in the ice house, a narrow rectangular one high up, above the level of the head, through which only the weakest shaft of light managed to pierce, though it was helped none by the burgeoning mist and a glowering of grey cloud that had filled the sky since early morning, portending fiercer weather to come. Even at this relatively early hour, visibility was thin outside. Inside it was practically nonexistent, and so there were shadows; that was my predominant impression of the ice house as I first dared to step across it's threshold, a congregation of shadows of subtly different hues.

What had I imagined? I don't know now, but it was not what I found. The room was bare, nothing more than four plain walls, a flat, clean floor, and a bench that ran around three sides of the four. Nothing ornate. No dais, no altar—was *that* what I had imagined? Perhaps it was-the wild queen laid out in state? But instead there was nothing but a hushed, mortuary sparseness—

—AND THE DARK shape of the body, laid out across the far wall, below a white sheet. It was the only thing clearly visible in the ice house, catching the dim light that seeped in. The sheet glinted. Ice crystals, I saw as I stepped closer; they coated it in a glimmering sheen that stiffened the fabric to the touch. I cautiously reached out to touch one corner and my brain experienced a flustered flip in discovered that the fabric felt beneath my fingers entirely unlike it appeared; it should have been pliable and soft, but was instead a rigid thing, frozen into shape by the veneer of ice that had formed over it, until the force of my touch broke the tension and rivulets of tiny cracks exploded from every crease and fold of it and it became newly pliable in my grasp.

Knowing if I tried to do it little by little my courage would fail me, I drew it back in one bold tug.

Her eyes were wide open and when the sheet whisked away they immediately met mine. It felt as if I had been thumped in the chest; I felt it like a physical thing, a brutal shock that slammed into me, and I leapt back involuntarily, colliding with the bench. She did not look like the painting— artistic license, perhaps, but the deviation was shocking. The painting gave her a wild beauty, haughty but with a certain natural warmth. Here there was nothing of the kind. She was made entirely of angles—taut, grey-white skin over sharp, angry points. In the painting she was made of willow trees, in person she was made of rocks.

But: the key still hung around her neck. I was *right*.

Never again has the distance of a few inches felt so far. That was all it was: a few inches for my arm to travel through the air, for my hand to hover above her chest, for my fingers to gingerly pick up the key and pluck it from it's chain. Yet those blue eyes watched me every step of the way and I froze involuntarily a hair's breadth away from the key. I was practically touching her—and suddenly *touch* seemed the most foul thing I could imagine. The very thought of my fingertips brushing against her cadaverous skin made the gorge rise in my through.

(Just a body. Pumps and chambers. Sinews and pulleys. Just a body.)

Would she be warm? Of course not, I knew, but like the rigid sheet the brain struggles to hold those two ideas together at once. A body should be warm, and her skin should be soft. *When I touch her, she will snap her head around, and she will reach out and wrap her fingers around my wrist, and-*

No.

No.

She will be cold.

She will be as cold as the snow that has buried her home, as the ice amongst which she is now kept, and when I touch her she will crack apart like that flower in my childhood garden, like a frozen lake collapsing in on itself, like the sheet across which the cracks had spread so easily, her body will crumble in front of me and—

(Stop!)

—I snatched the key.

There was resistance, and my panicked brain supplied hands scrabbling for mine to snatch back their property--but it was nothing more than the chain catching, then stretching, then breaking. I stumbled back, chest heaving.

All was still. The grey light didn't so much as waver. The body did not move an inch.

Just a body, I thought again. She could not hurt me. Her eyes could not see, her feet could not walk, her hands could not grasp. (Especially her hands, for they were wrapped around something. I peered closer, seeing only now what it was: a slender black cane, tipped at either end with silver.)

Thunk.

I heard the sound—heard it as the commanding rap of something sharp and hard against the door, and not simply as the treacherous sound of my own fearful heart striking the ribcage, and fled like a child.

<hr />

THERE WAS NO Hans at dinner. Perhaps he assumed I had done as he commanded and left, and therefore there was no point to attending; or perhaps he assumed I had *not* done as he had commanded, and therefore his absence was pointed. There was also no König—a fact that, on a basic level, was more problematic, as my heart-pounding venture to the ice house had left me ravenously hungry and there was no meal prepared in the breakfast room. I mooched around the kitchen rooting through cupboards and managed to scare up a makeshift dinner of cold meat and cheeses. The green door waited patiently in the corner, unremarkable in the last of the day's light. I considered unlocking it and exploring then, but I had other plans.

<hr />

THERE WAS NO Hans in the night either. I sat awake at the dressing table, alert and vigilant, until I felt the telltale trembling begin below the boards. I did not expect it, but found myself nonetheless hoping for a *rap-rapraprap-rap*, hoping that despite the day's anger he might still come running to me for comfort in the night and all our odds might be subsumed within the simplicity of a comforting embrace under the cover of darkness. But there was no knock until *the* knock.

Thunk—on Hans' door.

I waited, knowing he would ignore it. I would wait until *I* was called for. But no further knock was forthcoming, neither on his door nor mine, until I heard it sound further away down the corridor and knew all at once what I would see when I bolted to the door. Hans' door hung open, and I could see the shape of him receding away from me, the back of his shoulders visible hanging defeated and obedient. I followed him. He walked the same way as he had that first night, with the awkward gait of a sleepwalker as if he was moving not entirely of his own volition, but he was faster this time, as if his ability to resist the knocks that led him had diminished.

Thunk on the corner, *thunk* at the top of the stairs, and then descending *thunk thunk thunk* downwards. I could picture it so clearly now, the silver tip on each stair. His mother leading the way, Hans submissively in tow. Across the hall we went, down the kitchen corridor. I caught up with him there, Hans standing as he had done that first night, facing the corner like a naughty schoolboy. His hand rested on the doorknob; around him, the whole room shook, every item convulsing, a strident, dissonant orchestra of horrors striking up an accompaniment to our melodrama.

"Hans!" I called through the noise.

The line of his body changed; he had heard me, but he did not otherwise respond. I crossed to him, took his elbow, and he startled out of his vacant compliance, making a wordless sound of incomprehension.

I held up my hand and let the key fall and dangle on its broken, gossamer-light chain. "I know how to open it," I said.

He grabbed my wrist, fingernails cutting the skin. "No!"

I pulled free and slipped the key into the lock. It turned without so much as a whisper. The door fell open.

Panicked hands spun me about, and first I saw Hans' face close to mine, red and sweating, spittle cannoning from his mouth as he shouted something that was snatched away by the crescendo of noise that surged around us, and then another—a sharp, white face that should not have been there, all angles and bright, bright blue eyes. Fingers darted towards my face, striking my forehead, and then there was nothing but a sticky, viscid blackness opening beneath my feet to swallow me whole.

MASTER FISCHER—PLEASE forgive the intrusion of this letter. I know that you do not know me, but you were an acquaintance of my son. He has talked fondly of you, and in particular of your desire to become a trainer of horses. This is the reason I am contacting you. This summer at Bethlehem, our home near Zuabarnasshalt, we so happen to be graced with the presence of Luis Becker, an equine behavioural specialist, for the season, and so of course your name occurred to me, and I thought to perhaps extend you an invitation to stay with us for a short period? Herr Becker would be delighted to discuss your ambitions with you and perhaps set you upon the right path. We will of course be happy to pay for your travel. Yours in anticipation, Frau M. Krause, Bethlehem.

Master Stein—please forgive the intrusion of this letter. I know that you do not know me, but you were an acquaintance of my son. He has talked fondly of you, and in particular of your desire to master the art of calligraphy. This is the reason I am contacting you. This summer at Bethlehem, our home near Zuabarnasshalt, we so happen to be graced with the presence of Luis Becker, a specialist in illuminated manuscripts, for the season, and so of course your name occurred to me, and I thought to perhaps extend you an invitation to stay with us for a short period? Herr Becker would be delighted to discuss your ambitions with you and perhaps set you upon the right path. We will of course be happy to pay for your travel. Yours in anticipation, Frau M. Krause, Bethlehem.

Master Franke—please forgive the intrusion of this letter. I know that you do not know me, but you were an acquaintance of my son. He has talked fondly of you, and in particular of your desire to become a musician with the Reichsorchester. This is the reason I am contacting you. This summer at Bethlehem, our home near Zuabarnasshalt, we so happen to be graced with the presence of Luis Becker, the celebrated flautist, for the season, and so of course your name occurred to me, and I thought to perhaps extend you an invitation to stay with us for a short period? Herr Becker would be delighted to discuss your ambitions with you and perhaps set you upon the right path. We will of course be happy to pay for your travel. Yours in anticipation, Frau M. Krause, Bethlehem.

Master Fischer—please forgive the intrusion of this letter. I know that you do not know me, but you were an acquaintance of my son...

THERE WAS STILL black—a hot, glutinous murk like drowning in molasses, that stucky my eyelids together—but through it a sound, at first distant and then breathlessly near. It was the sound of a voice, ragged and choking, dispassionately repeating words like a rosary, Each repetition was the same but for a few small changes. Names. Occupations.

With some exertion, I opened my eyes. It felt like the morning after a hangover, bullying light and sound crowding in to overwhelm me. I was in the cellar, I could tell—or assumed, at least; I had a feeling of subterranea, of being underground, though with my vision swimming it was more sensed than seen. I was standing, but though nothing physically held me, I could not move of my own volition.

"We will of course be happy to pay for your travel. Yours in anticipation, Frau M Krause." A sob. "Bethlehem."

My vision swayed. A butterfly floated through the groggy shadows—no, not a butterfly. Paper. A letter. It floated to the ground.

Next.

Breath tickled my ear; someone (thing! corrected the panicked, primordial part of my brain that was clamouring at me to run—some*thing*) was right behind me.

Next! Sharp, spat, brooking no argument.

The recitation began again. "Dear Master Vogel..." It was Hans' voice, strangled almost out of recognition. "This summer at Bethlehem, our hosue near Zuabarnasshalt, we so happen to be graced..." My faculties were slowly regaining a footing. The cellar was not the overgrown hole in the ground I had imagined—quite the opposite. It was a machine. The whole room was filled with tanks and pistons, wheels and tracks, cantilevers and gauges whose purpose I couldn't parse. They were turning and spinning and grumbling and thrusting and *shaking*—enough, I understood, to shake the entire house that stood above it, quaking up from the rickety roots of the house, communicating their tremors and gyrations into every brick, board and nail of Bethlehem. The whole assemblage stank of cordite and copper— the sharp scent of photographer's flashbulbs, but magnified a hundred-fold. An enormous wheel turned ponderously in the centre of this chaotic jumble and with every cycle a voltaic throb expanded outwards, setting the hairs on my neck standing on edge (from where, alert and wavering, they quivered to the breaths that rasped across my skin from the unseen figure to my rear).

"Yours in anticipation..."

In the centre of all of this was a chair—nondescript, the kind you might find in an office or a cheap cafe, more horrifying in its banality than any of the apparata surrounding it. Held tight by straps was Hans. Wires snaked across the floor and disappeared somewhere behind it. Obscenely, the first though that that dawned on me was the perfect artistic composition of it, Hans framed so perfectly by the turning wheel, as if it was an enormous halo—but what card would this be? Hans the Coward? Hans the Victim? Hans the Sacrifice?

Next. An exhalation stirred the nape of my neck; I smelled mulch and dirt.

In Hans' lap lay a filthy, mud-caked biscuit tin, dented and bent. From its open lid spilled a pile of papers—letters.

Next!

The vines that choked the house were here too, winding amongst the machinery as if they themselves were the wires that connected circuit to circuit. *I'm in the ground now*, I thought, *down here amongst the roots themselves. Down below the dirt and the snow, down amongst the real bones of Bethlehem.* And then a second thought dawning right after: *down in the ground, where you were going to bury her.*

Hans bent his hands awkwardly to pluck the next letter from the pile. He began to read it, the same words with a new new name. And so the next, and the next, and the next after that, each time the voice commanding him until only one sheet of paper remained and a sheaf of letters lay at Hans' bound feet.

Stop. Obediently, he clumsily pushed the lid back onto the tin.

A shadow darted across my vision, from one shadow to another. I caught only a glimpse of its form—oblique, flitting shape something like a woman but also like something springy and elongated whipping across the room. The tin flew from Hans' fingers, clattering across the ground. I felt it rebound from my feet, though I was still powerless to move against it.

I warned you. I told you what happens to men like you. You know the Good Book as I do. Tell me, what happens to men like you?

Hans head hung pliant and flimsy against his chest. His eyes were squeezed shut, though whether tearful or fearful I couldn't tell.

Tell me!

Hans mumbled.

Louder!

He raised his chin infinitesimally. "Death."

And?

"Death and… torment."

I tried my best to move, to in some way draw his attention, to signal that he was not alone, to break whatever bond it was held me and rush to free him, but to no avail.

But not for you.

Hans shook his head. "Not for me." The words sounded practised, catechistic, as if he had spoken them a hundred times before.

Why not for you?

I read the response on Hans' lips rather than heard them—they came out as little more than an exhausted whisper utterly lost amongst tumult of the machines.

"Because my mother loves me."

Because your mother loves you. And you shall be grateful that despite being tested by your filthy habits, you have a mother who understands how to help you. You do want to be helped, don't you?

Neither Hans nor I moved; perhaps we were both in our own ways trapped and unable to move as we wanted.

Don't you?

His lips formed a 'Yes', and then that flicker of shadow again, that sensation of movement in my peripheral. *Then*, the voice scraped, *we shall begin.*

Hans pulled forward as far as his restraints allowed him, pushing his head down towards his knees. *Look!* the voice screamed. *Look!* and resignedly Hans lifted his head and looked straight into my eyes.

Are you aroused? The voice sounded disgusted; and with each of the questions it spat out a fresh blast of breath carried the putrid fetor of the rot. *Are you excited? Are you... upright?*

Reluctantly, Hans nodded.

Your mother loves you. There was a metallic clunk, a sizzle, and Hans screamed. Every hair on my body sprang to attention with an electric crackle, and opposite me Hans spasmed violently in the chair. The flashbulb smell, the wires, the chair—understanding shot through me, a kinder dose than what shot through Hans.

After a painfully long moment, it ceased, and Hans collapsed shaking back into his chair.

The shadow moved at my back. *You are in the window*, it said, and I knew somehow that it was no longer addressing Hans—these words were for me. My arm moved by itself, free of any bodily autonomy I might have applied to it. My fingers fumbled the button of my collar, clumsily loosening it, then descended, each button springing open. With the last button my nightshirt hung open, and I felt something plucking at my neck; the shirt slid down my shoulders and pooled at my feet.

Are you aroused?

Weakly, he nodded, and again: the clunk, the sizzle, the screaming. A wet patch bloomed between Hans' legs; so much electricity was shooting through him he had lost control of his body.

Your mother loves you.

"Please..." It was nothing more than a whimper from Hans. "Please, no more."

You are still in the window. Something scuttled down my spine. My own treasonous fingers pulled at the drawstring of my trousers.

When they too had sunk to the ground, I stood there exposed as Hans was subjected for a third time to the machine. (*Your mother loves you.*) He didn't scream out loud this time, just gritted his teeth and roared into the back of his own throat. When this bout was done he hung like a rag doll, held up only by the straps at his wrist.

Lips against my ear: *Turn around.*

I closed my eyes as I turned. I still, if nothing else, could control my eyes, and I had no desire to see what stood behind me. I already knew what face I would see.

Son, do you renounce? The smell—that graveyard smell, like vegetables left to rot forgotten in a cupboard—blasted into my face,

I heard nothing from Hans, though god only knew if by this point he was even capable of speaking.

Son, do you renounce?

No reply. Clunk. Sizzle. Scream.

Son, do you renounce?

No reply. Clunk. Sizzle. Scream.

Son. Do you renounce?

Finally, wheezing, broken, but clear: "No."

The shadow whipped away, and I dared to open my eyes.

No? It a furious, angry shriek that ripped through my eardrums, set every machine in the room singing with the word, bounced back from all sides: *no, no, no, no, no, no.*

"I... cannot."

My eyes adjusted to the darkness. There were stairs in front of me, stairs leading up to a green door.

You... cannot?

"No."

A sibilant, animalistic hiss: *Whyyyyyyyyyyyyyyyyyyyyyyyyyyy?*

"Because," said Hans (and then a long, rattling breath, this single moment that in my memory is a monstrous prolonging that stretches from here to our sunlit attic in Paris), "I love him."

The sounds of cycling and whirring faltered and slowed; the machines abated. The shadows tensed like living things and then released me; I had control of my arms and legs again, and unprepared I buckled. I landed painfully with the biscuit tin jabbing into my stomach, glimpsing a blurred flash of Hans slumped in the chair, a willowy figure standing over him. A coppery woosh of machinery zipped across my vision, and then nothing but the dark ceiling from which spiralled a single, glinting snowflake.

(Here you will have to forgive me if my narrative is less than clear; I am still not quite certain of how events unfolded myself, though I have done my best to piece them together since. Perhaps you will make more sense of it than I.)

The green door fell in, revealing behind it an enormous König-shaped bulk—and behind König: Hans' army.

They blew into the room on a gust of lancinating wind, cascading down the steps into the cellar. They poured around me, over me, descending on the chair. The shadow—Hans *mother*—was swept up amongst them, a single, bending bough powerless amongst their mighty storm, impotent to prevent the hands that lifted her and bore her up on their shoulders. The whole house shook anew, quaking with a ferocity I had not experienced before; the machines rocked and groaned; dials leaped, and gas jettisoned from burst gaskets, clouding the room with burning, shrieking steam. The ceiling flexed as if the entire foundations were agitated; vines tightened and stretched as everything shifted, and with them the pipes and components that held together the machine sprang loose of their moorings and collapsed in on themselves.

Through this barrelled König; he ripped open the bindings that tethered Hans and lifted him as easily as if he was a baby, and a moment later myself too, hauled up naked and flung over his shoulder. Up the stairs the phantoms surged, their prize born aloft, us in pursuit, bursting up into the kitchen like a flood bursting its banks.

The glass doors flew open, and off went Hans' army into the pitch-black night beyond.

A thick fissure shot across the kitchen slabs, darting from one to the next like an infection. Without a second's pause, König hauled us onwards, lurching up the corridor and into the hall. Here was even worse; the floorboards capered beneath our feet and I could hear the ping of nails as they ripped free. The floor dipped like a sea; the stairs sagged then gave way in one tumultuous rush. The first flight to the half-landing caved in as if was made of nothing more substantial than paper and vanished down into the earth.

The portrait of Hans' mother shook free of its hangings and plummeted. It landed on its bottom edge, and then titled slowly forward and plunged into the hole, and fair out in the grounds the sound of a bell cut through the rest of the noise. It chimed over and over, faster and faster as if a stamped was passing it, ringing and ring until with an anguished, arcing chime it soared free from its moorings and fell silent forever.

WE BURIED THE body the next morning without ceremony. Hartmann and Son were summoned and explained to in no uncertain terms precisely what they should do. Hans picked one of the gardens—a plain one, he said, with no buildings or adornments. Nothing more than a patch, really—that was the way he described it. The undertakers sank a hole six feet deep and the body, re-wrapped in nothing more than its icy sheet, was lowered into it. There was no coffin, no priest, and no words spoken. Hans waited just long enough to see the body into the ground, and then turned and walked away, leaving Hartmann Junior to shovel dirt back into the hole he left behind.

The house was split like an earthquake; much of it had survived, but a crater ran through the centre of the downstairs into which the remains of the stairs and landings wilted. We had retrieved our things from the upstairs rooms and, fearing a further cave in, had taken up residence in the drawing room and breakfast room.

The boys were waiting for us when we returned to the house. They sat around the table and watched us. They seemed to no longer be troubled by the daylight. *Draw until they breathe*, I thought, and wondered if perhaps this was my doing. But I suspected it was not.

WE BURIED THE boys with all the honour we could muster in the circumstances. When *that* night was over and everything was at last calm, I discovered that in our flight from the cellar I had been clutching the biscuit tin, and it seemed as fitting a coffin as anything. We gathered the drawings I had made, and passed solemnly through the grounds, through the maze, up past the now-empty ice house, to the hollow. The bell did not sound when we passed—after that night it was broken beyond repair.

Kneeling opposite each other amongst the pine-needles, Hans dug a hole in the centre. He sat cross-legged, holding the biscuit tin in his hands, staring at the lid.

I rested a hand on his shoulder. "Hans? Are you okay?"

He nodded pensively. "It's one thing to hate *her* for what she did to them," he said slowly. "But the thing I'll never forgive myself for..." He swallowed, and looked up at the dense canopy of trees encircling us. "After she... caught me, and had the doctor come—yes, that's what happened. I suppose you don't know the story. She found me with...a man. Luis, he was called. He lived in the town. And she had the men come and install the machine in the cellar, so she could—so that..." He tailed off. He seemed to be holding back tears, fixing his eyes up at the boughs to ward them off. "I had to do what she wanted. I had to 'renounce' it—that's what it was called. Renounce *them*." He traced his fingertips over the lid. "But she didn't even know there was a *them*. She knew about Luis, obviously, but none of the others before him. I knew I had to put them away, but I wanted them to... I don't know."

I squeezed his shoulders reassuringly.

"I wanted them to live on," he said eventually. "They couldn't be entirely gone. So I drew them as I remembered them, and I buried them where no one would find them, and that was enough." His hands tightened around the tin. "But instead *she* found them."

"She believed it was out of love," I said, though it was such a weak platitude that I couldn't evince even the slightest shred of belief into it.

"No she didn't," Hans said. "Not really. And do you know how I know that?"

I shook my head.

"Because she didn't try to save *them*—when she invited them here. When she wrote all those letters full of her horrid promises and lured them here. As monstrous as it is, if she'd strapped them to the chair and filled them full of electricity, I'd understand. But she didn't—she just had them murdered. As punishment."

Punishment for who? I wondered. Punishment for them, or for him?

"And then," he said bitterly, "she left the box for me to find, with all the letters. So I would know what she had done."

He sniffed and wiped away his tears. I didn't know what to say that could possibly make even a stone's ripple on the deep lake of sorrow that was dammed up inside of him right in that moment. Instead, I pressed the sheaf of drawings into his hand.

He lifted the first, and inspected it. "Jonas," he said. "He was the son of my French tutor." He folded it carefully into four, and lifted the lid off the tin.

Inside there remained a sheet of paper. He plucked it out, and unfolded it. One side of it was covered in close, neat handwriting. He scanned it, and as he did so he started to laugh.

"Well," he said, "at least another mystery is solved."

"What is it?"

"The will. And if further proof was needed that nothing was done out of love, this would be it." He smiled to himself and passed it across to me. "She didn't leave me the house." He pointed to a line in the second paragraph. "'The immediate sale of all property and assets, to be donated in full to the Nationalsozialistische Deutsche Arbeiterpartei for the benefit of the cause.'"

"Oh, Hans... I'm so sorry."

But he was beaming at me. "Don't be," he said. "I feel..."

He took a deep breath.

"I feel free."

One by one we worked through the drawings of the boys. Hans named them—names I recognised from the trunks in the locked hall room—and carefully folded each picture away into the tin. Then he set the lid firmly atop, lowered it into the hole he had made, and gently filled in the mud and needles atop it.

"May they finally rest their bones," I said, and Hans nodded solemnly.

But there was no such rest for them. When we returned to the house, we found them still waiting for us, ringed around the table, silent and utterly unmoving.

THAT AFTERNOON WE packed our things in our trunks, and elected to set out for a return journey away from Bethlehem. We looked for König in vain— we had seen hide nor hair of him since he had carried us up from the cellar.

"Do you blame him?" I said, when Hans began to fret. "I'm surprised he wasn't carried away by the boys along with your mother. Surely he *knew* about them too?"

"Perhaps," Hans said.

"And what about what she did to you? How could he stand by and say nothing?"

"He didn't," Hans said. "He spoke up for me. And then he never spoke again."

It took me a moment to understand. "You mean she—"

"Yes."

"My god."

"Yes."

"But he stayed?"

Hans shrugged. "He's the fifth generation of his family to serve at Bethlehem. Where else would he go?"

We searched the house—those parts that were still navigable—but turned up no sign of him, apart from his ring of keys hanging on a nail in the hallway. I couldn't say I blamed him—wherever we turned we'd find one of the boys, watching us with lachrymose, imploring eyes. They never said anything, but even a glimpse of one of them engendered a flood of guilt in me that we were preparing to leave them behind to haunt the ruins of Bethlehem alone. But what else could we do?

Finally admitting defeat, Hans took the key from the ring and led us out to the car. It took three attempts to get the exhausted old thing started. I hadn't known Hans could drive, and judging by his white-knuckled grip on the wheel I wasn't convinced he could, but at least we were moving. The rest of the trip did nothing to persuade me of his abilities; moments after our departure, a snowcloud broke and we were immediately lost in an impenetrable blizzard. We inched cautiously through the snow, the wheels spinning and slithering; Bethlehem had vanished in the rearview within a few feet's journey so thick was the snow, and it took us twenty minutes before we reached the main gate, a journey that should have taken only a few minutes. We fared no better on the road beyond, and within the hour we were hopelessly stuck at the bottom of a shallow incline that nonetheless was completely impassable in these abject conditions. No amount of engine revving nor us heaving against the back of the car with our boots skidding in the snow could coax the car forward, and eventually we had no choice but to give up and, wrapping ourselves tightly in our coats, trudge back along the deep tire tracks, underneath the iron roots with their thick metal letters, and up the long drive to the house and—as Christmas Eve darkened, seek shelter in Bethlehem once more.

The boys waited for us behind the front door, silently welcoming.

<hr />

WHICH WAS HOW we came to pass a Christmas with ghosts.

The storm hung overhead for five more days. Each morning Hans and I would wake on the mattress we had dragged downstairs, disentangle from each other, and dress. We'd make a breakfast from the remains of the larder that we had salvaged, and hole up in the drawing room. Sometimes we drew. Sometimes we drank. Sometimes I asked him to tell me about one of the boys—how he met them, what they had done together, how it had ended.

Sometimes the boys sat with us. They tended to herd together, but not always—we found they flocked to the warmth. In the mornings we might be eating breakfast with one of them in attendance, sitting beside Hans or I, watching us. By evening, when skies darkened and we stoked the fire, they usually gathered.

As the days wore on, we started to run out of things to talk about, and began to tell the boys tales of Paris. Hans lay on his back, describing the city to them—his favourite dive bars, the clubs he frequented with his friends, the petty rivalries of the showgirls he circulated amongst. He described our attics, and our street. He told them how free Paris was, how he and I could go there and know nobody would try and do to us what his mother did. How no one would hurt us in Paris like that ever again.

I listened to him tell these stories and wondered: was this how he really saw Paris? The picture he painted of freedom did not chime with the Hans who had crept away in the morning light every time he had slept in my bed.

<hr />

But now that I knew what had befallen him in the year before he had fled to Paris, I saw it all afresh. I saw Hans in his attic at night, knowing that there would be no knock of a cane on his door in the night and yet still unable to sleep, and I saw him rise from his bed and dance across the street, to take refuge with me, to rest his bones where he was safe.

I resolved: there was to be no more knocking on doors once we returned to Paris.

The talk of Paris reminded me of my portfolio of paintings, the multitude of Hans that hung in my attic. The idea of him as a jumble of different personalities had been juvenile, I realised, but now a new idea struck me. I dug up out a fresh pad and began to draw the boys all over again, and in the course of that night I laid out another new tarot, but this time instead of only Hans' face, I painted in each of the boys. Elias the Bard; Moritz the Blacksmith; Felix the Doctor; Benjamin the Scribe; until I had a full deck.

ONLY ON THE fifth night did I realise, and felt utterly foolish for not having done so before.

The trunks below the stairs had not been empty. They had all held something inside them, something about—I realised with horror—the weight and consistency of bones.

We filled the hollow, and covered it back over with our bare hands, and when we returned to the house there was nobody sat at the table any longer.

On the eighth day, finally the weather cleared, and clear skies dawned above Bethlehem, Hans and I decided that at last we dared to venture out. "Do you want to say your goodbyes to the house?" I asked Hans, but he shook his head. He'd already done that a week ago, and had no plans to do so again.

Free of snowstorms, the car was a depressingly short distance away from the house, and we managed with some effort to heave it out of its rut and persuade the engine begrudgingly to start. We trundled into town and left it parked on the curb by the train station.

I waited outside Hartmann and Sons while Hans delivered the will inside and watched the small village come sleepily to life. I saw someone braving the sleety square to knock on the surgery door, and remembering Hans' description of the town wondered idly whether the casualty was human or animal; moments later I spied a nervous-looking gentleman entering the greengrocers, and smirked to myself. A few moments later, Hans returned, looking cheerful. "And that," he said, "is that."

The train chugged into the station half an hour later, and I had the sensation drowning sailors must experience at first sighting sails on the horizon. The guard dragged our trunks aboard and we navigated ourselves to an empty compartment, settling in as the engine roared and Zuabarnasshalt accelerated away from the window. We vanished into pines, leaving everything behind us and far, far out of sight.

"*A boy, a boy, a boy so blue,*" I sang absently to myself, staring out of the window. The train shot into a tunnel, and with everything dark for a moment, I saw our faces reflected back, pale and alive, and behind us thirteen others, and then we were back in the light.

Hans hand crept into mine. "*A boy so blue with love for you,*" he sang back softly to me, and this time I let him.

STORY NOTES

THE LIBRARY OF LOST THINGS was written as a birthday present for my friend and publisher Steve Berman. His troubles with finishing the books and stories he was working on were the seed from which the idea of the Library came—and the reason S. Berman makes a cameo appearance. So truly in character that I could not provide a better example were I to care to try, he returned his birthday present to me the next day with editorial notes. He contributed some of the best lines in the story, but he was also strongly against the talking rats; I stood firm, and to this day we keep tally of the goodreads reviews that quote his lines, and the reviews that name the rats as their favourite part of the story.

This story was acquired for Tor.com by Ann Vandermeer, a fact which still astonishes me to this day, even though I have the acceptance email framed on my wall.

IN SEARCH OF STARS began as a follow-up to the story that follows it in the collection, a story about Dorian Gray set in the 1970s; after that was published I set sights on writing a collection of stories that took fantastic characters from Victorian literature and transposed them throughout the 20th century. *In Search of Stars* takes as it's so-barely-a-reference-point-I-feel-bad-even-calling-it-that a character named Alberto C from a *From the Earth to the Stars*, who invents a paint that nullifies gravity, a premise so suspiciously similar to Henry Cavor and the gravity-resistant Cavorite that I couldn't resist them making a brief appearance too. (I am also wildly indebted to *The Encylopedia of Fantastic Victoriana* by Jess Nevins while I researched the stories I planned for this collection. The rest never reached fruition, though somewhere there exists fragments of stories in which Peter Pan's shadow menaces the lost boys of the World War 1 trenches, the Bride of Frankenstein becomes a model for Andy Warhol, and Carmilla snacks on suffragettes. Maybe one day.)

GOLDEN HAIR, RED LIPS might be the fastest story I've ever written, one of those hallelujah moments in which a number of ideas collide fortuitously and the story flows. I am of an age and background in which the stories of gay culture that preceded me was not readily available—not passed down, not mythologised, not present, and in my mid-20s I sat down to consciously redressed the balance. I consumed every story I could—books, film, and documentary. 'Golden Hair, Red Lips' melds allusions to the tragic story of the Upstairs Lounge into the San Francisco that I learned about through the documentaries *We Were Here* and *How To Survive A Plague*. One particular thing in the latter of these stuck with me above everything else: a man who talked about how it was not uncommon to see someone move on with someone new swiftly after they had lost a partner, that it was not disrespect but a need to combat the fragility and brevity of life. This made it into the story in the form of its repetitions as Dorian Gray moves from one lover to the next—and as for Dorian himself, what better figure from queer literary canon could there be to juxtapose with the ravages of that era that one whose potency relies on his immortality and the unspoilability of his youth?

I submitted the story to Nightmare Magazine's *Queers Destroy Horror*, and was shocked to receive my first professional sale with it (and more than a little surprised to discover I wrote horror.) This story proved to me I could write the way I wanted to; a year later, 'The Library of Lost Things' proved to myself I could do it more than once.

CROAK TOAD started with a title, and it was too good a title to waste. It's also the most fun I've ever had—once I figured out how to write it. It had six false starts before I struck a voice and a format—each section is strictly 200 words long, and from restraint grows invention. *The Wind in the Willows* is also my mother's favourite book; not only has she not read this story, she won't even allow me to describe it's plot in case I ruin the book for her.

NOTHING TO WORRY ABOUT is the oldest story in the book, written and published more than ten years ago, and the only story I rewrote for the collection. Partly this was because it's tricky for any writer to look at something they wrote ten years ago and not want to pop the hood and tinker with the engine, but largely it was because when I wrote it, it's premise seemed considerably more dystopian than it does now. Coming in today's climate of heartbeat bills and rape-paternity cases, the original version of this accidentally read like a pro-life tract, and so it underwent revisions (and triage at the capable hands of the gay men's writing group to whom I belong.)

DIRECTOR'S CUT set out to take a trope and smash it up—in this case the longstanding rule that in early cinema for a homosexual to appear they must in some way be punished, something that lives on into the unspoken 'kill your gays' trope that sees gay characters so frequently killed off—or at bare minimum not permitted to continue to a happy ending--in mainstream media. For researching this story I have to point to *The Celluloid Closet* as an fascinating and useful resource.

THE CONCUBINE'S HEART was another case of restriction breeding invention, another story in which I couldn't figure out my angle until I started working within a formal structure. In this case I was working with a tight brief too: I was writing for a call that specified steampunk with an international focus, with disabled and/or queer characters. Of all the stories I have written, 'The Concubine's Heart' felt the most like I'd pushed out to sea and had no idea which way up to hold the paddle while I was writing it, and a sense of complete surprise that the boat hadn't sprung a leak by the time I got it to shore.

ANTONIA & CLEOPATRA is perhaps a departure from the rest of the stories in the collection: it's an unapologetically absurd, pulp story. The character of Cleopatra—the S&M brothel madam with a glass-bottomed brothel—is an alter-ego of a close friend (fear not—they named the character *and* specified the mode of transport themselves); Antonia is based on said friend's actual mother, a specialist in ancient languages who frequently was flown out to historical sites to translate in what I choose to believe was a string of female-Indiana-Jones-type adventures. This is by far the lightest story I've written, and was therefore absolutely torture to write (far more respect is deserved for those writers who can write a light soufflé of a story without any perceivable effort than they get; try it. It's fucking hard.)

BY CHANCE, IN THE DARK was written in a haunted manor house buried in mist deep in wild northern countryside, during a writer's retreat. We arrived in the dark, following arcane printed instructions (turn left at the Roman burial tump!) up a long, dark driveway only to discover the house locked, and the key not where it should be. Our mobile phone signal was long gone. "We should split up," someone suggested. "And someone should go knock at that creepy cottage up the road, and see if they have a key."

THE LAST DRAG SHOW ON EARTH is my love-letter (of a kind) to Manchester's Canal Street. A set of streets near the city centre on which all the gay bars are situated, it's been there for over 50 years. You're most likely to know it from Russell T. Davies' shows *Queer as Folk* and *Cucumber*. In an interview once, Davies said that the longer you were on Canal Street the stranger it became, how you'd see the same faces again and again, like ghosts, only getting older. That's what this story is about—the ghosts of Canal Street, rising up out of the water to reclaim the street. Tallulah Trout is a character who has herself ghosted in and out of a couple of my other stories, even though a drag queen friend, the redoubtable Donna Trump, declared that the name 'Tallulah Trout' was a really shit name for a drag queen.

NO SLEEP IN BETHLEHEM was meant to be three-thousand words long and finished in a week. It was, quite emphatically, neither.

ACKNOWLEDGEMENTS

First and foremost thanks has to go to the editors who published these tales in the first place: Wendy N. Wagner, who bought 'Golden Hair, Red Lips' for *Nightmare*'s *Queers Destroy Horror* and earned me my first professional sale; Ann VanderMeer who bought 'The Library of Lost Things' as my second, and helped cross several goals off my bucket list in one go; Keffy R.M. Kehrli; Benjanun Sriduangkaew; Sarah Hans; Graeme Shimmin, Craig Pay and Eric Steele; and John Joseph Adams.

Thanks to those who have read, tweaked, advised and revised, critiqued and immeasurably assisted in making my stories what they are, and those who have read and broadcast them: Steve Berman first and foremost, for a skillful red pen, and for not minding too much when I ignore his edits; Paul Magrs and everyone else at Fambles; Mark Ward; Jeff Mann; 'Nathan Burgoine; Jerry L. Wheeler; Quick Sip Reviews; Victoria Villasennor and Nicci Robinson with Bold Strokes UK; Nick Campbell; and to anyone who I've inadvertently forgotten my humble apologies. Many thanks also to the artists who provided beautiful work accompanying my stories in some of their previous appearances: Red Nose Studio, K.G. Schmidt and Jenna Fowler.

I promised a dedication for a first novel, and that debt remains owing — one day it will come around.

To my logical family who supported me while I wrote these stories, I'm eternally grateful. Thank you especially to MT & JC who, at my lowest ebb, pressed a word processor into my hands and told me to write; that story isn't in this book, but the ones that are wouldn't be here without it (and neither would Cleopatra Bonny and her glass-bottomed boat.)

PUBLICATION CREDITS

ABOUT THE AUTHOR

MATTHEW BRIGHT is a writer, editor and designer who's never too sure what order those should come in. His fiction has appeared in *Nightmare*'s *Queers Destroy Horror*, *Lightspeed*, Tor.com, *Glittership*, *Steampunk Universe*, *Queen Mob's Tea House*, *Wild Thymes on the Number 22*, and *Clockwork Iris* amongst others. Alongside co-author Christopher Black he is the author of the experimental novella *Between The Lines* (Roman Books). He is the editor of a number of anthologies, including *The Myriad Carnival: Queer and Weird Tales From Under The Big Top*, *Clockwork Cairo: Steampunk Tales of Egypt* and Lambda Literary Award finalist *Gents*. On the release of his first anthology, *Publishers Weekly* named him 'unequivocally an editor to watch' which is exciting or threatening depending on how you read it. He lives in England and pays the bills as a book designer.

@mbrightwriter | matthew-bright.com
@inkspiraldesign | inkspiraldesign.co.uk